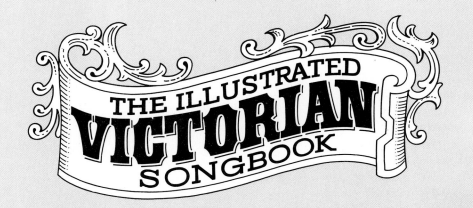

THE ILLUSTRATED
VICTORIAN
SONGBOOK

The Victorians' nostalgic view of medieval England is perfectly caught in Harmony (above) *by Frank Dicksee, first exhibited in 1877. The frontispiece* (opposite) *features the elaborate interior of the Canterbury Hall, prototype of Victorian music halls.*

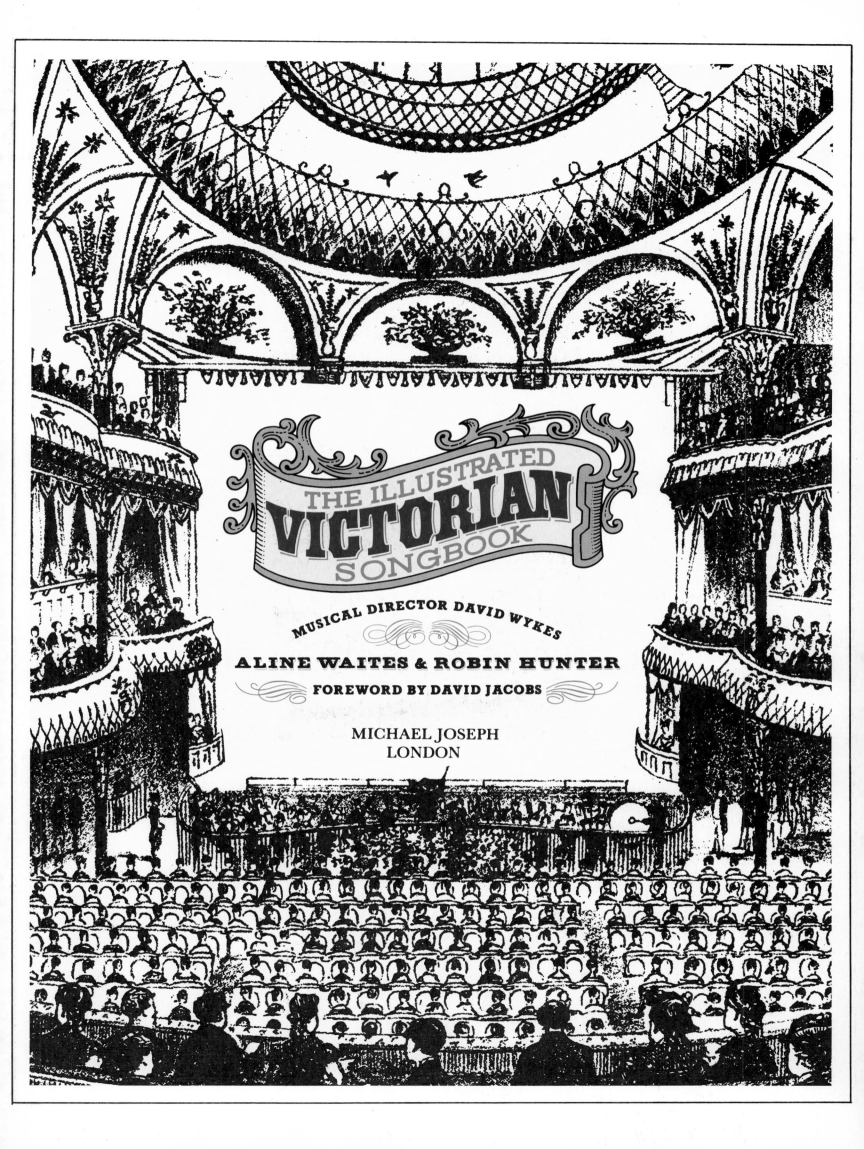

THE ILLUSTRATED VICTORIAN SONGBOOK

MUSICAL DIRECTOR DAVID WYKES

ALINE WAITES & ROBIN HUNTER

FOREWORD BY DAVID JACOBS

MICHAEL JOSEPH
LONDON

MISS LINA VERDI.

1891 A

ROTARY PHOTO. E.C.

DAN LENO

Impressionist, mimic and music
hall artiste, Lena Verdi
(above) won her first contract in
1898 at the age of 11 and began
her stage career just as the great
Dan Leno (above right) was
ending his. She was at the Grand
in Clapham when he forgot his
lines, a sad thing to see in an actor
whom George Bernard Shaw
described as "the lovable kind".
Lena Verdi also appeared (as the
contemporary cutting tells us) at
the Crown Theatre, Peckham
(right). It was later named the
Peckham Hippodrome and in
1912 became a cinema.

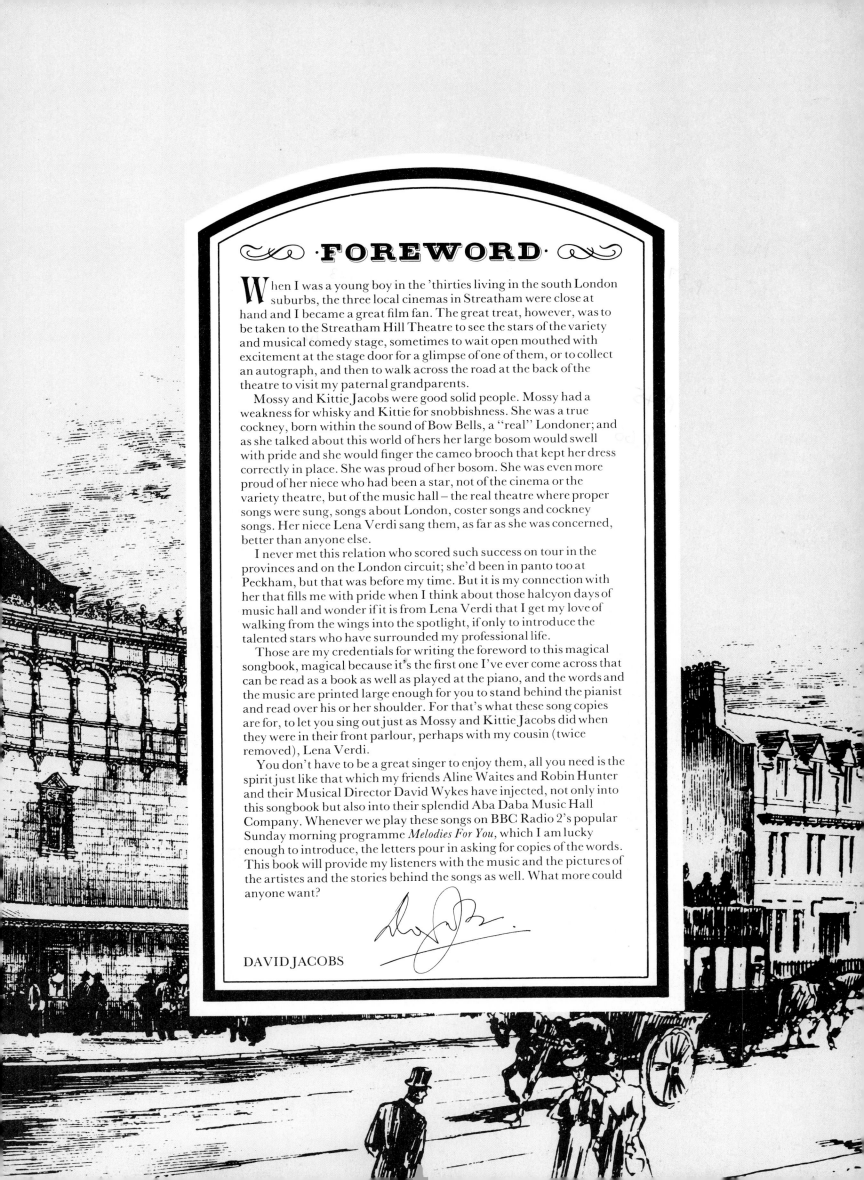

·FOREWORD·

When I was a young boy in the 'thirties living in the south London suburbs, the three local cinemas in Streatham were close at hand and I became a great film fan. The great treat, however, was to be taken to the Streatham Hill Theatre to see the stars of the variety and musical comedy stage, sometimes to wait open mouthed with excitement at the stage door for a glimpse of one of them, or to collect an autograph, and then to walk across the road at the back of the theatre to visit my paternal grandparents.

Mossy and Kittie Jacobs were good solid people. Mossy had a weakness for whisky and Kittie for snobbishness. She was a true cockney, born within the sound of Bow Bells, a "real" Londoner; and as she talked about this world of hers her large bosom would swell with pride and she would finger the cameo brooch that kept her dress correctly in place. She was proud of her bosom. She was even more proud of her niece who had been a star, not of the cinema or the variety theatre, but of the music hall – the real theatre where proper songs were sung, songs about London, coster songs and cockney songs. Her niece Lena Verdi sang them, as far as she was concerned, better than anyone else.

I never met this relation who scored such success on tour in the provinces and on the London circuit; she'd been in panto too at Peckham, but that was before my time. But it is my connection with her that fills me with pride when I think about those halcyon days of music hall and wonder if it is from Lena Verdi that I get my love of walking from the wings into the spotlight, if only to introduce the talented stars who have surrounded my professional life.

Those are my credentials for writing the foreword to this magical songbook, magical because it's the first one I've ever come across that can be read as a book as well as played at the piano, and the words and the music are printed large enough for you to stand behind the pianist and read over his or her shoulder. For that's what these song copies are for, to let you sing out just as Mossy and Kittie Jacobs did when they were in their front parlour, perhaps with my cousin (twice removed), Lena Verdi.

You don't have to be a great singer to enjoy them, all you need is the spirit just like that which my friends Aline Waites and Robin Hunter and their Musical Director David Wykes have injected, not only into this songbook but also into their splendid Aba Daba Music Hall Company. Whenever we play these songs on BBC Radio 2's popular Sunday morning programme *Melodies For You*, which I am lucky enough to introduce, the letters pour in asking for copies of the words. This book will provide my listeners with the music and the pictures of the artistes and the stories behind the songs as well. What more could anyone want?

DAVID JACOBS

First published in Great Britain by
Michael Joseph Ltd., 44 Bedford Square, London WC1B
3DU, 1984.

© Copyright 1984 Sheldrake Press Ltd.

Designed and produced by Sheldrake Press Ltd.,
188 Cavendish Road, London SW12 0DA.

Editor: SIMON RIGGE
Picture Editor: Eleanor Lines
Art Direction/Book Design: Ivor Claydon, Bob Hook
Assistant Editors and Caption Writers: Diana Dubens,
Mike Brown, Margot Levy, Julia Courtney, Sally
Crawford, Barry Anthony
Editorial Assistants: Mary Ann Colvile, Sally
Weatherill
Production Manager: Bob Christie

Copyright in the songs is acknowledged on page 252.
Typesetting by SX Composing Ltd.
Colour origination by Fotographics Ltd., London
Printed and bound in Spain by Printer Industria Grafica,
Barcelona. DLB 24778-1984

ISBN 0 7181 2488 X

THE AUTHORS

ALINE WAITES began her acting career at the BBC, playing Mrs Dale's daughter Gwen. In 1969 she started a theatrical company – Aba Daba – and has devised and directed over 500 shows in Europe, the USA and Canada as well as at the Pindar of Wakefield and other London and provincial theatres. With Robin Hunter she has written two satirical pantomimes, a melodrama, a London revue and a 'thirties musical comedy – all of which have been produced successfully at the Pindar and elsewhere. She lives in Hampstead.

ROBIN HUNTER, son of film actor Ian Hunter, spent his formative years in Hollywood. His association with music hall began in 1953 when he first appeared as Chairman at the Players Theatre. During a varied acting career, which has spanned all types of West End theatre from American musicals to Shakespeare, he has also found time to work extensively as a commercial writer. His writing partnership with Aline Waites began in 1982 when he joined the Aba Daba Company.

THE MUSICAL DIRECTOR

DAVID WYKES read physics at Cambridge and worked with the famous Footlights Revue. For 25 years he has been a public relations consultant, but in addition has been variously engaged as writer, composer, musical director and arranger in cabaret, radio, television and theatre. He joined the Aba Daba Company in 1970 and has worked closely with them in Britain and abroad.

CONSULTANTS

JACKY BRATTON sees herself as an analyst of popular culture with a keen interest in theatre and music hall. In addition to being Reader in English Literature at the University of London, she is a leading theatre historian and teaches theatre history at the Guildhall School of Music and Drama and the British Theatre Association. She is the author of several books on theatre history, music hall and Victorian children's literature.

TONY BARKER's passion for music hall was inspired when he started collecting original music hall recordings, sheet music and illustrations of the artistes. In 1978 he launched *Music Hall* magazine which has broken new ground in researching the lives and careers of music hall artistes. Tony Barker has been an adviser for several radio programmes about music hall, and is involved in the re-issue of old music hall records as well as a series about British music to be filmed for television. He plays guitar in the rhythm and blues band Ivor's Jivers.

First endpaper:
A programme from the London Pavilion, Piccadilly Circus, lists two major stars of music hall, Albert Chevalier and Lottie Collins with her famous number Ta-ra-ra Boom-de-ay.

Last endpaper:
On a bill from the Glasgow Empire Palace Theatre, one of H. E. Moss's highly successful chain of provincial music halls, the star turn is the Australian singer Florrie Forde.

This page:
A selection of sheet music covers displays the versatility of Victorian illustrators, whose designs may be seen as the equivalent of the visuals on modern record sleeves.

·CONTENTS·

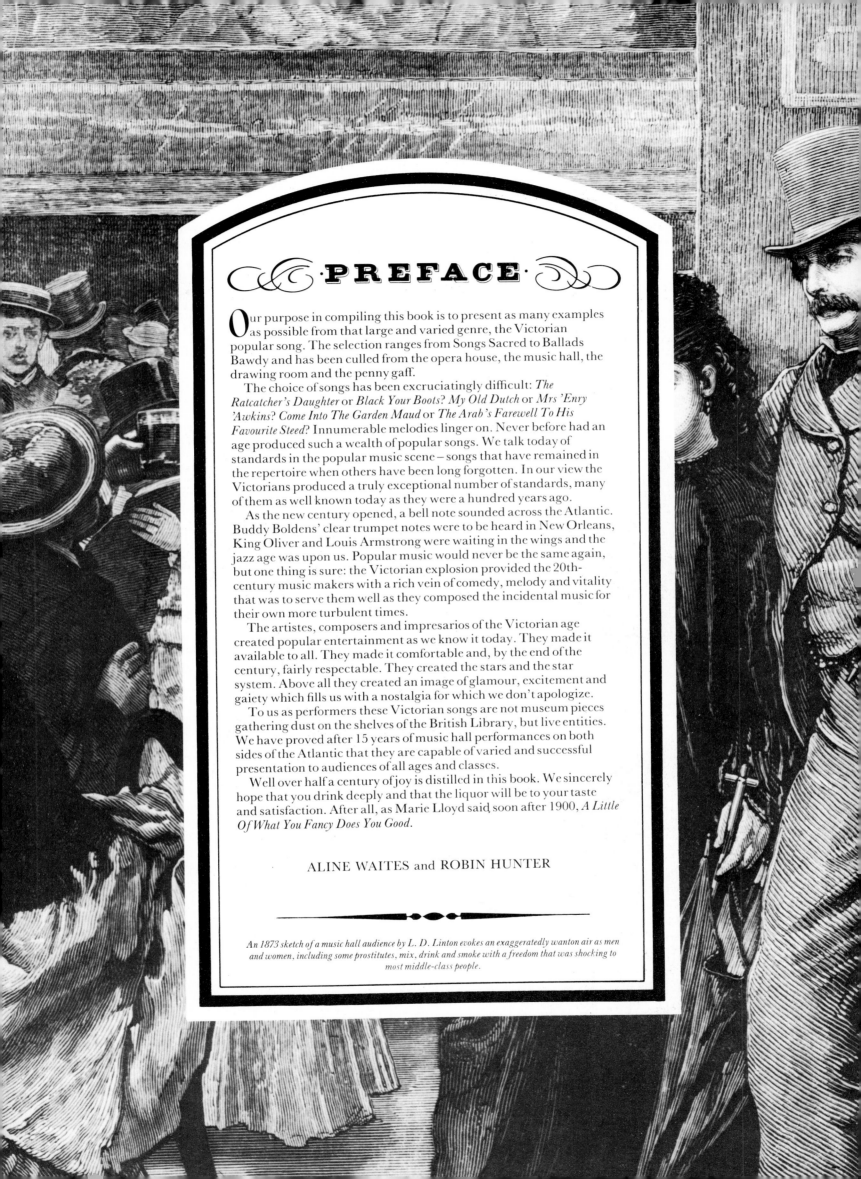

·PREFACE·

Our purpose in compiling this book is to present as many examples as possible from that large and varied genre, the Victorian popular song. The selection ranges from Songs Sacred to Ballads Bawdy and has been culled from the opera house, the music hall, the drawing room and the penny gaff.

The choice of songs has been excruciatingly difficult: *The Ratcatcher's Daughter* or *Black Your Boots? My Old Dutch* or *Mrs 'Enry 'Awkins? Come Into The Garden Maud* or *The Arab's Farewell To His Favourite Steed?* Innumerable melodies linger on. Never before had an age produced such a wealth of popular songs. We talk today of standards in the popular music scene – songs that have remained in the repertoire when others have been long forgotten. In our view the Victorians produced a truly exceptional number of standards, many of them as well known today as they were a hundred years ago.

As the new century opened, a bell note sounded across the Atlantic. Buddy Boldens' clear trumpet notes were to be heard in New Orleans, King Oliver and Louis Armstrong were waiting in the wings and the jazz age was upon us. Popular music would never be the same again, but one thing is sure: the Victorian explosion provided the 20th-century music makers with a rich vein of comedy, melody and vitality that was to serve them well as they composed the incidental music for their own more turbulent times.

The artistes, composers and impresarios of the Victorian age created popular entertainment as we know it today. They made it available to all. They made it comfortable and, by the end of the century, fairly respectable. They created the stars and the star system. Above all they created an image of glamour, excitement and gaiety which fills us with a nostalgia for which we don't apologize.

To us as performers these Victorian songs are not museum pieces gathering dust on the shelves of the British Library, but live entities. We have proved after 15 years of music hall performances on both sides of the Atlantic that they are capable of varied and successful presentation to audiences of all ages and classes.

Well over half a century of joy is distilled in this book. We sincerely hope that you drink deeply and that the liquor will be to your taste and satisfaction. After all, as Marie Lloyd said, soon after 1900, *A Little Of What You Fancy Does You Good*.

ALINE WAITES and ROBIN HUNTER

An 1873 sketch of a music hall audience by L. D. Linton evokes an exaggeratedly wanton air as men and women, including some prostitutes, mix, drink and smoke with a freedom that was shocking to most middle-class people.

·INTRODUCTION·

"Since singing is so good a thing, I wish all men would learn to sing," said William Byrd in the 16th century. His words were truly taken to heart by the Victorians. They were the pioneers of the choral society, the music teaching college, the expensively bound home *Musical Educator* and that self-styled system of "music for the people", Tonic Sol-Fa. They brought in the mass-produced upright piano and the harmonium, the popular hymn and the sentimental ballad. And from the fairgrounds, the pubs and the music halls there came that other tradition, the popular sing-along of the Victorian working class.

Victorian – what does that word conjure up today? To some people it means puritanical, prejudiced, stuffy, respectable; whereas mention Victorian music hall to those same people and they think of rude songs and Marie Lloyd. The patriot will think longingly of the glorious age of the British Empire, and the social historian will remember the enormous gap between rich and poor, the rise of the middle classes, the triumph of the factory system, the squalid social conditions as described by Dickens, Thackeray and Henry Mayhew.

The extraordinary diversity of those quick changing times was mirrored in the music, and a book on popular Victorian songs has to spread its net wide in order to create a true picture. In our selection the earthy vulgarity of the music hall contrasts vividly with the sentimentality of some of the minstrel airs. The rampant patriotism of songs like *Rule Britannia* sits strangely alongside the cynicism of the First Lord of the Admiralty in *HMS Pinafore*. Can the gay, sophisticated arias of operetta and musical comedy have lived in the same world as the plaintive tragi-comedy of the street ballads?

The answer is that the Victorian age lasted more than 60 years and that those years were the most revolutionary yet witnessed in the social history of Europe. The timespan of this book, give or take a few glances to either side, runs from 1837, when the 18-year-old Victoria came to the throne, to 1901 when she died, the matriarch of Europe, at Osborne House in the Isle of Wight. During that time factories replaced fields as the nation's chief source of income, railways superseded the stage coach, steamships created the opportunity of world travel and world-wide trade on an entirely new scale, and the population of the British Isles virtually doubled. In 1830 it was 24 million; by

Members of the so-called "upper ten thousand", the cream of Victorian high society, receive a formal welcome as they arrive at a ball during the London season. The illustration comes from the sheet music cover of a waltz called Belgravia, *after the Duke of Westminster's estate just off Hyde Park Corner which was developed in the 1820s and became one of London's most fashionable and aristocratic residential districts. This was the world that middle-class households in Bloomsbury or Chelsea loved to emulate.*

1901 it had passed 41 million. At the same time more and more people were leaving the land and living in the towns and cities where industry provided growing employment opportunities. At the beginning of Victoria's reign there were nine cities, apart from London, of 100,000 people or more; by 1891 there were 23. The population of London itself grew from just under two million to more than four million. With the progress of the industrial revolution, new working patterns, new lifestyles and new money created a demand for new forms of entertainment. The bourgeoisie, swollen in size, prosperity and pride, looked for gentility. It was an age of *nouveaux riches*. People who had come up from the working classes did not want to be reminded of it, and the kind of songs they preferred were as far removed from the back-yard squalor of their antecedents as they could possibly be. By the early 1850s no one above the rank of labourer or artisan would venture into a pub to buy a drink. Middle-class men repaired to the newly built clubs where they could enjoy their leisure in the surroundings of magnificent Italian-style *palazzi*. The gentlemen's discussion groups which had traditionally met in the club rooms of pubs became a thing of the past, replaced by local trade union meetings and "free and easy" or "harmonic meeting" clubs with their own vigorous popular songs. It was from these gatherings – neither expensive nor demanding of their audiences – that music hall was to emerge.

As the cities grew, particularly London, which contained a far bigger, more various and more footloose population than any other, large numbers of working-class people were in need of a convivial evening out in comfortable surroundings. Living conditions in the poorest districts of early Victorian cities were appalling. Rubbish was thrown out into the streets and left to rot. Whole families often lived in one room. It is not surprising that the metropolitan poor looked outside their homes for entertainment.

In country areas the traditional centre for leisure activity was the local inn, often with its own skittle garden, and the millions of new town and city dwellers looked for their amusement to the taverns, which did a roaring trade. Harmonic gatherings became more organized. In time good singers were singled out to sing solo, and became favourites with the patrons of the tavern. They soon demanded payment for their performances, and the landlords happily obliged in order to keep their clientele. The payment was probably no more than free beer or a pie or even a bob or two, but even so, the singers by demanding and receiving payment became professionals and were able to hire themselves out to other establishments. As landlords competed with one another to provide bigger and better forms of entertainment, many of them built on to their pubs a saloon theatre in order to provide a special place for their singers to perform. In time some publicans became more ambitious, presenting melodramas, burlesques and circus-style performances.

Saloon theatres were not allowed under the terms of their licence to present plays, that privilege being reserved exclusively for those theatres with a royal charter – Covent Garden and Drury Lane. But by presenting burlesque or comedy versions and adding music to them, the taverns were able to present dramatic entertainments without breaking the law. Such was the success of these performances that the legitimate theatres followed suit and in their turn presented operas, pantomimes, even variety shows and circuses. Wild beasts appeared on the stages of these hallowed buildings.

The 1843 Theatres Act introduced tougher regulations. Proprietors of saloon theatres either had to register their premises as theatres (in which case they could put on plays censored by the Lord Chamberlain, but lost the right to provide food and drink in the auditorium); or they had to stop presenting anything which could be described as dramatic entertainment and apply for a magistrates' licence for singing and dancing only; they would then be able to carry on serving food and drink to their customers. Some of the saloon theatres

*V*esta Tilley represented the acceptable face of music hall. Her career spanned 50 years. It began when music hall had a raw, working-class vitality and reached a climax with her appearance in the first Royal Command Performance in 1912, an occasion that put a final seal of approval on her once despised profession.

A devout American family sets off to attend Sunday Church, a regular fixture of respectable life on both sides of the Atlantic. The music of the organ or the humble harmonium, and of voices raised to God in the singing of popular hymns, was one of the most characteristic sounds of 19th-century everyday life. The harmonium, introduced in France in 1840, was the youngest of the Victorian keyboard instruments. Composers such as Sir Arthur Sullivan wrote ecclesiastical songs especially for this durable reed instrument and its larger, more velvety-toned cousin, the American organ.

became legitimate. Others chose to put on non-dramatic pieces and keep their pub status: in this way music hall was born, expanding rapidly in the 1850s and 1860s as enthusiastic entrepreneurs poured in high-risk capital to construct larger and better buildings.

In America the popular music explosion found another form of expression: the black-face minstrel shows. With their themes of romantic love and death and their total lack of vulgarity, the minstrel shows proved quite acceptable to English concert-hall audiences when exported. The 3,000 miles' distance added a certain charm to these presentations and helped to disguise the uneasy fact that they were based on the misery of an enslaved people. America also had its own version of music hall, generally called vaudeville, and a more vulgar type of performance known as burlesque. At Tony Pastor's Music Hall on Broadway and Weber and Fields' famous New York venue, burlesque shows were preceded by music hall performances similar to those across the Atlantic.

During the rise of the music hall, the middle classes were patronizing the concert hall and the legitimate theatre, with bills ranging from grand opera to popular ballads, or else making their own form of amusement in their homes, gathered round the family piano. In 19th-century home entertainment, the piano was king. The industrial revolution provided both the means to manufacture and the means to purchase, and the newly prosperous middle classes sought to demonstrate their respectability by buying a pianoforte for their drawing room. By the end of the century some families even boasted two.

When the young Victoria came to the throne she inherited a nation that was, in terms of musical and artistic appreciation, divided. For the very few there were the glories of classical music, of opera, poetry and drama. For the vast majority of her loyal and devoted subjects, Art with a capital A meant little or nothing at all. Their idols were the street singers and tavern performers of the day, their literature the broadsides and lampoons. By the time the old Queen died, she left behind a nation much more unified, if not in terms of wealth, certainly in terms of popular art. Jenny Lind would not have been a household name in Whitechapel in 1850. In 1900 Marie Lloyd was a household name throughout the land. In 1837 you would have been hard-pressed to compile a list of more than a handful of popular artists well known to all strata of the community. By 1900 the list would include: Dan Leno, Henry Irving, Little Tich, Johann Strauss, George Robey, Enrico Caruso, Marie Lloyd, Adelina Patti, George Grossmith, Ellaline Terriss and Seymour Hicks, Sir Henry Wood and so on in infinite variety.

Already by then the age of the gramophone, the movie and the wireless was coming in. The undisputed reign of King Piano was nearing its end. As music hall moved on to palace of variety and then cinema, and musical comedy ushered in the 20th century and the modern musical, the old world of entertainment died a lingering death. By the 1930s the last of the great Victorian music hall stars were giving their farewell performances, and it was all over.

But was it? The old days have been kept alive in the memories of those who sat in the audiences, through hearsay in the minds of their children and grandchildren, and in the piano stools and chests of drawers of millions of families on both sides of the Atlantic, ready to be dusted

The Grecian Saloon, headlined below in its own advertising typography, was one of London's best known saloon theatres. It stood in the grounds of the Eagle Tavern in City Road, and under the management of its proprietor, Thomas Rouse, offered musical entertainment with "Songs, serious and comic; Duets, Glees, Choruses, Overtures, etc., supported by a numerous and talented Company". In the tavern grounds wrestling contests were staged between the Cornish and Devonshire champions (below middle), while the florid Eagle Tavern itself (bottom), built by Rouse in 1821 to replace a country-style inn known as the Shepherd and Shepherdess, provided feasting and entertainment in its upstairs Long Room.

down and performed again. This book is both evidence of the revival of Victorian popular music and, we sincerely hope, a contribution to its continuing vitality.

In preparing the book we have delved into cupboards for old sheet music and now often out-of-print histories of the 19th-century theatre, disinterring quantities of material which have brought to life the concert hall, the music hall and above all the ordinary Victorian family in moments of lightheartedness as well as smugness and gloom. For the sake of appearance and authenticity, we have selected as far as possible the earliest editions of the songs, and these are what you see reproduced on our pages. A good deal of Victorian sheet music was badly printed, sometimes out of alignment, distorted, faded or over-inked, and the composers and arrangers committed some crashing blunders which seem to have slipped past the proof-readers. We have corrected the cardinal errors, but blemishes on printed pages which in a few instances are more than 150 years old remain to intrigue and occasionally astonish the eye.

What we have not been able to reproduce is the patina of age, the yellowing pages, the tears and dog ears, the brown blotches and thumb marks and above all the smell of old paper – all part of the pleasure of reliving old times. By way of compensation we have included among the illustrations a few colour photographs of some of the earliest typographical covers.

Over the years many of the songs have been published in numerous editions, often with different words and both minor and major variations in the tunes and accompaniments – a true indication of a song's popularity. Sometimes a later version of a song is now more familiar than the original (*After The Ball*, *Are We To Part Like This?* and *Champagne Charlie* are examples), and in *The Boy In The Gallery* we have thought it necessary to include the later tune alongside the original. We also publish for the first time new arrangements of two old street songs, *Sam Hall* and *She Was Poor, But She Was Honest*, which were not printed in any form until after the Victorian era.

It is often surprising how far back one can date some songs which still have an honourable place in the popular repertoire, and in the musical by-lines at the head of each song we have made a point whenever we have the information of giving not only the name of the writer and composer but also the date of first publication. Where the words and music were written at different times, we provide two dates, each separated by a comma from the name of the writer or composer to whom it applies. If a piece is known to have been written or composed before publication, the earlier date is given. Details of the edition from which the music has been reproduced are given in the source list on page 252, along with copyright notices for those songs which are still in copyright.

We have arranged the songs in nine sections which encapsulate the different forms of entertainment and chart the history of their development from the 1830s to the end of the century. Although we would have loved to stray into the Edwardian age in pursuit of a particular favourite such as "Dilly Dally" (*My Old Man Said Follow The Van*) or *Down At The Old Bull And Bush*, we have stayed loyal to our title and called a halt in the second year of the new century. We have, however, legitimately introduced many songs which originated long before Victoria came to the throne, but remained popular with our Victorian forebears and still figure in the modern repertoire of popular songs.

Clockwise from below: a cigarette card features Katie Lawrence (not Lillian as stated), singer of Daisy Bell; *the light comedian Charles Mathews appears in his role as Dazzel in Boucicault's* London Assurance; *the famous operatic star Adelina Patti graces a Victorian drawing room; among the pavilions and walks in the Eagle Tavern appears* (left) *a view of the imposing frontage of the Grecian Saloon.*

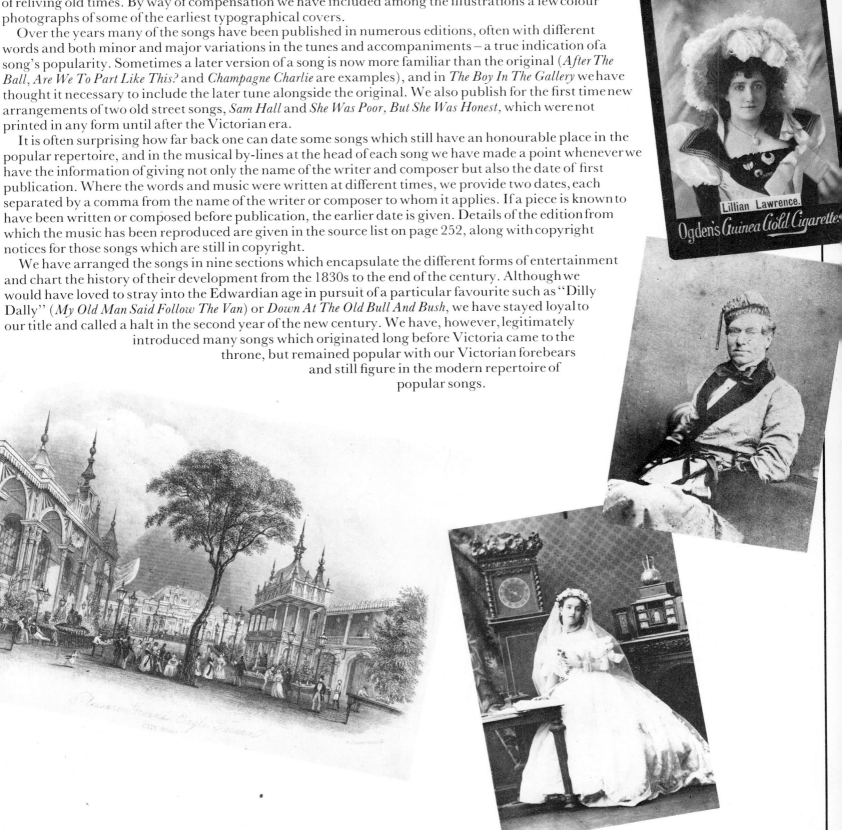

THE · DRAWING ROOM · SOIREE

Since the days of Jane Austen around the end of the 18th century, the ability to play the new, fashionable pianoforte had been an accomplishment expected of upper-class young ladies, who shed many a bitter tear in their attempts to master the instrument. The young gentlemen they were trying to impress would themselves cut a dash in their rendering of the latest ballads at the soirées which were such a feature of society life.

As the Victorian middle classes became more prosperous, they began to emulate the gentlefolk, adding prestige to the occasion by engaging professional singers like Harry Clifton to render moralistic songs such as *A Motto For Every Man* or *Up With The Lark In The Morning*. Later Clifton was to perform the same songs with surprising success in the rough and tumble of the music halls.

The music of the Victorian drawing room tended to be of a high moral tone with songs about God and Death, Patriotism and Temperance, and above all Love – pure and romantic, often tragic and unrequited. Nowadays the more soulful Victorian ballads can seem rather banal, but to prove that the Victorians were not lacking in humour, we have included one song, *The Baby On The Shore*, which pokes fun at the whole genre.

We have also chosen two songs which may be described as sacred and two rousing hymns in the hope that we can challenge Voltaire's statement, "The Most High has a decided taste for vocal music provided it be lugubrious and gloomy enough".

In The Concert *by the French-born artist James Tissot (1836-1902), members of high society gather for a violin recital during a musical evening at a large house.*

· HOME! · SWEET · HOME! ·

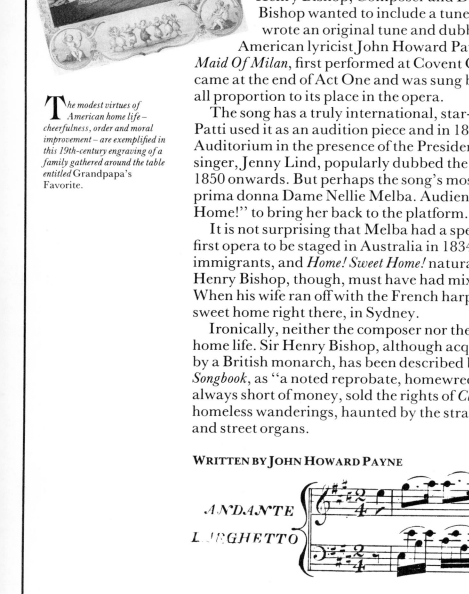

Of all the hundreds of songs we have considered for inclusion in this book, there has never been any doubt in our minds about which should have pride of place. *Home! Sweet Home!* was almost a sacred text for middle-class Victorians. It expressed a longing for peace and tranquillity at a time of rapid industrial growth and social upheaval, when millions of people were on the move from country to town and from the old world to the new. The home was a place of shelter, "not only from all injury," wrote John Ruskin, "but from all terror, doubt and division".

The melody of the song first appeared in 1821 in an album of national airs compiled by Henry Bishop, Composer and Director of Music at the Theatre Royal, Covent Garden. Bishop wanted to include a tune from Sicily, but was unable to find a suitable one. So he wrote an original tune and dubbed it Sicilian. Two years later he added words by the American lyricist John Howard Payne and put the resulting song into an opera, *Clari, or The Maid Of Milan*, first performed at Covent Garden on 8th May, 1823. *Home! Sweet Home!*, which came at the end of Act One and was sung by the soprano Maria Tree, quickly achieved fame out of all proportion to its place in the opera.

The song has a truly international, star-studded history. The great operatic soprano Adelina Patti used it as an audition piece and in 1859 performed it at the opening of the Chicago Auditorium in the presence of the President of the United States, James Buchanan. Another top singer, Jenny Lind, popularly dubbed the Swedish Nightingale, sang it in all her concerts from 1850 onwards. But perhaps the song's most famous performer was the distinguished Australian prima donna Dame Nellie Melba. Audiences around the world would chant "Home! Sweet Home!" to bring her back to the platform.

It is not surprising that Melba had a special place in her heart for this song. *Clari* had been the first opera to be staged in Australia in 1834, when most of the population were still first-generation immigrants, and *Home! Sweet Home!* naturally became part of the young colony's heritage. Sir Henry Bishop, though, must have had mixed feelings about the success of his song down under. When his wife ran off with the French harpist Nicholas Bochsa, the two of them made their home sweet home right there, in Sydney.

Ironically, neither the composer nor the writer of the song experienced the simple pleasures of home life. Sir Henry Bishop, although acquiring respectability as the first musician to be knighted by a British monarch, has been described by Michael Turner in his pioneering study, *The Parlour Songbook*, as "a noted reprobate, homewrecker and spendthrift". John Howard Payne, who was always short of money, sold the rights of *Clari* for £250 and spent most of the rest of his life in homeless wanderings, haunted by the strains of *Home! Sweet Home!* coming from cafés, cabarets and street organs.

The modest virtues of American home life – cheerfulness, order and moral improvement – are exemplified in this 19th-century engraving of a family gathered around the table entitled Grandpapa's Favorite.

WRITTEN BY JOHN HOWARD PAYNE — COMPOSED & ARRANGED BY HENRY R. BISHOP — 1823

though we may roam, Be it e _ ver so humble, there's no place like home! A

charm from the skies seems to hal _ low us there, Which seek through the

espress:

world, is ne'er met with else _ were. Home! Home! sweet sweet

pp

Largo

Home! There's no place like Home! There's no place like Home!

colla voce   *ten*   *Tempo 1mo*   *ff*

A NOTE ON
PERFORMANCE
The small grace notes (♪) in
this song should be sung
lightly, neither too clipped
nor too swooning. Other
notes in small type should be
given their full face value.
    The marking "*espress*" is
an open invitation to
legitimate licence on the part
of the singer during the
eight-bar refrain, where the
written-out *portamento* on
"There's" turns bar 4 into at
least 5/8. The small notes
prolong the trill into a
miniature *cadenza* which
further tests the tolerance of
the metronome-minded
pianist. At the end of the
song "*ad lib*" indicates a yet
more elaborate *cadenza*.
    The *ff* interjections reflect
the grandeur of the original
orchestral framework in the
opera house and should not
be interpreted literally: a
corresponding *fortissimo* on
the drawing room piano
would simply suggest
impatience.

This old, shingled cottage in
East Hampton, Long
Island, drawn in the 1890s when
the town still preserved a rural
charm, is where the writer of
Home! Sweet Home!, John
Howard Payne, spent his early
childhood.

17

Two vignettes illustrate the daily activities of a middle-class household in mid-19th-century Germany. The cosy, or gemütlich, nature of German home life was especially admired in England where Queen Victoria, Prince Albert and their nine children offered the perfect example of family togetherness.

SECOND VERSE. piu Animato

An Ex_ile from Home Splendour dazzles in vain Oh! give me my lowly thatch'd Cottage a___gain! The Birds singing gaily that came at my call Give me them with the peace of mind dearer than all. Home! Home! sweet sweet Home! There's no place like Home! There's no place like Home!

· IN · THE · GLOAMING ·

This charming song of noble renunciation was composed by Annie Fortescue Harrison who was the wife of the comptroller of Queen Victoria's household, Lord Hill. The story line is never clearly explained. How or why the lover "passed away in silence" we shall never know. However, the narrator assures us that it is all for the best, so we can take comfort in that.

WRITTEN BY META ORRED, 1874   COMPOSED BY ANNIE FORTESCUE HARRISON, 1877

In the gloam ....ing oh. my dar ....ling when the lights are dim and low — And the qui ... et sha........dows

Melancholy songs of courtship and parting appealed to the sentimental side of the Victorians. But there was also a more humorous, even saucy, side expressed in such songs as Not There!, from which this illustration comes. In the song, the girl's mother warns her daughter not to meet her lover at the stile: "Of rustic stiles you always should beware, Don't be too bold – you might catch cold – not there! my child, not there!"

The Victorian fondness for doleful sentiment extended not only to love songs but also to an enjoyment of sylvan settings touched with Gothic melancholy, well expressed in this drawing of Sherwood Forest from The Story of Some English Shires, published in 1897.

AID FOR THE AMATEUR PIANIST

The lyrics of this song do not specify the sex of the singer, and this edition in F is described as suitable for baritone or contralto. An alternative in A was available for tenor or soprano.

The publication of songs in multiple editions was a common practice a century ago. Music publishers had bigger markets before the mass production of gramophone records and could afford to be kinder to accompanists who could not transpose. There is no surer way for a pianist to become popular today than to cultivate the ability to transpose an accompaniment into any key to suit the singer.

In the gloam....ing oh! my dar....ling think not bit......ter....
...ly of me? Tho' I passed a.........
...way in si......lence left you lone.......ly

Rall:

set you free For my heart was

Cres:

*M*ost Victorian parlour songs were given their public baptism at concerts such as this one, held in 1885. If they proved successful with the audiences, the songs would quickly find their way into drawing rooms across the nation.

The theme of idealized love which lay at the core of Victorian romanticism is epitomized in this painting from about 1894 of a knight and his lady, by the minor Irish artist William G. Mackenzie. The painting of medieval subjects was a tradition which went back to the late-18th-century and flourished in mid- and High Victorian times. It was deeply influenced by the Pre-Raphaelite view of the Middle Ages as pure and valorous.

crush'd with long ......ing, what had been could ne.......ver be It was best to leave you thus dear best for you and best for me It was best to leave you thus............... Best for you and best for me...........

· K I L L A R N E Y ·

The composer of this beautiful air was an Irishman, Michael William Balfe, who was born in Dublin in 1808 (appropriately enough at 19, Balfe Street). In later years both he and Edmund Falconer, who wrote the words, became managers of the Theatre Royal, Drury Lane, and to this day Balfe's statue stands in the Rotunda with those of David Garrick, Edmund Kean and William Shakespeare. But it was at the Royal Lyceum Theatre that *Killarney* was first performed "with distinguished success", according to the standard sheet music puff, by Miss Anna Whitty.

Michael Balfe was the foremost composer of his day, winning a degree of popularity among Victorians that was rivalled only by Arthur Sullivan later in the century. Balfe was a facile and extremely accomplished tunesmith. He believed a good tune was everything, and was criticised by some lyricists for not showing off their words to best advantage. Nevertheless, he supported his melodies with effective accompaniments and composed the music for two poems by Longfellow which became Victorian standards: *I Shot An Arrow Into The Air* and the evergreen duet *Excelsior!*

Middle Lake, one of the three celebrated lakes near Killarney in Ireland's south-west county of Kerry, lies in a valley which the travel writer H. V. Morton described as a botanist's paradise. "Here grow cedars of Lebanon, arbutus, wild fuchsia . . . the scented orchid, which grows along the Mediterranean coast and in Asia Minor, the great butterwort, which is a native of Spain, and the 'blue-eyed grass', which you will see only in Canada".

WRITTEN BY EDMUND FALCONER   COMPOSED BY MICHAEL WILLIAM BALFE

1 By Kil lar_ney's lakes and fells ✻ Em'rald isles and
3 No place else can charm the eye With such bright and

winding 'bays   Mountain paths and   woodland dells   Mem'_ry ev__er
va_ried tints   Ev'__ry rock that   you pass by   Ver__dure broi__ders

fond_ly strays.   Bounteous na_ture loves all lands,   Beau_ty wanders
or besprints   Vir_gin there the green grass grows Ev'__ry morn springs

ev'_ry where,   Footprints leaves on ma_ny strands   But her home is sure_ly there!
na_tal day,   Bright hued berries daff the snows   Smi__ling win_ter's frown a__way

Briar roses and a pleasant coastal scene illustrated a song called Love's Summer Dream *which appeared in* The Girl's Own Paper, *a weekly magazine presenting poetry, readers' questions and romantic tales on a high moral plane.*

ORIGINAL
PUBLISHER'S
FOOTNOTE
✻ To sit on rocks to muse o'er flood and fell. 25 Stanza. 2nd Canto of Childe Harold's Pilgrimage.

NOTE
Killarney was published in two forms: with two verses (numbered 1 and 3 in our text), and with four verses (the two additional verses were numbered 2 and 4).

An-gels fold their wings and rest   In that E - den of the west,   Beauty's home Kil

An - gels oft - en pausing there   Doubt if E - den were more fair   Beauty's home Kil

-lar — ney Heav'n's re-flex Kil - lar - ney.

-lar — ney Heav'n's re-flex Kil - lar - ney!

2.

Innisfallen's ruin'd shrine

  May suggest a passing sigh,

But man's faith can ne'er decline

  Such God wonders floating by

Castle Lough and Glena Bay

  Mountains Tore and Eagles nest

Still at Mucross you must pray

  Though the monks are now at rest.

    Angels wonder not that man

    There would fain prolong life's span

    Beauty's home Killarney

    Heav'n's reflex Killarney.

4.

Music there for Echo dwells,

  Makes each sound a Harmony,

Many voic' the chorus swells

  Till it faints in ecstacy.

With the charmful tints below

  Seems the Heaven above to vie

All rich colours that we know

  Tinge the cloud wreaths in that sky.

    Wings of Angels so might shine

    Glancing back soft light divine

    Beauty's home Killarney

    Heav'n's reflex Killarney.

Wearing an expression of some unease, an amateur singer appears at a fashionable ballad concert in an illustration from The Strand Musical Magazine *of January 1895. Many young ladies of the period dreamt of a singing career despite the fact that they had too little talent to reach professional standards.*

· COME·INTO·THE· ·GARDEN·MAUD·

Undoubtedly the most notorious of all drawing room ballads, this Victorian favourite contains words from a much longer poem, *Maud*, written by the Poet Laureate, Alfred Lord Tennyson. It was set to music in 1857 by Michael Balfe and was the cause of a tremendous row between him and Tennyson who objected to the musical stress on the word "Come" which he felt utterly destroyed the accentuation of the first line.

Sims Reeves, for whom the song was written, approved Balfe's original draft with a scribbled "This'll do" over the first few bars. Tennyson's view, however, received strong critical backing. The song became an instant target for lampoon, and has remained controversial to this day. To keep the debate alive, we have included a defence of Balfe from our own Musical Director on page 33.

Poor Tennyson. In 1893, two years after his death, the song was again held up to ridicule – this time, according to legend, by the Queen of the Halls, Marie Lloyd. Marie is said to have been accused by a body of people calling themselves the Purity Party of singing obscene songs. The London County Council licensing committee summoned her to sing the offending songs in their presence, which she did with such sweetness, and so little expression, that the committee were forced to give her a clean bill.

Then in a fit of rage she gave a performance of *Come Into The Garden Maud* with all the double meanings and sexual innuendo she could find. At the end she swept out in triumph, announcing: "You see, it's all in the mind".

WRITTEN BY ALFRED LORD TENNYSON, 1855

COMPOSED BY MICHAEL WILLIAM BALFE, 1857

The etiquette of Victorian courtship is thoroughly lampooned in this scene illustrating a sheet music cover for the comic song Oh George! Don't Be So Forward – written, composed and sung by John Read – in which a woman makes a half-hearted attempt to ward off a clumsy admirer. "Tickling and squeezing you think is pleasing," she says. "I think myself Sir, it's awfully rude."

PIANO.

dolce.

Come into the gar _ den Maud, For the black bat, Night, has flown; Come into the gar _ den Maud, I am here, at the gate a _ lone. I am here, at the gate a _ lone. And the wood-bine spi _ ces are waft _ ed a_broad, And the musk of the ro _ _ ses blown, For a breeze of morn _ ing

BALFE.

The statue of Michael Balfe in the rotunda of the Theatre Royal, Drury Lane, commemorates a man who, although a successful writer of songs, was essentially a composer of opera. Among his output of 30 operas, the most successful were The Siege of Rochelle *(1835),* The Bohemian Girl *(1843) and* The Rose of Castille *(1858) which are rarely, if ever, performed today.*

moves, And the planet of love is on high, Be-

-ginning to **faint in** the light that she loves, On a bed of daffo-dil

sky, To faint in the light of the sun she loves, To

faint in the light and to die. Come! come!

One of the most dashing figures of the Victorian concert circuit was Sims Reeves (1818-1900) for whom the cavatina Come Into The Garden Maud *was composed. As an accomplished tenor, he was equally at home in opera – appearing in 1843 at La Scala, Milan, in Donizetti's* Lucia di Lammermoor *– as well as in the popular series of London Wednesday Concerts and Monday "Pops".*

ALFRED TENNYSON

Alfred Tennyson (1809-1892) was the foremost poet of the Victorian era, becoming Poet Laureate in 1850 in succession to William Wordsworth. Born in the Lincolnshire village of Somersby and educated at Trinity College, Cambridge, he wrote a vast amount of poetry mainly dealing with legendary and historical subjects. These included *Morte d'Arthur* (1842), *In Memoriam* (1850), inspired by the death of his close friend, the 22-year old Arthur Hallam, *Maud* (1855) and *Idylls of the King*, a series of poems on the Arthurian romance written between 1859 and 1885.

A demure woman watches for her husband from a flower-wreathed window in a sketch illustrating the sheet music cover of A Sweet Face At The Window. *At the heart of the Victorian man's dream was the faithful and loving wife, always there to greet the returning head of the household.*

Opposite:

The figure of Harry Clifton, a popular singer of music hall and theatrical songs, dominates a scene that mocks the sort of genteel musical party at which he frequently performed. The tableau illustrates a sheet music cover of an 1868 Clifton song, Jones' Musical Party, whose lyrics express the appalled sentiments of a professional singer surrounded by a band of amateurs.

dolce.

Rose of the rose-bud, Gar_den of girls, Come hither, the dances are

done; In gloss of satin and glimmer of pearls, Queen,

li_ly, and rose, in one. Shine out little head running

o_ver with curls, To the flowers and be ___ their Sun. Shine out! Shine

A decorative sticker suitable for adorning gifts, bouquets and love letters carries what one might think was a perversely self-contradicting legend: "Your charm needs no adornment". It was printed in 1880 as part of a range of fancy goods and greeting cards for every occasion whether seasonal, religious or romantic.

Your charms need no adornment.

THE ORIGINAL *MAUD*

Tennyson completed his poem *Maud*, from which the words of *Come Into The Garden Maud* were taken, two years before the publication of the song. Tennyson called the poem a monodrama. Its febrile, complex plot traces the spiral into madness of the narrator whose father has committed suicide, leaving him poverty-stricken and bitter.

His love for Maud, daughter of the lord of the manor, has him eaten up with jealousy of both her brother (an "oil'd and curl'd Assyrian Bull"!) and the man she is to marry. At the poem's end, Maud dies and the narrator, deranged with despair, rushes off to fight in the Crimean War where he meets an unknown fate.

The song itself highlights an incident during a ball at the manor house where the narrator stands outside, uninvited, pleading for Maud to meet him at the garden gate.

*C*ane seating, pot plants, carpet and fountain bring a typically Victorian ambience to the verandah at Painshill, a country home in Surrey photographed in about 1900. Its garden, created by the Hon. Charles Hamilton in the 1740s, ranked among the finest landscaped gardens in England and was especially noted for its air of picturesque decay.

In a wistful scene from Tennyson's poem Maud, *drawn by the early 20th-century English illustrator, Eleanor Fortescue-Brickdale, the narrator is shown fulfilling his dream of meeting Maud by the garden gate – something that never actually took place.*

A MUSICAL POSTSCRIPT

The controversy surrounding Balfe's setting of *Come Into The Garden Maud* is more than a disagreement between Balfe and Tennyson. It is also one between musicians and poets generally.

According to the great Irish composer Sir Charles Villiers Stanford, Lord Tennyson once complained to him that "so many composers made the notes go up when he wanted them to go down, and go down when he wanted them to go up". He was particularly indignant that Balfe's setting of this song fell from the word "Come" instead of rising to the word "garden".

That is the poet's view, but from the musicians' side the judgement is open to question. There is more to accentuation than pitch. Harmonic tension puts the emphasis firmly on the word "garden", underlined by the indication "*dolce*" over the word "Come" and the heavy accent over the "gar-" of "garden" – markings which have been lost in careless editions.

Some listeners have been puzzled by the word "queenlily", a mis-hearing of "Queen, lily" (*page 30*). Here is a reminder to singers of the importance of punctuation as well as diction in making sense even of nonsense.

33

·COME·HOME, FATHER·

This is a typical temperance song with the familiar characters of the Sick Mother, the Dying Baby and the Innocent Child trying to lure the Drunken Father away from the sinful taverns. It was performed in a temperance melodrama *Ten Nights In A Bar Room*, produced in New York in 1858. In the play the Innocent Child does eventually persuade the Father to come home, but is then struck on the head by a drinking glass which was aimed at the Father – and little Mary expires with Poor Weeping Mother and Contrite Father beside her. The writer of the song was the Connecticut Yankee Henry Clay Work, who was variously: printer, inventor of machines and toys, abolitionist, prohibitionist, self-taught musician and songwriter. He also wrote *Marching Through Georgia, Ring The Bell Watchman* and *My Grandfather's Clock*.

Temperance songs of this kind were intended for a theatre or drawing room audience, but also evoked a satisfyingly tearful response from the intemperate patrons of the music halls. They may have affected the audience, but not the beer sales. Maybe the only cure for such heart-rending emotion is strong drink!

WRITTEN & COMPOSED BY HENRY CLAY WORK

1858

THE DEMON DRINK

Victorian social theorists considered drunkenness a major problem, especially amongst the urban "lower orders", many of whom doubtless discovered that a bottle of cheap gin was "the quickest way out of Manchester".

The Nonconformist conscience was particularly outraged by insobriety. Nonconformists fought the demon drink both through the emotional propaganda of the Temperance Movement and by political means, through their influence in the Liberal Party. Gladstone blamed his 1874 election defeat on the Licensing Act of 1872, which limited opening hours. "We are borne down by a torrent of gin and beer", he lamented when a Conservative distiller turned him out of his own constituency of Greenwich.

The Tory Home Secretary R. A. Cross, who was also active in trades union legislation, proceeded to ease licensing restrictions, provoking this comment from a grateful wag:
"For he's a jolly good fellow,
Whatever the Rads
    [Radicals] may think –
For he has shortened the
    hours of work
And lengthened the hours of
    drink."

poor bro-ther Ben-ny so sick in her arms, And no one to help her but me...... Come

home! come home! come home!... Please fa-ther, dear fa-ther, come home!....

2

Father, dear father, come home with me now
  The clock in the steeple strikes two ;
The night has grown colder and Benny is worse,
  But he has been calling for you.
Indeed he is worse, Ma says he will die,
  Perhaps before morning shall dawn !
And this is the message she sent me to bring—
  " Come quickly, or he will be gone."
          Come home, etc.

3

Father, dear father, come home with me now !
  The clock in the steeple strikes three :
The house is so lonely, the hours are so long
  For poor weeping mother and me.
Yes, we are alone, poor Benny is dead,
  And gone with the angels of light ;
And these were the very last words that he said
  " I want to kiss Father, good night."
          Come home, etc.

In the 1870s and 1880s the Temperance Movement mounted a campaign to beat the music halls at their own game by setting up temperance music halls. In 1880 the Old Vic was taken over and converted into the Royal Victoria Hall and Coffee Tavern (bottom left). The Great Central Hall, Bishopsgate, was another temperance hall, and in 1897 The Illustrated London News published a series of sketches publicizing its attractions (below).

In the top picture (1) a woman pays for a bottle of ginger ale from a refreshment counter. In the centre (2), a man recites from a suitably uplifting poem. On the centre left (3) a member of the audience signs the pledge that will bind him to a teetotal future. On the centre right (4) members of the audience quench their thirst with cups of tea – "the Cup which Cheers but not Inebriates", in the words of a copy-writer from the Old Vic. At the bottom (5) working men and their wives enjoy a comic song from a top-hatted entertainer. Buns and soft drinks are prominently on show.

In An Anxious Hour, painted by Alexander Farmer in 1865 and exhibited at the Royal Academy, a mother keeps watch over her feverish child as he lies asleep. At a time when child mortality was high, any ill-health was regarded with concern and this painting records just such a worrying moment.

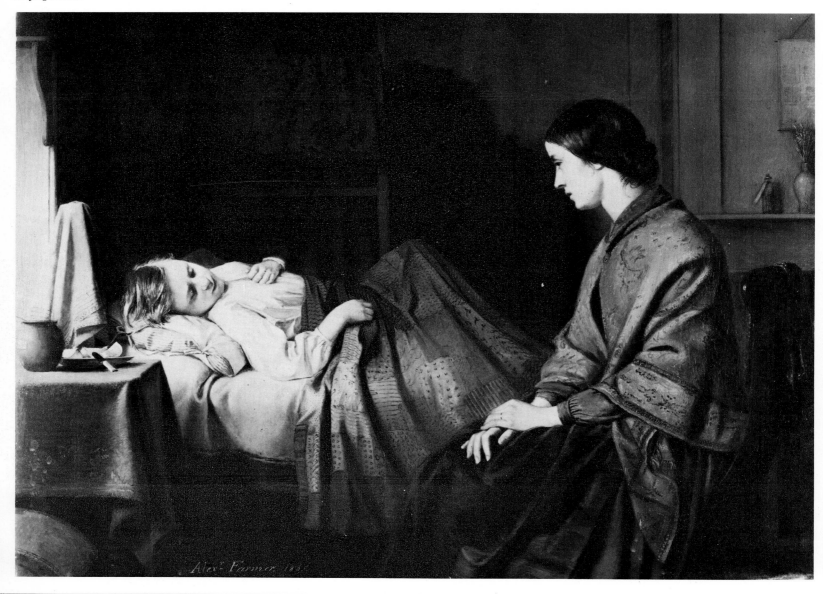

LOVE'S OLD SWEET SONG

When Clifton Bingham wrote a poem in 1882 containing the now familiar words "Just a song at twilight", he was inundated with offers from composers to set the piece to music. James Molloy, who put his offer in a telegram, beat them all to the gun, got the commission and wrote the haunting tune which turned a few lines of verse into an evergreen classic. Arthur Sullivan was once accused of using the first few bars of the tune in one of his operas. He shrugged it off by saying that there were only eight notes to choose from.

Molloy, who was born in Dublin in 1837, was by training a barrister, but neglected the law in favour of singing his own ballads at St. James's Hall in London. He was a thoroughly professional entertainer, polishing and revising up to the moment of performance. *The Kerry Dance* was another of his successes and embodies the same dreamlike nostalgic flavour which became his trademark.

Love's Old Sweet Song, however, was introduced to the public by a bigger name, the American-born soprano Antoinette Sterling. She was perhaps the most popular ballad singer of the day – Sullivan's *The Lost Chord* was written for her – and as such was able to claim the lion's share of the royalties from music publishers in return for her undoubted ability to ensure the success of their merchandise.

WRITTEN BY C. CLIFTON BINGHAM   **COMPOSED BY J. L. MOLLOY**   **1884**

**ANTOINETTE
STERLING**

The American soprano Madame Antoinette Sterling, portrayed here in the kind of prim, high-necked dress she insisted on wearing at her recitals, was the first to sing *Love's Old Sweet Song* in America where it was received with rapturous acclaim.

Born in New York State in the early 1840s she started singing in churches, studied in Paris and returned to New York City to sing German *lieder* as well as more popular songs. She made her English debut at a Promenade Concert in London in November 1873. A year later she sang before Queen Victoria. While she never appeared in music halls or even an opera house, she was a success at the more respectable concert halls. She lived in England until her death in the early 1900s.

Once in the dear dead days be-yond re-call, When on the world the

mists be-gan to fall, Out of the dreams that rose in hap-py throng

Low to our hearts Love sung an old sweet song; And in the dusk where

A NOTE ON PERFORMANCE

This is one of the very few songs in this book with even rudimentary pedal instructions. One of them says "*sempre Ped.*": a useful pointer. The Victorians used the pedal a hundred times in a song. It was, to quote the authorities, "the soul of the piano", "the accompanist's best friend".

But playing in the period style you have to look out for contrary indications: rests, *staccato* signs, lighter textures or crisper rhythms. By letting up on the pedal at the right spots you can successfully "orchestrate" the accompaniment.

The earnest pretensions of a musical soirée are gently mocked in this Punch *cartoon of the 1890s by George du Maurier. Entitled* Music At Home, *it has Jones, "an eligible Bachelor", tenderly whispering to the woman in yellow beside him: "I should have been Married long ago, if it hadn't been for too much Music! Whenever I'd screwed up my Pluck to the pitch of Popping the Question, somebody always began to Sing, and of course I had to –". His chatter is broken into by a chorus of "SHSHSHSHSH!" from annoyed bystanders.*

fell the firelight gleam, Softly it wove itself in _ to our dream.

a tempo.

Just a song at twilight, when the lights are low, And the flick'ring shadows

softly come and go, Tho' the heart be weary, sad the day and long,

Still to us at twi_light comes Love's old song, comes Love's old sweet song.

A NOTE ON THE MUSIC

This is a particularly bad example of the distortion that commonly marred Victorian sheet music. A common reason for a splayed or curved line was that the printer, having set up the type in the frame, would put the wedges in too tight, causing the whole page to bend.

A smart crowd attends a symphony concert at St. James's Hall in Regent Street, London, in an engraving from The Illustrated London News *of 10th April, 1858, the year the building opened. The hall had fine acoustics and served as the capital's principal concert venue until its closure in 1905. Ballad singers and, from the early 1880s, minstrel troupes, performed in a side hall.*

E _ ven to-day we hear Love's song of yore, Deep in our hearts it

dwells for e _ ver_more Foot_steps may fal _ _ter, weary grow the way,

Still we can hear it at the close of day, So till the end, when

life's dim shadows fall, Love will be found the sweetest song of all.

Just a song at twilight, when the lights are low, And the flick'ring

In an engraving by J. Cook, a Victorian family listens to the evening hymn sung by two of the children. In many well-to-do middle-class homes this was one of the few times of the day when children were allowed through from the nursery, well groomed and presented, to be with their parents.

THE · BABY · ON · THE · SHORE

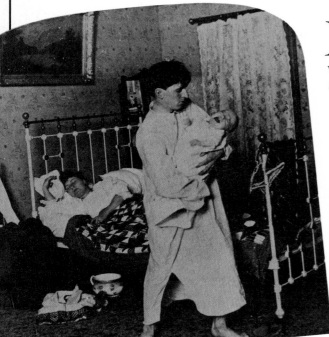

Macabre, witty and quirky, *The Baby On The Shore* is just one of the 600 songs and sketches the extraordinary entertainer George Grossmith wrote and performed in his remarkable career. It came from his musical sketch *How I Discovered America* and is a spoof on sentimental ballads in general and the American composer Stephen Foster (*page 81*) in particular.

Grossmith first came into prominence as John Wellington Wells in the Gilbert and Sullivan Opera *The Sorcerer*, produced by D'Oyly Carte at the Opera Comique in 1877. Never very ambitious, he was reluctant to take the part – firstly because he didn't think he was good enough, and secondly because he was quite happy doing solo performances of his own material at private houses and provincial clubs.

However, W. S. Gilbert managed to persuade him that he was needed and he stayed with the D'Oyly Carte Company for 12 years. In 1889 he managed to extricate himself and resumed his career as solo entertainer. After seven months on his own he had earned £10,000, while his salary with the D'Oyly Carte had been only £2,000 per year. Grossmith managed to be funny without stooping to vulgarity and appealed to all levels of society. In 1892 he and his brother Weeden completed one of the best loved books in the English language, *The Diary of a Nobody*.

In a scene punningly entitled A Knight of Labour!, a young husband lets his exhausted wife sleep while he takes his turn at pacifying the baby. This serio-comic tableau was staged in 1897 and photographed by Strohmeyer & Wymen of New York for use in a stereoscope – an optical device that allowed the viewer to gain a three-dimensional impression from two photographs taken from slightly different angles.

WRITTEN & COMPOSED BY GEORGE GROSSMITH

The phrase "the old folks at home" which George Grossmith slipped into his parody of ballads and minstrel songs is of course the title of one of Stephen Foster's most enduring songs. As this postcard depicts, The Old Folks At Home recounts the memories of a slave who has been sold and sent away far from his family.

On a postcard of around 1900, a dejected figure by the roadside dreams of his cottage on the banks of the Swanee River. By this time, the name Swanee River, taken from the central refrain of Foster's Old Folks At Home, had become the song's alternative title and butt of numerous parodies.

2 In the far, far west the sun was setting, Yes, setting as it never sat be-
3 The moon was slow-ly rising, Yes, rising as it never rose be-

-fore; We were thinking of the old folks at home, And we
-fore; We were feel-ing weary, ve-ry weary, And we

found the ba-by on the shore. Yes, we found the ba-by on the
sat up-on the ba-by on the shore. Yes, we sat up-on the ba-by on the

shore, A thing which we've nev-er done be-fore; So,
shore, A thing which we'd nev-er done be-fore; If you

This Raphael Tuck postcard of George Grossmith was personally autographed in ink by the songwriter, who established himself as one of the most popular society entertainers in late Victorian England. His autobiography of 1888 was aptly titled A Society Clown. He retired in 1908 and died in 1912 at the age of 65.

This illustration by Harry Fenn of the Porcupine Islands in Frenchman's Bay on the coast of Maine comes from Picturesque America, a descriptive survey edited by W. C. Bryant and published in 1894. Grossmith's musical impression of America, of which The Baby On The Shore forms part, was paralleled at this time by a nationwide interest in the geography of the United States, newly opened up by railroads and steam boats, and well produced travel books were much in vogue.

get...... the pipes and whiskey ready, And we'll feed the ba_by on the
see the mother, tell her gen_tly, That we sat upon her ba_by on the

shore. Yes, we'll feed the ba_by on the shore, A thing which we've never done be_
shore. The baby's qui_et_ly sleeping, A thing which it never did be_

fore; Oh, way down the old Swannee river, We will feed the ba_by on the
_fore; So, af_ter all it is better To leave the ba_by on the

shore. _____
shore. _____

A drawing of Leveson's New Imperial Car appeared in the English magazine The Sketch on 4th December, 1895, accompanied by a glowing account of this latest Victorian pram. The perambulator would, according to the article, "be greeted with delight by the nurse, for, owing to the novel arrangement of the shafts, she is brought nearer to the car, and has, therefore, more control over it, while, as it stands on all four wheels at once, it does not require tilting".

Sun-scorched palmettos cluster thickly around the mouth of the St. John's River, Florida, in an illustration from Picturesque America. The writer and artist negotiated Florida's inland waterways in a steamer whose "general outline was that of an ill-shaped omnibus" and whose "smoke-pipe, the engine, pilot-house, and all other of the usual gear of steamers, were housed, for the excellent reason of protecting them from being torn away by the overhanging limbs or protruding stumps everywhere to be met with in the narrow and difficult navigation of the swamps."

· ABIDE · WITH · ME ·

No collection of drawing room songs would be complete without a hymn or two, and this one has surely stood the test of time. The Rev. Henry Fromer Lyte wrote the words after witnessing the death of a close friend. The poem was discovered after his death in 1847 and published in 1850. It was set to the music of *Eventide* by William Henry Monk and became one of his many contributions to *Hymns Ancient and Modern*, published in 1861.

This great collection, which marked the late conversion of the Anglican Church to popular hymn singing, was not thoroughly revised until 1904; in those 53 years 60 million copies were sold.

Until well into the television age, *Abide With Me* was the finale of the Cup Final sing-along at Wembley Stadium conducted by "the man in the white suit", as he was always known, waving aloft his *Daily Express* songsheet. This charming tradition was eventually destroyed by the fans themselves who refused to join in, preferring their own supportive chants.

A postcard from the "Songs" series by Bamforth & Co. Ltd. illustrates the second verse of Abide With Me, *juxtaposing a sad little scene of earthly change and decay with the comfortable words: "O Thou who changest not, abide with me." Cards with religious themes were both varied and popular, icons brought by mass production to the faithful of the industrial revolution.*

"ABIDE WITH ME" (2).

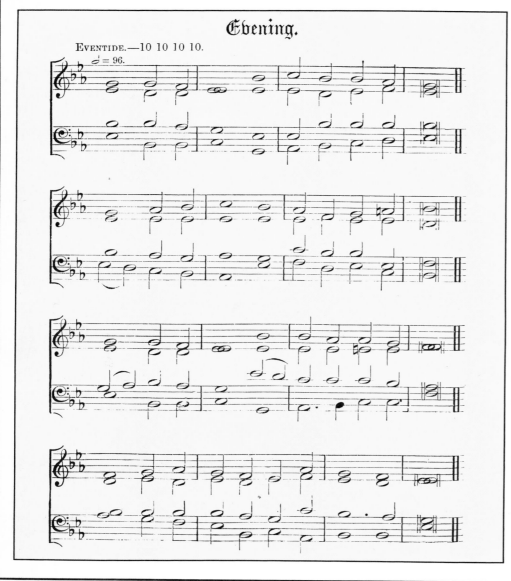

Evening.

EVENTIDE.—10 10 10 10.

♩ = 96.

WRITTEN BY REV. HENRY FRANCIS LYTE, c.1847
COMPOSED BY WILLIAM HENRY MONK, 1861

" Abide with us ; for it is toward evening, and the day is far spent."

mf ABIDE with me ; fast falls the éventide ;
      The darkness deepens ; Lord, with mé abide ;
      When other helpers fail, and cómforts flee,
f   Help of the helpless, *(p)* O abíde with me.

p   Swift to its close ebbs out life's líttle day ;
      Earth's joys grow dim, its glories páss away ;
      Change and decay in all aróund I see ;
mf O Thou, Who changest not, *(p)* abíde with me.

mf I need Thy Presence every pássing hour ;
cr What but Thy grace can foil the témpter's power ?
      Who like Thyself my guide and stáy can be ?
f   Through cloud and sunshine, Lord, *(p)* abíde with me.

f   I fear no foe with Thee at hánd to bless ;
      Ills have no weight, and tears no bítterness ;
      Where is death's sting ? Where, Grave, thy víctory ?
      I triumph still, if Thou abíde with me.

p   Hold Thou Thy Cross before my clósing eyes ;
cr Shine through the gloom, and point me tó the skies ;
f   Heav'n's morning breaks, and earth's vain shádows flee ;
      In life, *(p)* in death, O Lord, *(cr)* abíde with me.

A - men.

·ETERNAL·FATHER,· STRONG·TO·SAVE·

Waves threaten a sailing ship in a scene taken from the long-running series, The Musical Bouquet. *Published by Sheard & Co. from 1846 until they were taken over by the Herman Darewski Music Publishing Company in 1918, the series finally contained thousands of titles which were sold in numbered songsheets for – in 1900 – a mere 3d. a copy. Many people had them bound in large volumes.*

John Bacchus Dykes was memorably christened after the Roman god of wine in Hull in 1823 (begging comparison with another prominent Victorian, the Rev. Dionysius Lardner, author of a standard history of the steam engine, whose parents apparently preferred the equivalent Greek god). Forty years later Dykes, while Precentor of Durham Cathedral, wrote *Melita*, the tune to Eternal Father. With words by William Whiting, it has become known as the Navy's Hymn. It has a timeless appeal which was recognized by no less a composer than Benjamin Britten when he incorporated it as the stirring climax of his setting of the medieval play *Noye's Fludde*. Dykes was a prolific composer. When *Hymns Ancient and Modern* was being compiled, he submitted seven tunes. They were immediately accepted and more were requested. In the end at least 60 tunes by Dykes were included. Six remain in the modern version of the hymn book: Eternal Father, *Holy, Holy, Holy, Jesu Lover Of My Soul, Nearer My God To Thee, O Come And Mourn* and *Our Blest Redeemer*.

WRITTEN BY WILLIAM WHITING
COMPOSED BY REV. JOHN BACCHUS DYKES 1861

"These men see the works of the Lord, and His wonders in the deep."

mf ETERNAL FATHER, strong to save,
    Whose arm hath bound the restless wave,
    Who bidd'st the mighty ocean deep
    Its own appointed limits keep ;
p   O hear us *(cr)* when we cry to Thee
dim   For those in peril on the sea.

mf O CHRIST, Whose voice the waters heard
p   And hush'd their raging at Thy word,
cr   Who walkedst on the foaming deep,
dim And calm amid the storm didst sleep ;
p   O hear us *(cr)* when we cry to Thee
dim   For those in peril on the sea.

mf O HOLY SPIRIT, Who didst brood
    Upon the waters dark and rude,
    And bid their angry tumult cease,
    And give, for wild confusion, *(p)* peace;
    O hear us *(cr)* when we cry to Thee
dim   For those in peril on the sea.

mf O TRINITY of love and power,
    Our brethren shield in danger's hour ;
    From rock and tempest, fire and foe,
    Protect them wheresoe'er they go ;
cr   Thus evermore shall rise to Thee
f   Glad hymns of praise from land and sea.

A - men.

For those at Sea.

MELITA.—8 8 8 8 8 8.
♩ = 80.

THE · HOLY · CITY ·

This wonderful stirring tune was composed by a well known baritone of the day, Michael Maybrick. He also composed *Star Of Bethlehem*, both works being published under the pseudonym, Stephen Adams. The words to *The Holy City* were by Frederic Weatherly, a versatile lyricist whose best known works include *Thora, Nirvana, Roses Of Picardy* and the definitive words to *The Londonderry Air, Oh Danny Boy*, published in 1913 and sadly, therefore, outside the scope of this book.

Edward Lloyd, a great Wagnerian tenor of the day, often included *The Holy City* in his concerts.

The 50-foot high Tower of David, capped by a 17th-century minaret, rises above a crusader citadel in this lyrical view of Jerusalem's Old City by the English topographical artist David Roberts. Based on drawings he made during his trip to the Middle East in 1838, the lithograph was published in July 1841 in the first of six huge volumes entitled Holy Land, Egypt and Nubia.

WRITTEN BY F. E. WEATHERLY

COMPOSED BY STEPHEN ADAMS 1892

Last night I lay a sleep_ing, There came a dream so fair, I

One of the most heartfelt of religious poems, later turned into a popular hymn, was Lead, Kindly Light, written by the one-time vicar of St. Mary's Church, Oxford, Cardinal Newman (1801-90). On this postcard the words are given a crude Messianic flavour by an over-dramatic scene with an idealized heavenly city in the background. They were actually written to express the crisis of faith which Newman suffered after a near-fatal fever in Sicily in 1833.

Hush'd were the glad Ho-sau-nas The lit-tle chil-dren sang. The

sun grew dark with mys-te-ry, The morn was cold and chill, As the

sha-dow of a cross a-rose Up-on a lone-ly hill, As the

cantabile

sha-dow of a cross a-rose Up-

rall:

-on a lone-ly hill. Je-

D. %

The singing of sacred songs at Christmas and throughout the year involved children from an early age, offering plenty of opportunity for talent to shine. Michael Maybrick, composer of The Holy City, was one of many infant prodigies who emerged from the thriving world of Victorian music. He was appointed organist of St. Peter's, Liverpool, at the young age of 14.

SACRED AND NOT SO SACRED MUSIC

Church music and the organ have been intimately related since the Middle Ages. Surprisingly, the organ's relationship with popular, secular music goes back almost as far.

During the Civil War of the 1640s, when the Puritan objection to elaborate church music was at its height, organs were among "superstitious monuments" removed from churches. These organs were bought by tavern keepers, and so laid the early foundations of music hall in the pubs.

A French traveller complained: "They have translated the organs out of the Churches to set them up in taverns, chaunting their dithyrambics and bestial bacchanalias to the tune of those instruments which were wont to assist them in the celebration of God's praises".

Oliver Cromwell, who liked music anywhere except in church, removed the organ from Magdalen College, Oxford, to Hampton Court where he employed an organist to teach his daughter and play for his own pleasure.

During the Victorian period organs not only came back into the churches but reached an apex of popularity in concert halls and middle-class homes, reflecting the religious flavour of so much polite singing.

The reed organ or harmonium, like the piano, was widely bought for home music making. Some families had one of each instrument. This heavily ornate, solid black, walnut Windsor Organ six feet nine inches high was advertised in the 1895 sales catalogue of Montgomery Ward & Co., Chicago, the largest mail order business in the United States, "supplying every trade and calling on earth".

In an 1841 lithograph by David Roberts entitled Mount Calvary, priests of the Church of the Holy Sepulchre in Jerusalem assemble in a chapel built on the presumed site of the Crucifixion. According to legend, Christ's cross stood in a hole under the altar, rimmed with a circlet of gold, and two holes on either side held the crosses of the thieves who were crucified with him.

·THE·LOST·CHORD·

Frederick Sullivan, who sang the part of the judge in the first Gilbert and Sullivan comic opera *Trial by Jury*, died at the early age of 39. During the vigil at his bedside, his brother Arthur was inspired to compose the tune of *The Lost Chord*, based on a poem by Adelaide Proctor who also died young in 1864.

By a surprising coincidence, shortly after the tune was written, the soprano Antoinette Sterling called on Sullivan with a copy of the same poem and said, "Why not set this to music?" Sullivan was able to deliver on the spot what has come to be regarded as the archetypal Victorian ballad.

Musically the words "I struck one chord of music, Like the sound of a great Amen" are nonsense: it takes more than one chord to make an Amen. But as Sullivan said, there is only one *Lost Chord*, and it earned him royalties of about £10,000.

This edition of the song was available in as many as five different keys, from E flat to A, to suit every possible voice – an indication of its enormous popularity.

WRITTEN BY ADELAIDE A. PROCTOR, 1858   COMPOSED BY ARTHUR SULLIVAN, 1877

As the flowery typographical cover of the songsheet indicates, this edition of The Lost Chord in F came with an optional harmonium part which added greatly to the effect. For reasons of space the entire accompaniment has not been printed here; in any case, where are the homes now with both piano and harmonium?

COMPOSER'S FOOTNOTE
The pedal marks should be very carefully observed.

A pen and ink drawing from Melody Magazine of 1896 depicts a Gothic church. The Gothic of the Middle Ages, according to leading critics and architects such as Ruskin and Pugin, had been the supreme architecture. The Victorian revival set the stamp of Gothic on everything from churches to parlour organs.

COMPOSER'S FOOTNOTE
When harmonium accompaniment is also used, the pianoforte is silent from this mark ✽ in page [56] to this mark ✽ in page [57].

cresc: — — — — — — — *dim:*

Psalm, And it lay on my fe_ver'd spi _ _ _ rit, With a

cresc: — — — — — — — *dim:* — — — —

Ped | ✳

touch of in_fi_nite calm, It qui_et_ed pain and

cresc: — — — — — — *dim:*

sor _ row, Like love o_ver_com_ing strife It

cresc: — — — — — — — *dim:*

seem'd the har_mo_nious e _ _ _ cho From our dis_cord_ant life, It

p *P tranquillo.*

tranquillo sempre.

link'd all per_plex_ed meanings, In_to one per_fect peace, And

An angel of glad tidings, accompanied by two others, holds "a robe of light" in an illustration from The Strand Musical Magazine *of January 1895. Published monthly, the magazine presented a varied line-up of songs, piano pieces, interviews with musicians and articles for a broad readership at a modest price of sixpence.*

THE LOST CHORD (2).
It flooded the crimson twilight,
Like the close of an Angel psalm,
And it lay on my wearied spirit.

A celestial hierarchy of angels floods the church in this tinted 1907 postcard of The Lost Chord, *giving it a veneer of religious experience. The angel figured strongly in Victorian iconography, symbolizing a palatable image of divinity, or at least, of virtue incarnate.*

poco a poco piu animato.

trembled a_way in_to si_lence, As if it were loth to

cresc: *animato.*

agitato.

cease; I have sought, but I seek it vain_ly, That

agitato.

one lost chord di__vine, Which came from the soul of the

or_gan, And en__ter'd in__to mine.

cresc:____ molto ____

Grandioso.

It may be that Death's bright An_gel, Will

____ ritard: *ff*

speak in that chord a_gain; It may be that on_ly in

Heav'n, I shall hear that grand - A _ men. It

may be that Death's bright An _ _ _ gel, will speak in that chord a _ _

_gain It may be that on _ ly in Heav'n I shall hear that

grand A _ _ men...........

The success of The Lost Chord *gave postcard publishers a field day, as this wonderful example shows, to indulge in orgies of posed photography. The result was reminiscent of, but laughably inferior to, the classical and Byzantine paintings of artists like Sir Lawrence Alma-Tadema.*

THE·SONG·AND·SUPPER·ERA

The form of entertainment known as music hall did not acquire its name until about 1850 when Charles Morton and others like him built halls on to their pubs in order to present organized evening performances. But many elements of music hall had been in existence long before. Street singers, drawing-room ballad singers, makeshift theatres known as penny gaffs, pleasure gardens and tavern glee clubs or "free and easies" all generated songs and comic turns which provided material for the early music halls.

During the first 15 years or so of Victoria's reign there were some 250 glee and ballad singers in the streets of London. They sang songs from cheaply printed "broadsides", written about events such as a sensational murder or public execution, told in doggerel and set to a traditional tune, or else relied on "nigger" songs, sailor's songs, patriotic songs and even French songs – *The Marseillaise* was particularly popular.

But by the 1840s cheap entertainment was already moving indoors, to pubs and to the song and supper rooms where the young gentlemen of the town gathered to dine, drink and join in the bawdy entertainment provided by the landlord, who also acted as chairman and chucker-out. The most famous of these song and supper rooms was Evans's in Covent Garden. The notorious Cider Cellars and Coal Hole nearby produced many songs that were consigned to the Victorian moralists' bonfire as well as some, like *Sam Hall* and *Villikins And His Dinah*, which went on to become music hall successes.

Staged eruptions of a model Mount Vesuvius, firework displays and concerts were among the entertainments provided in the 15-acre Surrey Zoological Gardens in Kennington, south London.

· SHE · WAS · POOR, · · BUT · SHE · WAS · HONEST ·

This is probably one of the most successful anonymous songs in the world. The tune repeats throughout the verses and the chorus, and is therefore exceptionally easy to pick up. The words have been parodied again and again. From the many versions available we have chosen a set of verses which gives a good clear story line.

The story is a burlesque melodrama of the kind so popular with 19th-century street singers. Unlike the better-off, who took their tragedy very seriously, the poor had to laugh at their troubles. They had no other cushion against disaster. Most of the songs in this section deal with death, ruin, poverty, suicide, unrequited love – and all were billed as comic songs.

Poor but honest factory girls gather outside the mill in The Dinner Hour, *painted by Eyre Crowe in 1874. For most of the century factory work, domestic service or marriage were the only alternatives to that much damned but widespread Victorian calling, a life of sin and shame.*

TRADITIONAL   **ARRANGED BY DAVID WYKES, 1984**

She was poor, but she was

Moderato

PIANO

FORTE

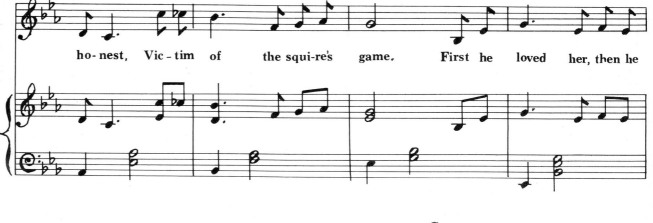

ho-nest, Vic-tim of the squi-re's game. First he loved her, then he

left her, And she lost her ho-nest name. "It's the same the whole world

CHORUS

o - ver, It's the poor what gets the blame. It's the rich what gets the

plea-sure Ain't it all a bleed-in' shame?"

last time

shame. Ain't it all a bleed - in' shame?"

A NOTE ON PERFORMANCE

The large number of short verses in pre-music hall songs of this kind, and the simplicity of the music, tempt the pianist into varying the accompaniment to suit the action. *She Was Poor, But She Was Honest*, with its quick inter-cutting between gutter and grandeur, urban corruption and country idyll, and its mock-melodramatic suicide, offers more temptation than most. The story moves more quickly if the chorus is not repeated after every single verse. One satisfactory solution is to sing the chorus after every two verses.

Any girl who threw herself off Westminster Bridge in 1872, the year Gustave Doré published this engraving, would have had little chance of survival. Despite improvements, the River Thames was still heavily polluted with the London sewage which, during the hot summer of 1858, caused such a stench that river traffic had to be suspended and Parliament adjourned.

2.

Then she ran away to London,
For to hide her grief and shame,
There she met another squire,
And she lost her name again.

3.

See her riding in her carriage,
In the park and all so gay.
All the nibs and nobby persons
Come to pass the time of day.

4.

See the little old world village
Where her aged parents live,
Drinking champagne what she sends 'em,
But they never can forgive.

5.

In the rich man's arms she flutters,
Like a bird with broken wing.
First he loved her, then he left her,
And she hasn't got a ring.

6.

See him in his splendid mansion,
Entertaining with the best
While the girl what he has ruined,
Entertains a sordid guest.

7.

See him in the House of Commons,
Making laws to put down crime,
While the victim of his passion,
Trails her way through mud and slime.

8.

See him riding in his carriage,
Past the gutter where she stands.
He has made a stylish marriage,
While she wrings her ringless hands.

9.

Standing on the bridge at midnight,
She cries, "Farewell blighted love".
There's a scream—a splash—Good Heavens!
What is she a-doing of?

10.

Then they dragged her from the river,
Water from her clothes they wrang.
For they thought that she was drownded,
But the corpse got up and sang:

It's the same the, &c.

· SAM · HALL ·

The drama of a man condemned to death for murder is told in the first person. It gives his story, from his conviction and incarceration to his dreadful journey in a cart to the gallows at Tyburn. The fact that he is almost illiterate, unable to articulate more than a few words at a time, interspersed with curses against those who brought him to the final degradation, gives this song an uncanny power and strength. There is no trace of the glamorous Robin Hood or Dick Turpin image. Sam Hall is just a wretched human animal going to legal slaughter in front of a gaping crowd.

There were many earlier versions of this song. In one, the protagonist was Jack Hall, condemned to death for selling candles short of weight, and the original was about Captain Kidd, the early 18th-century pirate who did exist and did hang. But it is Sam Hall who lives on, thanks to the performance of W. G. Ross. Ross was an unsuccessful actor until he leapt into prominence in the Cyder Cellars with this number. His face blackened so that he resembled an unshaven chimney sweep, he sat astride a chair, his hands gripping the back of it like prison bars, and snarled and spat out the words, demonstrating in an electrifying way the horror of public executions. Ross was offered other roles in the legitimate theatre, but he never threw off the infamous character he had created and he never sang his song in the music halls.

TRADITIONAL   **ARRANGED BY DAVID WYKES, 1984**

2.

I killed a man they said, so they said,
I killed a man they said, so they said,
I hit him on the head with a bloody great lump of lead,
And I left him there for dead, Damn his eyes!

3.

They put me into quod, into quod,
They put me into quod, into quod.
They put me into quod and they tied me to a log,
And they left me there by God, Damn their eyes!

4.

Oh the preacher, he did come, he did come.
Oh the preacher, he did come, he did come.
Oh the preacher, he did come and he talked of kingdom come.
He can kiss my bloody bum, Damn his eyes!

5.

I goes up Holborn Hill in a cart,
I goes up Holborn Hill in a cart.
I goes up Holborn Hill, at St. Giles I takes my gill,
And at Tyburn makes my will, Damn my eyes!

6.

Oh the hangman, he comes too, he comes too.
Oh the hangman, he comes too, he comes too.
Oh the hangman, he comes too with all his bloody crew.
And he tells them what to do, Blast their eyes!

7.

So it's up the steps I go, wery slow,
So it's up the steps I go, wery slow,
So it's up the steps I go and you bastards down below
All standing in a row, Damn your eyes!

8.

I sees Molly in the crowd, in the crowd,
I sees Molly in the crowd, in the crowd.
I sees Molly in the crowd, and I hollers out aloud,
"Molly ain't you bleedin' proud?" Damn your eyes!

9.

So this shall be my knell, be my knell.
So this shall be my knell, be my knell.
This is my funeral knell, and I'll see you all in hell
And I hopes you frizzles well, Damn your eyes!

As a mixed quartet of glee singers performs on stage, a waiter serves his customers with hot punch, brandy or bottled beer at Evans's Song and Supper Room in King Street, Covent Garden. Evans's in its early days was a late-night haunt of bucks and rakes and the entertainment, according to a theatre historian of the 1890s, consisted of songs "of the erotic and Bacchanalian order". But by 1864, when this print was published, the bill had been sufficiently cleaned up for women to be admitted to the auditorium.

A famous New Smutty Song.

Air—THE UMBRELLA COURTSHIP.

'Twas on a summer's night, O dear,
   That, far away from home,
Susan the milkmaid did repair
   To the meadows with young Tom.
As they tripped it light, along,
   Tom felt in such a glow,
He longed to—do a certain thing;
   But she said, "No, No, No!"

"Oh, you cruel maid," said Tom,
   "My passion to defy!
You've set my blood in such a glow,
   I'm certain I shall die;
Only just taste a little bit,
   You needn't swallow all, you know.
Besides, there's no one here to see!
   Shall I?"—Still 'twas "No, No, No!"

Thus they walked up to a hill,
   Which Tom, so frisky, raced her down;
But, luckless maid, her foot it slipped,
   And all her little charms were shown.
Tom could not this sight resist;
   But by her side himself did throw,
And put a something in her fist;
   But still she answered, "No, No, No!"

"Oh, get you gone!" the damsel cried,
   This monstrous form fills me with dread;
And what would mother say," she sighed,
   "If I should lose my maidenhead?"
"You silly girl," the swain replied,
   "To praise you she could not be slow;
For, I'm sure, if she saw one like this,
   She would not answer 'No, No, No!'"

Susan now grew still more tender,
   As Colin's treasure met her sight;
Half inclined to surrender,
   And in his arms to seek delight.
Colin saw her, panting, throbbing,
   And in his arms her form did press;
And when she once had tasted Robin,
   Her tune was changed to "Yes, yes, yes!"

After the first round was done,
   Susan, panting, longing, lay;
And said, "I do so like the fun,
   I wish at it you'd once more play!"
Full six times they'd it in clover,
   And Susan really liked it so,
She fairly tired Colin over.
   Who was forced to cry out "No, No, No!"

Entitled Colin And Susan, this is an example of the bawdy songs popular in the song and supper rooms. It comes from a set of erotic songbooks published in the 1830s which were found in the British Museum in the 1970s.

Two bills publicize different entertainments at the Cyder Cellars, a stifling underground tavern likened in its day to the Black Hole of Calcutta. The harmonic meeting (far left) was an occasion for bawdy song-singing. The other bill (left) advertises one of the infamous Judge and Jury trials. These burlesque lawsuits originated in Dublin and were brought to London in 1841. They concerned "cases" of rape and general sexual depravity, with male actors playing the parts of both sexes and the public acting as the jury, and were one of the reasons the Cyder Cellars had such a bad name.

·VILLIKINS·AND· ·HIS·DINAH·

Villikins (cockney dialect for Wilkins, and capable of various spellings) is the ill-starred lover of the equally ill-starred Dinah. By the end of the song they have both been laid to rest in the same grave. Adapted from an old street ballad dating from before Elizabethan times, Villikins is a burlesque melodrama parodying the Victorian obsession with blighted love and unnatural death.

The first singer was Frederick Robson, a well known actor who was famous for his lightning changes of mood from comic to pathetic. Robson told this story of cruelty, anguish, suicide and despair in such a way that it had the audience convulsed with laughter. It is said that he would stop in mid-sentence and remark gravely, "This is not a comic song," which encouraged the audience to fresh paroxysms of laughter.

The tune is well known in America as *Sweet Betsy From Pike*, a song sung by professional entertainers who toured the mining camps in the California Gold Rush of 1849.

In an engraving taken from an original photograph by Herbert Watkins of Regent Street, Frederick Robson is dressed in the formal if flamboyant style suited to an established actor. He first made his mark at the Grecian Saloon, in the pleasure gardens of the Eagle Tavern, Islington, starring in selections from Shakespeare as well as in melodramas and comediettas. One of these, The Wandering Minstrel, *transferred to the Royal Olympic Theatre and the Canterbury Hall in 1853 with* Villikins And His Dinah *among its numbers, and it was then that Robson brought the song to popular attention.*

TRADITIONAL

CON GUSTO, AND RATHER RITOORALLANDO.

mf

It is of a rich merchant I am going for to tell, Who had for a daughter an un-kimmon nice young gal; Her name it was Di-nah, just sixteen years old, With a wer-ry large for-tin in sil-i-ver and gold. Singe-in, Too-ral-li, too-ral-li, too-ral-li, da.

Chorus. (Which I sings by myself.)

Singe-in, Too-ral-li, too-ral-li, too-ral-li, da.

Singe-in, Too-ral-li, too-ral-li, too-ral-li, da.

Singe-in, Too-ral-li, too-ral-li, too-ral-li, da.

W. HOLLAND

William Holland, best known as the manager of the Canterbury Hall (pp. 92 and 93), also promoted the North Woolwich Gardens with its concert hall, scenic lake, maze and zoo – although all he mentions in this publicity handout is the Aquarian Clown and four geese! Such places were modelled on the 18th and early-19th century pleasure gardens at Vauxhall, Ranelagh and Cremorne where Londoners could enjoy a high standard of music, singing, dancing and fireworks.

II.

Now, as Dinah was a wal-i-king in the garding one day,
Spoken—(The front garding.)
The father comed up to her, and thus to her did say :—
'Go, dress yourself, Dinah, in gor-ge-us array,
(Take your hair out of paper.)
And I'll bring you home a hus-i-band both gal-li-ant and gay.'
Singein too-ral-li, &c.

Chorus. (In favour of the parient's desire, and the wedding-breakfast he was about to order of the pastry-cook round the corner.)
Too-ral-li, &c.

III.

Spoken.—Now this is what the daughter said to the prophetic parient, in reply.
'Oh, father, dear father,' the daughter she said,
'I don't feel incli-ned to be mar-ri-ed ;
And all my large fortin' I'll gladly give o'er,
If you'll let me live single a year or two more.'
Singein too-ral-li, &c.

(Wheedling and persuasive Chorus on behalf of the offspring's remonstrance to the author of her being.) Too-ral-li, &c.

IV.

Spoken.—Now this here is what the paternal parient said agin to the daughter, and tells you what the parricidal papa parenthetically and paregorically pronounced, with all the parabolical particulars.
'Go, go! boldest daughter,' the parient he cried,
'If you don't feel incli-ned to be this young man's bride,
Spoken confidentially—(He was a merchant pieman from Abyssinia, and exported baked taturs to Timbuctoo for the Hottentots.)
I'll give all your large fortin to the nearest of kin,
And you shan't reap the benefit not of one single pin.
Singein (In a Californian tone) too-ral-li, &c.

Chorus (of the enraged parient against his progeny)—
Too-ral-li, &c.

V.

Spoken. Now this is the most melancholy part of it, and shows what the progeny was druv to in consikvence of the mangled obstropolosness and ferocity of the inconsiderable parient.
Now, as Willikind was a wal-i-king the garding all round,
Spoken—(This was the back garding)
He spied his dear Dinah laying dead upon the ground,
With a cup of cold pison all down by her side,
And a billet-dow, which said as how—'twas by pison she died.
Spoken—(The label was marked 'British Brandy.')
Singein too-ral-li, &c.

(Mournful and desponding Chorus of the sympathizing sparrows, the sad and smoke-dried spectators of this malignant and misanthropic case of unfortunate severicide.)
Too-ral-li, &c.

VI.

Spoken. This here is what the lovyer did on the diskivery
Then he kissed her cold corper-ses a thousand times o'er,
And called her his dear Dinah, though she was no more ;
Then he swallowed up the pison, and sung a short stave—
Spoken—(Neither agreed with him.)
And Willikind and his Dinah were laid in one grave.
Singein (together) too-ral-li, &c.

(Dismal duplicated Chorus, in consequence of the double event.)
Too-ral-li, &c.

MORI-AL.

Now, all you young men, don't you thus fall in love, nor
Do that not by no means disliked by your guv'nor ;
And, all you young maidens, mind who you claps your eyes on
Think of Willikind and his Dinah—not forgetting the pison
Singein too-ral-li, &c.

Moral Chorus—(Powerfully impressed.) Too-ral-li, &c.

In this vignette drawn for the cover of a dance variation, the Vilikins and Dinah Waltz & the Vilikins Galop, *Frederick Robson appears as Jem Bags, the lead part in Mayhew's comedietta* The Wandering Minstrel. *Scenes of parental authority and suicidal remorse provide suitable illustrations to complete the melancholy triptych.*

"*The Rising Generation taking their lessons*" *was the artist's caption to this scene inside a penny theatre, or gaff. Frequented by children as young as eight, such places were the rough end of the market, "where juvenile Poverty meets juvenile Crime", as Blanchard Jerrold and Gustave Doré put it in their* London. A Pilgrimage. *Salacious songs, grotesque imitations of the West End swell and caricatures of the police were the chief fare, enlivened with pickpocketing and good-humoured rioting in the pit and boxes.*

GARDENS OF DELIGHT

Many of London's outdoor amusements from the late 17th to 19th centuries centred on the grand pleasure gardens which grew up on what was then the rural periphery of the capital.

The first to open, in 1661, was Vauxhall Gardens, just south of the Thames, where acres of leafy, lamp-lit walks, arbours, music and refreshments set the pattern for future gardens.

In the evenings, shows of a music-hall style were put on in the Rotunda, a large circular building decorated inside with mirrors, chandeliers and statuary.

Vauxhall was seriously rivalled between 1742 and 1803 by the fashionable Ranelagh Gardens, laid out in 1690 next to the Royal Hospital in Chelsea. Concerts and masquerades held in its own galleried Rotunda, 185 feet across, drew a more elegant society. Visitors included Dr Johnson and, in 1764, the eight-year-old Mozart; such was the Rotunda's fame that it was painted by Canaletto. His picture now hangs in the National Gallery.

The last of the famous pleasure gardens, Cremorne Gardens, opened in 1845 on the site now occupied by Lots Road power station, west of Battersea Bridge. It lasted until 1877, 14 years after the Vauxhall gardens had closed.

EXTRA VERSES, only recently recovered from the original Chaldean MSS. in the British Museum.

Spoken.—Now, this is the superlatively supernatural wisitation which appeared to the parient at midnight, after the *disease* of his only progeny.

(Phantasmagorean and sepulchral Chorus, to astonish the weak nerves of the parient.)

IX.

Spoken.—The Parient's fate, and what he thought he would do, but didn't.

Now the parient was struck with a horror of home,
So he packed up his portmanteau, all around the world to roam;
But, as he was starting, he was seized with a shiver,
Which shook him to pieces, and ended him for iver.

Spoken.—And those who came to pick up the bits could only sing   Too-ral-li, &c.

(Sympathetic Chorus for the parient's fragments, though the verdict was 'Sarved him right.')   Too-ral-li, &c.

X.

Spoken.—Now this is not a comic song, you will observe, so we will take a return-ticket back again to the subject, and finish with

ANOTHER MORI-AL—NUMBER TWO.

Now the moral is this—number one is not reckon'd—
So this is the first moral, though it comes second:—
You may learn from my song, which is true, ev'ry word,
All this wouldn't have happened if it hadn't have occurr'd.

Spoken.—And there would have been no occasion for singe-in   Too-ral-li, &c.
Nor for the comprehensive and categorically conclusive Chorus of   Too-ral-li, &c.

The RATCATCHER'S DAUGHTER.

The Serio-Comic Ballad,

Immortalized by PUNCH.

ARRANGED, WITH HARMONIZED CHORUS,

FOR THE

PIANOFORTE.

LONDON: PUBLISHED BY C. SHEARD, MUSICAL BOUQUET OFFICE 192, HIGH HOLBORN.

CITY WHOLESALE AGENTS; E. W. ALLEN, 11, AVE MARIA LANE; & F. PITMAN, 20, PATERNOSTER ROW.

THE·RATCATCHER'S· ·DAUGHTER·

Unlike the cover on the previous page, which features the pretty sprat seller and her lover, this songsheet illustration by W. A. Barrett portrays the rakish ratcatcher himself, a Dickensian figure complete with cudgel and black eye and, in the surrounding heraldic device, a trapped rat. Sometimes a ratcatcher would have a tamed rat nestling in his coat pocket or running about his shoulders.

Using the cockney dialect popularized by Charles Dickens, this doleful ditty tells the story of two costermongers, she a seller of sprats and he of lily white sand (for bird cages, knife cleaning and suchlike), who fall in love and meet a sad end. The lyrics are by a clergyman, the Rev. E. Bradley, and the tune is ascribed to the song's first singer, Sam Cowell. It is probably an adaptation of an earlier song sung in the supper rooms of Covent Garden in the 1820s.

A free and easy character, Cowell was noted for his unpunctuality. But no matter how late he arrived, his audience gave him an ovation. The manager of Evans's Song and Supper Room was infuriated. Finally, his patience exhausted, he shouted to the audience, "You have made Mr Cowell your god, gentlemen, but by God he shan't be mine", and dismissed him.

Cowell went straight to the Canterbury Hall where Charles Morton was willing to pay £30 a week instead of the 30s. paid by Evans.

WRITTEN BY REV. E. BRADLEY   **TRADITIONAL**

Not long a-go, in Vestminstier, There liv'd a rat-catcher's daughter,—But she didn't quite live in Vestminstier, 'Cause she liv'd t'other side of the va-ter;—Her father caught rats, and she sold sprats, All round and about that quar-ter; And the gentlefolks all took off their hats, To the put-ty lit-tle ratcatcher's

A young street musician entertains a little audience in a back street in 1875. Henry Mayhew in his London Labour and the London Poor divided street musicians into two classes: "the tolerable and the intolerable". Some were skilled players, others sought merely to attract attention and solicit money.

daughter! Doodle dee! doodle dum! di dum doo-dle da!

2ND VERSE

She vore no 'at upon 'er 'ead,
 No cap nor dandy bonnet,
The 'air of 'er 'ead all 'ung down her back,
 Like a bunch of carrots upon it;
Ven she cried 'Sprats!' in Vestminstier,
 She 'ad such a sweet loud woice, sir,
You could hear her all down Parliament Street,
 As far as Charing-Cross, sir!
                    Doodle dee, &c.

3RD VERSE

Now, rich and poor, both far and near,
 In matrimony sought her;
But at friends and foes she turn'd up her nose,
 Did the putty little ratcatcher's daughter.
For there was a man, sold lily-vite sand,
 In Cupid's net had caught her;
And right over head and ears in love
 Vent the putty little ratcatcher's daughter!
                    Doodle dee, &c.

4TH VERSE

Now lily-vite sand so ran in her 'ead,
 As she vent along the Strand, oh!
She forgot as she'd got sprats on her 'ead,
 And cried, 'D'ye vant any lily-vite sand, oh!'
The folks, amaz'd, all thought her craz'd,
 As she vent along the Strand, oh!
To see a gal vith sprats on her 'ead
 Cry, 'D'ye vant any lily-vite sand, oh!'
                    Doodle dee, &c.

5TH VERSE

Now ratcatcher's daughter so ran in his 'ead,
 He could't tell vat he was arter,
So, instead of crying 'D'ye vant any sand!'
 He cried, 'D'ye vant any ratcatcher's darter?'
His donkey cock'd his ears and laughed,
 And couldn't think vat he was arter,
Ven he heard his lily-vite sandman cry,
 'D'ye vant any ratcatcher's darter?'
                    Doodle dee, &c.

6TH VERSE

They both agreed to married be
 Upon next Easter Sunday,
But Ratcatcher's daughter she had a dream
 That she wouldn't be alive on Monday;
She vent vunce more to buy some sprats,
 And she tumbled into the vater,
And down to the bottom, all kiver'd up vith mud,
 Vent the putty little ratcatcher's daughter!*
                    Doodle dee, &c.

*Considering the state of the Thames at the present moment,
what must she have swallowed?

7TH VERSE

Ven Lily-vite Sand 'e 'eard the news,
 His eyes ran down with vater,
Said 'e 'In love I'll constant prove;
 And—-blow me if I'll live long arter.'
So he cut 'is throat vith a pane of glass,
 And stabb'd 'is donkey arter!
So 'ere is an end of Lily-vite Sand,
 Donkey, and the ratcatcher's daughter!
                    Doodle dee, &c.

8TH VERSE

The neighbours all, both great and small,
 They flocked unto 'er berrein',
And vept that a gal who'd cried out sprats,
 Should be dead as any herrein'.
The Corioner's Inquest on her sot,
 At the sign of the Jack i' the Vater,
To find what made life's sand run out
 Of the putty little ratcatcher's daughter!
                    Doodle dee, &c.

9TH VERSE

The verdict was that too much vet
 This poor young voman died on;
For she made an ole in the Riviere Thames,
 Vot the penny steamers ride on!
'Twas a haccident they all agreed,
 And nuffink life self-slaughter;
So not guiltee o' fell in the sea,
 They brought in the ratcatcher's daughter!
                    * Doodle dee, &c.

*Well, ladies and gentlemen,—arter the two bodies was
resusticated—they buried them both in one seminary—
and the epigram which they writ upon the tomb-stone
went as follows—Doodle dee, &c.

[The Spoken passages may be used or not, at the option
of the Vocalist.]

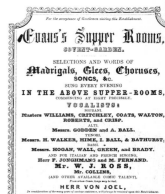

A decorative tile that formed part of Evans's Song and Supper Room is one of the few surviving relics of a once-famous London institution. Formerly as Joy's Hotel it had been much patronized by the nobility and it became known in its new guise as Evans's (late Joy's). In 1844 a magnificent new hall 72 feet long was built on at the back with a carved and painted ceiling and galleries supported on columns with ornamental capitals. The hall was the first to have a platform for the performers.

A handbill from Evans's advertises the entertainments which began at 8 and went on until after midnight. Madrigals, glees, ballads and operatic selections were sung by a choir of men and boys, with piano and harmonium accompaniment.

A troupe of busking minstrels perform at the seaside, the starting place for many young hopefuls with their eye on the London stage and the home of such provincial troupes as those led by Old Bones at Margate or Alf Allan at the Happy Valley, Llandudno.

·POLLY·PERKINS·OF· ·PADDINGTON·GREEN·

Harry Clifton had this song published under his own name in 1863. At about the same time another song was published in the North of England by George Ridley. Although it was called *Cushie Butterfield* and the words were different, it obviously had the same tune. There was instant war between North and South as to whose song was the original. In fact both writers appear to have used the tune of a well-known street ballad, *Nightingales Sing*. Certainly the folk song style shines through in this story of the broken-hearted milkman and the heartless Polly Perkins.

WRITTEN BY HARRY CLIFTON　　　　　　　　**ARRANGED BY J. CANDY**　　1863

Born in 1824, Harry Clifton made his name in middle-class drawing rooms singing "motto" songs that expressed acceptable wisdoms such as Paddle Your Own Canoe *or* Work Boys Work And Be Contented. *He later sang the songs with success on the halls.*

A busker accompanies a children's dance, turning the handle of his barrel-organ with his right hand. He would have had a regular route so that his customers in each street knew when to expect him.

maid; Who liv - èd on board wa - - - ges, the
house to keep clean, In a gen - - - tle - - - man's
fam' - ly near Pad - ding - ton Green. Oh! she was as

To be sung ad lib:

A dairy maid is chosen to demonstrate a lightweight cream separator in this illustration from a contemporary advertisement. Operating dairy equipment was among the everyday home skills expected of servants in a large Victorian household. They were not overpaid. Mrs. Beeton's Household Management, published in 1861, suggested that a maid-of-all-work should earn from £9 to £14 a year, plus free board and lodging.

2.
Her eyes were as black as the pips of a pear,
No rose in the garden with her cheeks could compare,
Her hair hung in 'ringerlets' so beautiful and long.
I thought that she lov'd me, but found I was wrong.
                    Oh! she was as, &c.

3.
When I'd rattle in a morning, and cry "milk below"
At the sound of my milk cans her face she would show,
With a smile upon her countenance and a laugh in her eye,
If I thought she'd have lov'd me, I'd have laid down to die,
                    For she was as, &c.

4.
When I asked her to marry me, she said, "Oh what stuff"
And told me to "drop it for she'd had quite enough
Of my nonsense" At the same time I'd been very kind,
But to marry a milk man she didn't feel inclin'd.
                    Oh! she was as, &c.

5.
"Oh the man that has me must have silver and gold.
A chariot to ride in, and be handsome and bold;
His hair must be curly as any watchspring.
And his whiskers as big as a brush for clothing."
                    Oh! she was as, &c.

6.
The words that she utter'd went straight thro' my heart,
I sobbèd, I sighèd, and straight did depart
With a tear on my eyelid as big as a bean,
Bidding good-bye to Polly and Paddington Green.
                    Ah! she was as, &c.

7.
In six months she married this hard-hearted girl,
But it was not a 'Wicount', and it was not a 'Nearl',
It was not a 'Barronite' but a shade or two 'wus'
'Twas a bow legg'd Conductor of a Twopenny 'Bus.
                    In spite of all she was as, &c.

The music hall in the Surrey Gardens, opened in 1856, had a seating capacity of 10,000 and was used among other things for the gigantic concerts of the impresario M. Jullien and the evangelical prayer meetings of Charles Haddon Spurgeon.

Opposite:

On this cover illustrated by Alfred Concanen, the unfortunate milkman of the song clutches his broken heart while his beautiful Polly Perkins waves to the bowler-hatted bus conductor she is soon to marry. In his rustic costume of smock and boots the milkman is portrayed as a simple, pure-hearted yokel easily hurt in the rough-and-tumble of big city life.

A Note On The Music

Victorian sheet music exhibits a marvellous lack of consistency, and Polly Perkins is no exception. There are frequent indications, as here, to sing two choruses after every verse, but the repeat signs DC, DS, ℅ and double bars with dots are muddled up without regard for style or uniformity. Frequently repeats are unmarked and left to the intelligence of the accompanist.

On this page the double bars with dots and the ℅ sign indicate a repeat of the chorus, but after the little "symphony" or ritornello that follows the chorus, there is no repeat mark to guide the performers back to the beginning of the next verse.

Extensive piano introductions and interludes between verses were popular. The interludes and the repeats of the chorus can simply be omitted if they become tedious.

An ascent by the French brothers Joseph and Jacques Montgolfier, pioneers of the hot-air balloon, was one of the attractions staged in the Surrey Zoological Gardens, along with concerts and masked balls in the giant music hall. The hall burnt down in 1860, only four years after it was built, but the gardens survived until 1878, when they were developed for housing.

POLLY PERKINS
OF
PADDINGTON GREEN,

OR THE
BROKEN HEARTED MILKMAN.

She was beautiful as a butterfly,   As proud as a Queen,
Was pretty little Polly Perkins   Of Paddington Green.

WRITTEN & SUNG WITH TUMULTUOUS APPLAUSE BY

HARRY CLIFTON.

Pr 2/6.

LONDON, HOPWOOD, & CREW, 42, NEW BOND ST W.

THE · BLACK-FACE · MINSTRELS

Minstrel shows ran alongside music hall as one of the most popular entertainments of the Victorian era. Based on the negro songs and dances of the plantations in the American South, they were performed almost entirely by white actors wearing burnt-cork make-up. Their life span very nearly coincides with the time scale of this book. From 1843 when Britain was visited by the first regular troupe formed in America, the Virginia Minstrels, the so-called "coon shows" were all the rage, spawning scores of troupes on both sides of the Atlantic. And yet, although the black-face tradition lived on well into the 20th century, the minstrel companies had virtually disappeared by the early 1900s.

From the 1920s, revivals of both the black and white varieties enlivened early wireless programmes, and in the 'fifties and 'sixties came the surprise success of the *Black and White Minstrel Show* on BBC Television and in live theatres across Britain. The show bore little resemblance to the originals, and pancake make-up replaced the traditional burnt cork, but it did give a new lease of life to many of the minstrel songs, not least those by Henry Clay Work and the great Stephen Foster.

The minstrel shows had one thing the halls could never claim: respectability. They were looked upon with favour by the Church, and the Minister and his family would be seen in the front row. With such heavenly sponsorship, no soirée could be complete without an item from the Ethiopian repertoire.

Bales of cotton from a plantation bordering the Mississippi River are loaded on to a paddle steamer in this 1870 lithograph by the American firm Currier and Ives.

·OH! SUSANNA·

During his brief career, Stephen Collins Foster wrote more than 200 songs including many which have since become folk songs. We have chosen two: *Oh! Susanna*, one of his earliest, and *Beautiful Dreamer*, his last. *Oh! Susanna* illustrates his command of the bright, lively minstrel style. It was adopted by the gold seekers on their way to California in 1849, and Henry Mayhew records it as being sung on the streets of London in his book on London life, published in 1851.

WRITTEN & COMPOSED BY STEPHEN C. FOSTER   1848

I'm gwoin' to A-la-ba-ma, Wid my ban-jo on my knee; I came from Lou-si-a-na, My true lub for to see. It rain all night de day I left, De wedder it war dry; De sun so hot I froze to deff;— Su-san-na, don't you cry.

The following Refrain to be sung after each Verse.

Oh! Su-san-na, Don't you cry for me; I'm gwoin' to A-la-ba-ma, Wid my ban-jo on my knee.

CHORUS.

1st Voice. Oh! Su - - san - na, Don't you cry for me; I'm gwoin' to A - la -

2nd Voice. Oh! Su - san - na, Don't you cry for me; I'm gwoin' to A - la -

3rd Voice. Oh! Su - - san - na, Don't you cry - for me; I'm gwoin' to A - la -

ba - ma, Wid my ban - jo on my knee.

ba - ma, Wid my ban - jo on my knee.

ba - ma, Wid my ban - jo on my knee.

THE ROAD TO BLACK FREEDOM

The rise to popularity of minstrel entertainment occurred during a period when Britain and the United States were involved in the struggles that led to the end of slave trading and slavery.

English anti-slavery campaigners, led by William Wilberforce, achieved their first major victory in 1807 when Britain – until then the foremost slave-trading nation – "utterly abolished, prohibited and declared to be unlawful" all dealing and trading in African slaves by British subjects. In 1833 slavery as an institution in the British colonies was finally abolished by Act of Parliament.

The Royal Navy, however, continued to comb the seas in an effort to wipe out slave trading by ships of other nations.

In the United States, the southern cotton- and tobacco-growing states still practised slavery, a fact which became an issue of great economic, political and moral dimensions. The publication in 1852 of Harriet Beecher Stowe's novel *Uncle Tom's Cabin* helped to stir up abolitionist fervour in the north, and in 1860 South Carolina, followed by the ten other Confederate States, seceded from the Union rather than give up the institution of slavery.

Five years of civil war followed during which, on 1st January, 1863, President Lincoln issued the Emancipation Proclamation, freeing all slaves in the rebellious territories. After the victory of the North in 1865, the proclamation was confirmed by the 13th Amendment prohibiting slavery anywhere in the United States of America.

V. 2. I jump'd on board de Telegraff,
    And floated down de ribber;
De 'lectric fluid magnified,
    And kill'd five hundred nigger!
De bulgine bust, de hoss ran off,
    I really tought I'd die;
I shut my eyes, and held my breff;—
    Susanna, don't you cry!
          Oh! Susanna, &c.

V. 3. I had a dream de oder night,
    When eb'ry ting was still;
I tought I saw Susanna dere,
    A-comin' down de hill.
De buck-wheat cake was in her mouth,
    De tear was in her eye;
Says I, "My lub, I'm from de south,—
    Susanna, don't you cry!"
          Oh! Susanna, &c.

V. 4. Now when I get to New Orleans,
    I mean to look around;
And if I see Susanna den,
    I'll fall upon de ground.
And if dat she should married be,
    Dis Nigg will surely die;
And when I'm dead and buried,
    Susanna, don't you cry!
          Oh! Susanna, &c.

Plantation workers busy in a cotton field in 1895 continue the long tradition of everyday life in the Deep South which had changed little in the 30 years since the end of slavery. The idealized negro of the minstrel songs was seldom seen picking cotton or man-handling bales on Mississippi landing stages. The songwriters tended to concentrate on his love life, his nostalgia for the past or – as in Oh! Susanna – his sense of humour.

· BEAUTIFUL · DREAMER ·

JACKSON'S EDITION.

WITH TONIC SOL-FA.

Beautiful Dreamer

Song

BY

S. C. FOSTER.

LONDON:
R. JACKSON & Co.,
46. RYE LANE. PECKHAM, S.E.
PUBLISHERS OF "THE GOBLINS' WEDDING," A BRIGHT PRETTY PIANO SOLO BY LEONARD GAUTIER.
THE PRETTIEST COMPOSITION OF THIS FAVOURITE COMPOSER—POST FREE 13 STAMPS.

Written shortly before Foster's death, *Beautiful Dreamer* is probably the best song of his declining years. The extraordinary clarity and purity of his work is as bright as ever, despite the miserable circumstances into which he had fallen. Much of his work he sold outright, and he was plagued by money troubles throughout his life. A disastrous marriage and a drink problem added to his woes. In 1864, suffering from TB and alcoholism, he fainted in the boarding house bedroom where he was living alone, fell against the wash basin, and gashed his throat. Two days later he was dead. His songs sold millions. He died with just 38 cents in his pocket.

Out of his marriage to Jane McDowell, a doctor's daughter, came one of his most beautiful compositions, *Jeanie* (originally Jennie) *With The Light Brown Hair*. After his death the copyright in the song was renewed so that she and her daughter could reap some benefit from the royalties after years of struggle. Ironically, the song ceased to be popular. In the ensuing 19 years it sold 19 copies. The royalties amounted to 75 cents.

Among Foster's other songs were *Camptown Races*, *My Old Kentucky Home*, *Massa's In The Cold Cold Ground* and *The Old Folks At Home*, now the official song of the State of Florida, which he sold to Edwin P. Christy of the Christy Minstrels for $15. It is strange to think that although Foster wrote so evocatively of the Deep South before the Civil War, he only once travelled south of the Mason Dixon Line. He never saw the Swanee River, and was never one of the Old Folks At Home.

*I*n this edition of the song Tonic Sol-Fa is prominently advertised for singers who had difficulty reading music. For more information on Tonic Sol-Fa, turn to page 108.

*P*oor Old Joe, *from which this cover illustration comes, was one of Foster's double-edition songs. It is virtually identical to his* Old Black Joe. *Probably he altered a few words and notes so that more than one publisher could issue the same song.*

WRITTEN & COMPOSED BY STEPHEN C. FOSTER 1864

Stephen Collins Foster was born near Pittsburgh in 1826 and died in the charity ward of New York's Bellevue Hospital at the age of 37. He started as a black-face minstrel in an amateur group when he was nine. Having seen the great T. D. Rice perform he tried to sell him songs, but his association with minstrel music was frowned upon by his family and his early work was published without his name.

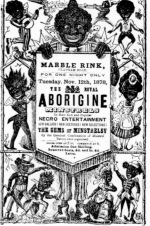

The Royal Aborigine Minstrels were one of innumerable black-face troupes which had sprung up in Britain by the 1870s. Several rejoiced in names that were probably more inventive than their routines, among them Harry Templeton's Original African Opera Troupe, Montague Roby's Midget Minstrels and Andy Merrilee's Armour Clad Amazon Female Christys.

A NOTE ON PERFORMANCE

In this song the last four bars of the accompaniment may be used as an introduction, which the arranger or editor seems for once to have forgotten.

·THE·GIPSY'S·WARNING·

A wonderful piece of Victorian middle-class morality, this minstrel song stands in clear contrast to the down-to-earth vulgarity of *She Was Poor, But She Was Honest*. Unlike music hall, which always retained an honest vulgarity, the minstrel shows were pure as driven snow. They melted away in the Naughty Nineties although the black-face performer lived on into the 20th century.

We have been unable to trace the original singer of *The Gipsy's Warning*, but this song with its famous first line "Do not trust him gentle lady, Tho' his voice be low and sweet" appears to have needed no star performer and is still familiar today. It has been parodied many times. In the 1920 revue *Whirligig* Violet Loraine sang a version called *The Gypsy Warned Me*: "I thought he'd buy a wedding ring for me I must admit, But all the bounder gave me was two passes for the pit, Because I didn't take the gypsy's warning".

WRITTEN & COMPOSED BY HENRY A. GOURD

A dark-eyed suitor woos a gentle maiden in an illustration from another popular minstrel song, Time May Steal The Roses, Darling. *He uses just the kind of gentle words the gipsy warned against: "Time may steal the roses, darling, From thy cheeks so fair and bright . . . Still whatever may betide us, fond and constant I will be".*

IMPRESSIVO.

Do not trust him gen-tle la___dy, Tho' his voice be low and
Do not turn so cold_ly from me, I would on_____ly guard thy

sweet, Heed not him who kneels be_fore you, Gen_tly plead_ing at your
youth, From his stern and with'_ring pow_er, I would on___ly tell thee

A jug with minstrel decoration was one of the many souvenirs produced to exploit popular enthusiasm for the black-face art. The early British black-face singer, J. A. Cave, wrote that "there were Jim Crow hats, Jim Crow pipes – in fact, Jim Crow everything". Later this merchandizing craze diversified into cast-iron negro money boxes and clockwork minstrel dancers.

Waterborne minstrels (below) ply their trade at a smart regatta. Following the appearance of Wilson and Montague's Minstrels before Queen Victoria in 1868, black-face acts became acceptable at social functions of all kinds. Minstrel performers could be relied upon to be inoffensive, and their costumes became increasingly grand and colourful, originating from the picturesque, sometimes bizarre outfits of the clown Joe Grimaldi, the early comic negro melodists Charles Dibdin and E. W. Mackney and the American performer Joel Sweeney. Another minstrel fashion was Georgian court dress.

3

Lady, once there lived a maiden,
  Pure and bright, and like thee, fair;
But he woo'd, and woo'd, and won her,
  Filled her gentle heart with care.
Then he heeded not her weeping,
  Nor cared he her life to save,
Soon she perished, now she's sleeping
  In the cold and silent grave.

4

Keep thy gold, I do not wish it,—
  Lady, I have prayed for this,
For the hour when I might foil him,
  Rob him of expected bliss,
Gentle lady, do not wonder
  At my words so cold and wild,—
Lady, in that green grave yonder,
  Lies the gipsy's only child.

· RING · THE · BELL · SOFTLY ·

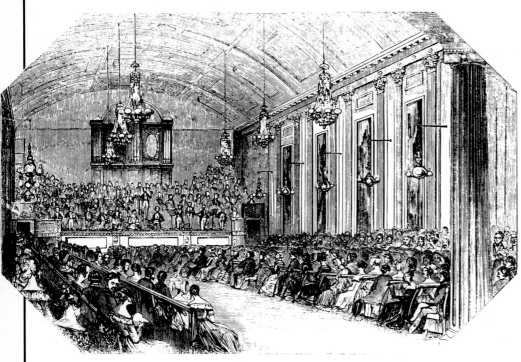

The Victorians were painfully aware of death, especially the death of little children. Loved ones went over to "the other side" with an alacrity unknown in our modern age. In the middle of the last century 15 in every 100 children never reached their first birthdays, and a married couple could expect to have five or six babies in order to ensure two surviving children. A stroll through any Victorian churchyard brings these statistics graphically to life with rows upon rows of sentimental inscriptions and tell-tale dates.

Mourning songs like *Ring The Bell Softly* offered the bereaved families an outlet through which they could express their grief while maintaining a stiff upper-lipped exterior. The minstrel troupes regularly performed such songs. Among their offerings on the fleetingness of children's lives were *The Angels Are Waiting For Me*, *Keep Pretty Flowers On My Grave* and *Beneath The Willow She Is Sleeping*.

The fashionable Hanover Square Concert Rooms were the chosen venue on 21st January, 1846, for the first London appearance of the American minstrel troupe, the Ethiopian Serenaders (see page 89). The entertainment, obviously aimed at a middle-class audience, was described as being "on a high plane" and the 2/- admission charge would have effectively excluded the lower orders.

WRITTEN BY DEXTER SMITH

COMPOSED BY E. N. CATLIN

MODERATO

Graves like this were going up at the rate of four a week in the West London and Westminster Cemetery, Fulham, when it opened in 1840. Churchyards alone could no longer cope with the dead of the rapidly expanding capital.

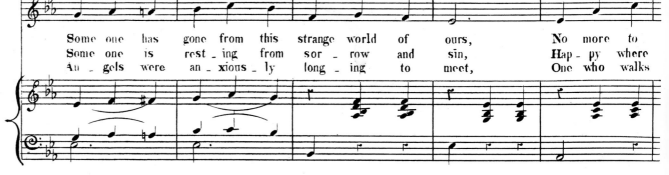

Some one has gone from this strange world of ours,   No more to
Some one is rest _ ing from sor _ row and sin,   Hap _ py where
An _ gels were an _ xious _ ly long _ ing to meet,   One who walks

ga _ ther its thorns with its flow'rs,.....   No more to lin _ ger where
earth's con _ flicts en _ ter not in,........   Joy _ ous as birds, when the
with them in Hea _ ven's bright street;......   Loved ones have whis _ per'd that

sun _ beams must fade, / Where, on all beau _ ty, death's fin _ gers are
morn _ ing is bright, / When the sweet sun _ beams have brought us their
some one is blest, / Free from earth's tri _ als, and ta _ king sweet

laid; / Wea _ ry with min _ gling life's bit ter and sweet,
light, / Wea _ ry with sow _ ing and ne _ ver to reap,
rest, / Yes! there is one more in an _ ge _ lic bliss,

Wea _ ry with part _ ing and ne _ ver to meet, / Some one has
Wea _ ry with la _ bour and wel _ com _ ing sleep, / Some one's de _
One less to che _ rish, and one less to kiss, / One more de _

gone to the bright gol _ den shore. / Ring the bell soft _ ly, there's
_ part _ _ ed to Hea _ ven's glad shore.
_ part _ _ ed to Hea _ ven's bright shore.

crape on the door, / Ring the bell soft _ ly, there's crape on the door.

_fz_ _fz_ _p_

In one of the most famous of all Victorian deathbed scenes, Little Nell, Dickens' "dear, gentle, patient, noble Nell", lies at rest in an illustration from The Old Curiosity Shop. Like most of his work, the book was published in instalments, and great public attention centred on the fate of the delicate little orphan girl as she wandered about the countryside with her bankrupt grandfather and eventually, in a melodramatic but moving scene, dies. Dickens himself grieved over her, and when the ship delivering the latest instalment to America approached the New York docks, a crowd was waiting on the quayside, shouting "Is Little Nell dead?".

THE STORY OF JIM CROW

The American minstrel show has its origins in a one-man song and dance act devised by the entertainer Thomas "Daddy" Rice and first performed on a Baltimore stage in 1828.

According to tradition, Rice based his routine upon the contorted movements of an elderly and physically handicapped black man he had noticed, who chattered nonsensically to himself as he worked in the livery stable near the theatre.

Struck by his zany mannerisms, Rice adapted them into a solo act. Dressed in ragged clothes, he transformed the old man's steps into a ludicrous dance, at the same time singing a verse that ran:
"Wheel about an' turn about
An' do jis so;
Eb'ry time I wheel about
I jump Jim Crow".

As soon as he cried the words "jis so", he would leap into the air to the audience's delighted surprise. They loved it and the show spawned a thousand black-face imitators organized in scores of competing troupes. In 1832, Rice won 20 encores for his "Jim Crow" act at the City Theatre in Louisville, Kentucky.

"The Last Visitor", no doubt keen for a quiet stretch of beach at the end of the season, receives an enthusiastic welcome from some underemployed minstrels in a scene drawn in 1892. By now the minstrel craze was on the wane, and the black-face troupes were beginning to disband.

OH DEM GOLDEN SLIPPERS.

R Childs.

James Bland who wrote this song (the music starts overleaf) was a black American. Born in 1854, he attended High School in Washington and entered Howard University to study law. During his education he learned to play the banjo and earned himself some pocket money performing in Washington hotels.

While at the university he met a lot of ex-slaves who were working on the campus and became fascinated by their style of music – so much so that he abandoned his studies in order to black up as a minstrel. Ludicrous though it may seem now, it was required for black people to assume make-up when they appeared in minstrel shows. Bland performed in this way with several black troupes, including Billy Kersans', Sprague's Georgia Minstrels and Callender's Coloured Minstrels, run by "Colonel" Jack Haverly, until in 1881 he left for Europe where he performed without the burnt cork.

He wrote at least 600 songs both for himself and other minstrel performers, some of whom published his work as their own. When he arrived back in America in 1900, the vogue for minstrel shows was over and he died penniless in 1911. In 1940 his song *Carry Me Back To Old Virginny* was adopted as the state song of Virginia.

WRITTEN & COMPOSED BY JAMES A. BLAND

1879

MODERATO.

1. Oh, my gold_en slippers am laid a_way, Kase I don't 'spect to wear 'em till my weddin' day, And my
2. Oh, my ole ban_jo hangs on de wall, Kase it aint been tuned since way last fall, But de
3. So, it's good bye, children, I will have to go Whar de rain don't fall or de wind don't blow, And yer

long-tail'd coat, dat I loved so well, I will wear up in de chariot in de morn; And my
darks all say we will hab a good time, When we ride up in de chariot in de morn; Dars ole
ul_ster coats, why, yer will not need, When yer ride up in de chariot in de morn; But yer

long white robe dat I bought last June, I'm gwine to git changed Kase it fits too soon, And de
Brud_der Ben and Sis_ter Luce, Dey will tel_e_graph de news to Un_cle Bac_co Juice, What a
gold_en slippers must be nice and clean, And yer age must be Just sweet six_teen, And yer

ole grey hoss dat I used to drive, I will hitch him to de chariot in de morn.
great camp meetin' der will be dat day, When we ride up in de chariot in de morn.
white kid gloves yer will have to wear, When yer ride up in de chariot in de morn.

An illustration from a contemporary minstrel song cover portrays a black couple in grotesque caricature typical of the genre. The minstrel show of the late-19th century had become so remote from its roots in American slave society that it no longer had much in common with real life. James Bland, who wrote Oh, Dem Golden Slippers!, was one of the very few American blacks to break into this curious market.

A selection of songs arranged for the piano contained this reminder of the instruments used by minstrels. First and foremost was the banjo, originally a four stringed instrument constructed from a gourd. Later the American performer Joel Sweeney created one from a halved cheese box and, despite his attempts to keep the design secret, the instrument soon became an essential part of the minstrel's act. Then there were the bones, the tambourine and the violin, punningly celebrated by G. H. Chirgwin in his sentimental song My Fiddle Is My Sweetheart, And I'm Her Faithful Beau.

POPULAR SONGS
FOR THE
PIANO-FORTE,
WITH CHORUSES.

THE JIM CROW LAWS

Eight years after their defeat in the American Civil War, the Southern states began introducing legislation designed to segregate blacks from whites, to deny them the same privileges as whites and, in effect, to reduce them to inferior status.

The first of these so-called "Jim Crow" laws – named after the black character of the popular minstrel shows *(page 85)* – was passed by Tennessee in 1873. In 1881, Tennessee was again first in passing a law segregating railroad coaches. It set a precedent that was followed throughout the south, and the Jim Crow laws became synonymous with racial segregation.

In 1896 – contrary to the spirit of the 14th and 15th Amendments – the Supreme Court of the United States upheld racial segregation in Louisiana in a "Separate but Equal" ruling which allowed blacks to be provided with segregated facilities for education, transportation and accommodation. Justice John Horland declared "The Constitution is color blind", but the ruling set off a wave of new segregation measures that designated drinking fountains, public benches, rest rooms, hospitals, sections of theatres and even cemeteries "Colored" or "Whites Only".

Segregation remained entrenched in Southern life until 1954 when the Supreme Court ruled against enforced separation in education – and, it followed, in all else. Whites were reluctant to comply until 1957 when President Eisenhower sent 1,000 US paratroopers to Little Rock, Arkansas, to enforce the entry of nine black students into the Central High School.

The Ethiopian Serenaders were one of the first socially accepted minstrel troupes in America, appearing at the White House as early as 1844. After their triumphant London debut at the Hanover Square Concert Rooms in 1846, they appeared at Vauxhall Pleasure Gardens and Evans's Song and Supper Room, creating an archetype for all subsequent minstrel troupes. They split up in 1900.

ON·THE·HALLS·
POPULAR CHORUSES

Chorus songs were the very essence, the life blood of music hall, providing the audience participation on which it so heavily relied. In this category we present songs in which the chorus is very much the dominant feature; sometimes the verses are completely incidental and the story line negligible. This form of composition was quite common among songwriters of the day. Vast numbers of songs had to be churned out to keep the star clients supplied with new material. A popular, catchy chorus was priority number one. If a witty first verse could be supplied, well and good. After that, ingenuity often ran out.

With the exception of *Oh! Mr Porter*, which we would describe as an integrated song with a beginning, middle and end, the verses to these songs are now little known. The choruses on the other hand are still part of everyday life. The strains of *Champagne Charlie* can be heard on Sunday mornings when the Salvation Army is out on parade. *Dear Old Pals* is second only to *Nellie Dean* in the repertoire of pub sing-alongs. And *Two Lovely Black Eyes* still crosses class boundaries, as it did when Charles Coborn introduced it in 1886. Within a week of its launch, he recorded seeing "parties of girls and lads of the coster fraternity, all of a row, arm in arm, shouting out my chorus at the top of their voices" Later, in the West End, he counted seven peers sitting round one little side table at the Trocadero, lustily joining in the same chorus.

Walter Lambert's imaginary scene Popularity, *set at "Poverty Corner" on the Waterloo Road, south London, includes the identifiable portraits of 226 music-hall performers.*

·CHAMPAGNE·CHARLIE·

Champagne Charlie was one of George Leybourne's most famous character songs, and an example of an early advertising song. Leybourne sang it brandishing a bottle of Moët & Chandon and lived up to the part both on and off stage. He dressed in the height of fashion and drove to engagements in a brougham with coachman and four white horses provided by the management of the Canterbury. Leybourne's great rival was Alfred Vance whose song *Cliquot* was written in direct competition to *Champagne Charlie*. Leybourne responded with a song called *Cool Burgundy Ben*, and they went on down the wine list, picking up hand-outs along the way, until Alfred Vance arrived at *Beautiful Beer*.

The chorus tune of *Champagne Charlie* was later adopted by the Salvation Army following their motto: "Why should the devil have all the best tunes?"

WRITTEN BY GEORGE LEYBOURNE   **COMPOSED BY ALFRED LEE**   c.1868

In a portrait by a leading illustrator of the time, Alfred Concanen, George Leybourne appears characteristically attired in immaculate evening dress. Leybourne was born in Gateshead in 1842 and worked as an engine fitter before finding his métier in the Free and Easies, the informal sing-songs that were popular in pubs. He made his music hall debut at the Canterbury in 1865.

Opened in 1852, and rebuilt double the size in 1854, the Canterbury at 143, Westminster Bridge Road was one of the first purpose-built music halls. Its founder and first chairman was Charles Morton who later managed several West End music halls, including the Oxford and the Tivoli, and became known as the Father of the Halls.

1. I've
2. The

seen a deal of gai-e-ty through-out my noi-sy life, With
way I gaind my ti-tle's by a hob-by which I've got, Of

all my grand ac-_com-_plish_ments I ne'er could get a wife The
ne-_ver let-ting o-thers pay, how-_e-_ver long the shot Who-

thing I most ex _ cel. in is the P. R. F. G. game, A
_ e _ ver drinks at my ex _ pense are trea _ ted all the same; From

CHORUS.

noise all night, in bed all day, and swim _ ming in Cham _ pagne. For
Dukes and Lords to Cab _ men down, I make them drink Cham _ pagne. For

ff

This label was current at the time Leybourne was singing Champagne Charlie. By subsidizing his performances, Moët & Chandon secured publicity and a place in the history books as an early commercial sponsor. They provided Leybourne with a retainer and free champagne to lavish on his audiences.

Well lit by gas chandeliers, the enlarged hall of the Canterbury could seat 1,500 people in comfort. The entertainers performed on an open stage and the audience could eat and drink during the show. This was where the management made their profit; admission cost only sixpence. In 1878, when theatres and music halls were required by law to have a proscenium arch and safety curtain, and drinking in the auditorium was banned, this type of hall died an instant death.

3.
From Coffee and from supper rooms, from Poplar to Pall Mall,
The girls on seeing me exclaim "Oh! what a Champagne swell!"
The notion 'tis of ev'ry one, if 'twere not for my name,
And causing so much to be drunk, they'd never make Champagne.
> For Champagne Charlie, &c.

4.
Some epicures like Burgundy, Hock, Claret, and Moselle,
But *Moët's Vintage* only, satisfies this Champagne swell;
What matter if to bed I go, and head is muddled thick,
A bottle in the morning sets me right then very quick.
> For Champagne Charlie, &c.

5.
Perhaps you fancy what I say is nothing else but chaff,
And only done, like other songs, to merely raise a laugh;
To prove that I am not in jest each man a bottle of Cham
I'll stand fizz round — yes that I will, and stand it—like a Lamb.
> Champagne Charlie, &c.

The image of the swell, the high-living, hard-drinking man-about-town, was one of the most popular of the music-hall stage. This figure appeared on the cover of The King Of The Strand, a song written in 1893 which owed an obvious debt to the champagne theme made so profitable by Leybourne.

93

On the original sheet music of Champagne Charlie, George Leybourne appears in the costume of what became known as the "heavy swell". According to the theatre critic Chance Newton, he was "one of the handsomest fellows I ever saw. In fact, he was quite an Apollo among men, and able to carry the most distinguished apparel".

Champagne Charlie is my name...... Champagne Charlie is my name......

Good for a_ny game at night, my boys, good for a_ny game at night, my boys,

Champagne Charlie is my name...... Champagne Charlie is my name......

Good for a_ny game at night, boys, who'll come and join me in a spree.

·DEAR·OLD·PALS·

This song, written by G. W. Hunt in 1877, may not have the greatest verses ever penned, but the chorus has been sung at reunions all over the world for more than a century. It is the traditional finale at the Players Theatre in Villiers Street, off the Strand, where Victorian music hall is still kept alive. G. H. Macdermott, with George Leybourne and Alfred Vance, was one of the Lions Comiques, trend-setters who steered music hall away from the traditional folk songs of the streets and taverns and into the more sophisticated world of topical and political satire.

Macdermott's first song at the Grecian Saloon in the 1860s, was *The Scamp*, written by the satirist and resident dramatist Henry Pettit. This poked fun at Brigham Young, the Mormon leader, and the so-called Tichborne Claimant *(see page 125)*, and its success led Macdermott to establish a reputation for impudence based on his lampoons of public figures of the day. In *Dear Old Pals*, however, Macdermott is all sweetness and light.

G. H. Macdermott, drawn here by Alfred Concanen, was billed sometimes as The Great Macdermott and at other times simply as Macdermott. He had a legendary ability to handle an audience. He specialized in descriptive and topical songs, commenting on the politics of the day. One ran "Charlie Dilke spilt the milk taking it home to Chelsea", and referred to a much publicized divorce involving the MP Sir Charles Dilke.

WRITTEN & COMPOSED BY G. W. HUNT

1877

I like my share of plea _ sure, and I'll have it while I can, I love a lov _ ing wo _ man, and Res _ pect an hon _ est man; I like to find true friend _ ship in The

A feature of the music hall magazine The Entr'acte was the weekly caricature of a theatrical or political personality by Alfred Bryan. This drawing of G. H. Macdermott plays up his waxed moustachios and silk topper, all part of the act for his satirical sketches of the West End gentry. The get-up was equally well suited to his serious songs about patriotism, Queen and country.

life that's roll _ _ ing by, And

such is al _ _ ways found be _ _ tween, My

old Pal Tom and I.

In an illustration from the long-running series the Musical Bouquet, two old pals take a drink in a mid-century Scottish tavern. Comradeship was high on the list of music hall virtues, though frequently in danger from the vicissitudes of life: Tom Costello's Comrades (page 185) had their friendship tested at school and on the battlefield, and the old pal in It's A Great Big Shame (page 137) discovered he had lost his best friend at the altar.

2
We've tasted of the "Ups" of life,
  We've also felt its "Downs,"
Sometimes our pockets held bright gold,
  And sometimes only "browns"
And be our drink bright sparkling "Cham,"
  Or merely humble beer,
The grasp of friendship's been the same,
  Through each succeeding year.
Chorus. Like dear old pals, &c.

3
We do snug little dinners, and
  They pass off very nice,
I put my old pal in the chair,
  He makes me take the vice;
We toast her Gracious Majesty,
  We don't forget "the gals,"
But *the* toast of the evening is
  "Success to true old pals!"
Chorus. We're dear old pals, &c.

4
It's ever been my maxim, yes,
  And so it ever shall,
To help a stranger when I can,
  But never desert a pal!
And after winning life's hard fight,
  What sweet reward is found,
In a conscience clear, a heart that's light,
  And dear old pals around!
Chorus. Still dear old pals, &c.

Macdermott was a particular favourite at both the old London Pavilion, built in 1861, and the new hall, reproduced here from Harper's magazine, which opened in 1885. As befitted its prominent position in Piccadilly Circus, the Pavilion presented some of the largest and most star-studded bills seen in London, and was a rendezvous for men-about-town until its closure as a music hall in 1918.

LAMBETH REMEMBERED BY A STAR

The colourful personalities of London's music-hall world made a deep impression on one boy who grew up in their midst: Charles Chaplin. Born in 1889, he was the younger son of two popular music-hall artistes whose marriage broke up a year after his birth.

In his autobiography *My Early Years*, Chaplin recalled the vaudeville stars of his childhood who frequented a pub on the Kennington Road, south London, close to the garret where he lived with his mother and brother in 1901.

"As a boy of twelve," he wrote, "I often stood outside the Tankard watching these illustrious gentlemen alight from their equestrian outfits to enter the lounge bar, where the élite of vaudeville met, as was their custom on a Sunday to take a final 'one' before going home to the midday meal.

"How glamorous they were, dressed in chequered suits and grey bowlers, flashing their diamond rings and tie-pins! At two o'clock on Sunday afternoon, the pub closed and its occupants filed outside and dallied awhile before bidding each other adieu; and I would gaze fascinated and amused, for some of them swaggered with a ridiculous air."

How ironic it is that the envious young Charles Chaplin should have become the big star of the new medium which spelled music hall's doom.

CHORUS. *TEMPO DI VALSE.*

We're dear old pals, jol_ly old pals,

Cling_ing to_gether in all sorts of weather, Dear old pals,

jol_ly old pals, Give me the friendship of dear old pals.

*D*erby Day was an event that united all classes as countless dear old pals jammed the road to Epsom in private carriages, horse-drawn charabancs, and even the humble donkey-cart, seen here in an 1885 Punch cartoon. The downs by the racecourse were full of merry-makers and itinerant musicians, and many songs were written about the occasion, including J. W. Rowley's Going To The Derby.

TWO·LOVELY· BLACK·EYES!

This is one of the most famous of all music hall choruses, but the verses are virtually unknown, and it comes as a surprise to discover that the song was about politics. It was written in 1886, a year of high political passion when Gladstone was forced to resign·over his attempt to give Home Rule to Ireland. The "two lovely black eyes" in question came from praising the Conservatives "frank and free" to an ardent Liberal, and pressing the merits of Gladstone to "a Tory true"

Charles Coborn tried the song out at the Paragon in the Mile End Road, with instant success. When he sang it at the Trocadero, the original two-week booking was extended to 14 months. As with *Champagne Charlie*, the Salvation Army recognized a catchy tune when it heard one, and included it in its repertoire with the words "My Jesus has died".

WRITTEN BY CHARLES COBORN   **ARRANGED BY EDMUND FORMAN**   1886

PIANO.

Charles Coborn, drawn here by H. G. Banks, was born in 1852 and started his career at the Alhambra on the Isle of Dogs – the East End namesake of the famous Leicester Square hall – where he was a vocalist, waiter, chucker-out and chairman. He sang his two greatest successes, Two Lovely Black Eyes *and* The Man That Broke The Bank At Monte Carlo, *throughout his long career, and lived to see his later performances filmed. He died in 1945 at the age of 93.*

Strolling so happy down Beth - - - nal Green,

This gay youth you might have seen,

Tompkins and I with his girl be - tween,

Oh what a sur - prise........ I

BENJAMIN DISRAELI

"Failure, failure, failure, failure, partial success, renewed failure, ultimate and complete triumph," said Lord Randolph Churchill, summing up the career of Benjamin Disraeli. Born into a comfortably-off Jewish family, the flamboyant young Disraeli found it hard to establish himself as a politician. His maiden speech in 1837 was drowned by hisses and boos, and Disraeli concluded with the prophetic words, "I will sit down now, but the time will come when you will hear me".

Not until 1868 did he "reach the top of the greasy pole" by becoming Conservative Prime Minister. By then he was a successful novelist – "when I want to read a novel I write one" – and was happily married to Mary Anne Wyndham Lewis, a "rattle" in Victorian parlance, unable, as she confessed, "to remember which came first, the Greeks or the Romans".

Queen Victoria, who detested Gladstone, got on well with Disraeli, possibly because he nicknamed her "the Faery" and flattered her assiduously though not entirely insincerely. He died in 1881 at the age of 76, having refused a deathbed visit from his sovereign: "It is better not. She would only ask me to take a message to Albert".

2

Next time I argued I thought it best,
To give the Conservative side a rest,
The merits of Gladstone I freely pressed,
　　When oh, what a surprise!
The chap I had met was a Tory true,
Nothing the Liberals right could do,
This was my share of that argument too,
　　Two lovely black eyes!
(Chorus.) Two lovely black eyes, &c.

prais'd the Con _ ser _ _ vatives frank and free,

Tompkins got an _ gry so spee _ _ _ di _ lee,

All in a mo _ ment he hand _ ed to me,

Two love _ ly black eyes . . . .

W. E. GLADSTONE

The Liberal leader William Ewart Gladstone was known as the Grand Old Man of Victorian politics; when he retired in 1894, 61 years had passed since he made his Maiden Speech in the House of Commons. A great reforming Prime Minister, he led four administrations and split his party by his conversion to Home Rule for Ireland. He was famous for his delight in felling trees on his estate at Hawarden in Flintshire.

Gladstone and his opposite number, Benjamin Disraeli, were personal as well as political rivals. The expanding electorate of the 19th century participated eagerly in the contest; they were able to buy souvenirs such as the Gladstone and Disraeli cruet — unfortunately history does not record which statesman contained salt and which held pepper — and doubtless they appreciated jokes like this:

Q. Why is Gladstone like a telescope?
A. Because Disraeli draws him out, sees through him and shuts him up.

3
The moral you've caught I can hardly doubt,
Never on politics rave and shout,
Leave it to others to fight it out,
    If you would be wise.
Better, far better it is to let,
Lib'rals and Tories alone, you bet,
Unless you're willing and anxious to get,
    Two lovely black eyes!
    (*Chorus.*) Two lovely black eyes, &c.

CHORUS.

Two love_ly black eyes ...... Oh what a sur_prise .... On_ly for tell_ing a man he was wrong, Two love_ly black eyes ......

The black eye, or "shiner", was a convention of slapstick comedy which got easy laughs from an audience and was often employed in music hall and variety. H. G. Banks used it here as an illustration for a songsheet. It later became a popular device of the silent screen.

"No more politics for me" is the caption to this departing figure of Coborn taken from the cover of Two Lovely Black Eyes. W. S. Gilbert made his own comment on the theme when he wrote in Iolanthe: "I often think it's comical, How Nature always does contrive, That every boy and every gal, That's born into the world alive, Is either a little Liberal, Or else a little Conservative!"

·TA-RA-RA-BOOM-DE-AY!·

"Ta-ra-ra" was sung on both sides of the Channel, as this French version confirms. In 1892 Lottie Collins took the song to America on a seven-month tour from Boston to San Francisco. When she died in 1910, her obituarist in The Performer *suggested that Ta-ra-ra-Boom-de-ay! was known and sung everywhere, even by the natives of Colombo.*

The Nineties certainly came in with a bang – perhaps we should say with a boom! A whole generation of people were bent on kicking over the traces and fighting to escape Victorian restraints and they adopted *Ta-ra-ra-Boom-de-ay!* as their theme song. The song caused a sensation when Lottie Collins sang it in *Dick Whittington* at the Grand Theatre, Islington. With the chorus she did an "Abandon" dance "after the French Style" which consisted of a whole series of dramatic high kicks – not easy in a long skirt, tight stays and a large feathered hat. She was encored again and again, sometimes fainting in the wings from sheer exhaustion.

There are many different versions of the words, and three claimants to the tune: the American Henry Sayers, the Englishman Alfred Moor King, and the Frenchman E. Déransart. Richard Morton who wrote the words for the Lottie Collins version, believed the tune was a Balkan folk song, taken to America by emigrants. One version of the song named *Ting-a-ling-boomderay* was featured in the New York minstrel show *Tuxedo*, where it was probably picked up by Lottie Collins.

WRITTEN BY RICHARD MORTON   **ARRANGED BY ANGELO A. ASHER**   **1891**

Not too strict, but ra_ther free, Yet as right as

right can be! Ne_ver for_ward, ne_ver bold,—

Not too hot, and not too cold, But the ve_ry

thing, I'm told, That in your arms you'd like to hold!

LOTTIE COLLINS 1903

On this postcard of Lottie Collins the sender wrote only one simple and self-explanatory message: "Ta-ra-ra-boom-de-ay". Lottie was born in 1866 and played the halls from the age of 11. She first appeared with her two younger sisters in a dancing sketch called Skiptomania, then went on to minstrel acts, comedy turns and burlesque. "Ta-ra-ra" rocketed her to fame in 1891.

THE MUSIC HALL JOURNALS

In the years before 1850, when purpose-built music halls were still in the future, the press rarely mentioned the entertainments on offer in the taverns or song and supper rooms. As music hall began to evolve and flourish, however, several journals covering or specializing in the subject began to appear.

The first to include accounts of the music-hall scene was the *Era*, a Sunday newspaper founded in 1838, which became one of the top papers reporting on music hall in the late 1860s.

The *Magnet* emerged from Leeds in 1866. It was followed, in 1870, by *The Entr'acte*, which styled itself "The Illustrated Theatrical and Musical Critic and Advertiser. A consulting paper for all amusements."

Two other magazines, the *Music Hall* and *Encore* appeared in 1889 and 1892 respectively. There were many other short-lived publications but those mentioned here lasted into the 20th century. With the decline of the halls these journals disappeared and none was functioning by the end of the Second World War. Variety journalism was then in the hands of the *Performer* (1906-57) and the venerable *Stage* which covered all branches of theatre.

2.

I'm not extravagantly shy,
And when a nice young man is nigh,
For his heart I have a try—
And faint away with tearful cry!
When the good young man, in haste,
Will support me round the waist;
I don't come to, while thus embraced,
Till of my lips he steals a taste!—

CHORUS.—Ta-ra-ra, &c.

3.

I'm a timid flower of innocence—
Pa says that I have no sense,—
I'm one eternal big expense;
But men say that I'm just immense!
Ere my verses I conclude,
I'd like it known and understood,
Though free as air, I'm never rude,—
I'm not too bad, and not too good!

CHORUS.—Ta-ra-ra, &c.

High kicks had quite a history. The can-can, advertised here in its more proper British version by the Prince of Wales' Theatre, dated from the Paris of the 1840s and was particularly popular with British and American tourists willing to pay for their thrills. In the most famous version of the dance, the music comes from the overture to Orpheus and the Underworld by Jacques Offenbach, the king of Parisian operetta. At the end of the century, the dance came to symbolize the age known as the Naughty Nineties.

The magazine Pick-Me-Up carried this drawing of Lottie Collins with a review of a performance at the London Pavilion, describing her as a popular favourite "quite beyond individual praise". Earlier she had told an interviewer how she put the Boom into Ta-ra-ra-Boom-de-ay!: "It was, I think, the mad rush and whirl of the thing that made it go. I got round a 40-foot circle twice in eight measures. I first sang it at a matinée and such a storm of applause followed it I didn't know what I'd done."

CHORUS.
Tempo di Marcia.

Ta_ra_ra Boom-de_ay, Ta_ra_ra Boom_de_ay, Ta_ra_ra
Boom_de_ay, Ta_ra_ra Boom_de_ay; Ta_ra_ra Boom_de_ay,
Ta_ra_ra Boom_de_ay, Ta_ra_ra Boom_de_ay, Ta_ra_ra
Boom_de_ay!

· DAISY · BELL ·

Katie Lawrence, dressed as she appeared on the cover of Daisy Bell, *first sang the song in London in 1893. "Miss Katie Lawrence seems to have vaccinated all England with the lymph of* Daisy Bell*", commented* The Entr'acte, *"and in all cases it has taken".*

MUSIC FOR THE AMATEUR

Earlier this century, teachers of vocal music had to learn two completely different methods of writing down music. One was the traditional staff notation with notes on five-line staves; the other was Tonic Sol-fa, a method whereby each of the notes of the scale are given a syllabic name, doh being the keynote or tonic. A tune could be written (and what is more, sight-read) unambiguously in Tonic Sol-fa, complete with metre, rhythm, rests, chromatic notes and modulations. The key was simply indicated at the beginning of the piece and at each subsequent modulation. Those brought up on Tonic Sol-fa had no difficulty with transposition.

The system is now familiar from its use to teach the children in *The Sound Of Music* their scales the easy way with "Doe . . . a deer, a female deer, Ray . . . a drop of golden sun".

Tonic Sol-fa was introduced in the 1840s by John Curwen the publisher. It was a development of an earlier Italian system and such was his belief in the solid English musical renaissance of the late-19th century, that he promoted it with an almost missionary zeal. He founded the Tonic Sol-fa College in 1863 with the motto "Music for the people". His mission was successful. Tonic Sol-fa, as an aid to the wholesome enjoyment of music by the masses, became as essential as guitar chords were to become for a later generation.

Daisy Bell, we would suggest, is as catchy a chorus now as when Harry Dacre wrote it in the 1890s. Since 1867 when the modern bicycle appeared, cycling had become all the rage. According to one story of the song's origin, Dacre took his bicycle with him when he travelled to America and was charged duty on it at the customs shed. A friend remarked, "Lucky you didn't have a bicycle made for two – you'd have been charged double". The incident stuck in his mind and the result was *Daisy Bell*.

In spite of the craze for tandems, Dacre had no luck selling the song to an American publisher. It was Katie Lawrence, then visiting America, who liked the song, bought it and took it back to London. She made it her most popular success. Soon errand boys were whistling it in the street.

Cycling encouraged women to discard their long skirts in favour of the fashion pioneered in the US by Mrs Amelia Bloomer in the 1850s – with little success at the time. She called it "Rational Dress" but it was known universally as "Bloomers". Now for the first time trousers were worn in the street by respectable women, although they were still considered daring. Katie Lawrence wore them legitimately; she adopted the character of Daisy Bell's lover and dressed as a boy.

WRITTEN & COMPOSED BY HARRY DACRE　　　　1892

Dai - - - - sy! Planted one day by a glanc - ing dart,

Planted by Dai - - sy Bell!...... Whe-ther she loves me or

loves me not, Sometimes it's hard to tell;...... Yet I am

long-ing to share the lot Of Beauti-ful Dai - - sy Bell!......

The Middlesex Music Hall Drury Lane was popularly known as the Old Mo after the Mogul Tavern from which it sprang. It was attended by a more humble class of patron than the plusher West End halls but John Pennell's drawing featuring a popular song and dance artiste of the time demonstrates its intimate nature.

A young lady in bloomers sets the new liberated style. "Of course I had to buy her a 'bike'," sings her "Dear old Guv", in That's My Baby, the song from which this illustration comes. He also had to buy her a piano and listen to her "a-yapping out the French" and concludes: "It's your blooming education that's spoilt my little kid!"

2.
We will go "tandem" as man and wife, Daisy, Daisy!
"Ped'ling" away down the road of life, I and my Daisy Bell!
When the road's dark we can both despise P'liceman and "lamps" as well;
There are "bright lights" in the dazzling eyes Of beautiful Daisy Bell!

Chorus

3.
I will stand by you in "wheel" or woe, Daisy, Daisy!
You'll be the bell(e) which I'll ring, you know! Sweet little Daisy Bell!
You'll take the "lead" in each "trip" we take, Then if I don't do well;
I will permit you to use the break, My beautiful Daisy Bell!

Chorus

In a whimsical illustration dated 1869 two light-hearted day trippers speed off into the countryside on a "bicycle for two persons". Probably this machine never left the drawing board as the tandem did not become commercially successful until the 1890s at the time of Daisy Bell. The design is modelled on the velocipede or "boneshaker", so called because it ran on tyreless iron rims.

·OH! MR PORTER·

Unlike the majority of Marie Lloyd's songs which were too topical to travel through time, *Oh! Mr Porter* remains one of the best loved chorus songs. The song portrayed the hazards of railway travel for the unaccompanied young woman, and Marie made the most of it. Her saucy wink was her trademark and she had the ability to extract sexual innuendo from the most innocent of lyrics. The actions which she suited to the words of *Oh! Mr Porter* were said to be highly salacious.

Marie Lloyd, whose real name was Matilda Wood, made her first appearance under the name of Bella Delmere at the Royal Eagle Music Hall in 1885. She had an early, and short-lived success with Nelly Power's song *The Boy In The Gallery (see page 159)*, but she soon became famous for the songs that were written specially for her.

Being a true cockney, born in Hoxton, she cashed in heavily on the craze for coster songs at the beginning of her career with *The Coster Girl In Paris* and *Garn Away*. Later on she aspired to a more elegant style with songs like *When I Take My Morning Promenade* and *Every Little Movement Has A Meaning Of Its Own*. Rather later in her career came *My Old Man Said Follow The Van*, perhaps the song most closely associated with her. She died at the age of fifty-two, reportedly of a broken heart, but more likely from drink, hard work and ill treatment by her third husband.

She was an international star, popular in Paris, Berlin, Australia, Africa and America, and without doubt one of the greatest stars created by the music hall. Sarah Bernhardt described her as "the only woman of genius on the British stage", and when asked what she liked most about London, she listed the Tower, the Crystal Palace – and Marie Lloyd.

On the cover of Oh! Mr Porter *the young Marie Lloyd appears as the innocent country girl prey to moral dangers. Her reputation for "blueness", described by all and sundry, including herself, as "ceruleanism", and her very public private life kept her off the bill for the Royal Command Performance held at the Palace in 1912. Marie staged her own show that same night at the London Pavilion and the posters proclaimed: "Every performance by Marie Lloyd is a Command Performance By Order of the British Public".*

WRITTEN BY THOMAS LE BRUNN   **COMPOSED BY GEORGE LE BRUNN**   1893

THE RAILWAYS

As well as bringing travel within the reach of a growing population, the expansion of the railways brought steady employment at a time of economic uncertainty. The London and North Western Railway was formed in 1846 as an amalgamation of three smaller railways – the London to Birmingham, the Grand Junction and the Liverpool and Manchester – to provide a main line service connecting London with the North by the West Coast route. It would thus have been the line that caused confusion in *Oh! Mr Porter.*

Late_ly I just spent a week with my old Aunt Brown,

Came up to see the wond'rous sights of famous Lon_don Town........

Just a week I had of it, all round the place we'd roam_____

Was_n't I sor_ry on the day I had to go back home?.....

Worried a_bout with pack_ing, I ar_rived late at the sta_tion,

Marie Lloyd poses with grapes tumbling out of her hat and two cherries and a stalk held teasingly between her teeth. Affectionately known as "our Marie" to her public, her love of life and singular lack of inhibition left behind the legend of a warm, loving person with a fine sense of humour.

Dropped my hat-box in the mud, the things all fell a

bout,———— Got my tick_et, said 'good-bye,'

Right a_way!" the guard did cry, But I found the

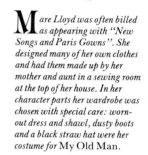

Mare Lloyd was often billed as appearing with "New Songs and Paris Gowns". She designed many of her own clothes and had them made up by her mother and aunt in a sewing room at the top of her house. In her character parts her wardrobe was chosen with special care: worn-out dress and shawl, dusty boots and a black straw hat were her costume for My Old Man.

2

The porter would not stop the train, but laughed and said "You must
Keep your hair on, Mary Ann, and mind that you don't bust!"
Some old gentleman inside declared that it was hard,
Said "Look out of the window, Miss, and try and call the guard."
Didn't I, too, with all my might I nearly balanced over,
But my old friend grasped my leg, and pulled me back again,
Nearly fainting with the fright, I sank into his arms a sight,
Went into hysterics but I cried in vain:—

(CHORUS.)

In his illustration for the Dear Old Gentleman scene in Oh! Mr Porter, H. G. Banks faithfully portrayed the luggage rack, window blind and leather buttoned seats of the 1st-class carriage of the day. The late Sir John Betjeman who once travelled in a carriage of this kind on the London Tilbury & Southend Railway, recalled with nostalgic pleasure that the compartment "smelt and felt like the interior of a family brougham".

3

On his clean old shirt front then I laid my trembling head,
"Do take it easy, rest awhile," the dear old chappie said.
If you make a fuss of me and on me do not frown,
You shall have my mansion, dear, away in London town.
Wouldn't you think me silly if I said I could not like him?
Really he seemed a nice old boy, so I replied this way,
I will be your own for life your imay doodleum little wife.
If you'll never tease me any more I say.

(CHORUS.)

train was wrong, and shout _ ed out:............

CHORUS.

Oh! Mister Por _ ter, what shall I do?.......... I want to go to

Birmingham and they're taking me on to Crewe. Send me back to Lon _ don as

quickly as you can,........ Oh! Mis _ ter Porter, what a sil _ ly girl I

1st time. 2nd time.

am. am......

Maidens in distress on trains provided a fertile theme not only in Oh! Mr Porter, as illustrated here, but in numerous other songs, including one called Bradshaw's Guide, in which another kind gentleman meets a lady who "could not recollect the town to which she'd wish'd to ride". She ends up going back to his quarters, "And all the live-long day, then both of us, we tried to find the town she wanted in my Bradshaw's Guide".

Victorian travellers, faced with getting themselves and their often bulky luggage from place to place, were at the mercy of "Mr Porter" – shown below in a satirical cartoon version. In 1871, the year before the railway guard shown on the opposite page appeared in a series of portraits of British workmen, Great Britain boasted 13,500 miles of railway and carried 360,000 passengers and 166,500,000 tons of freight annually.

THE BRITISH WORKMAN, 1872

THE · LILY · OF · LAGUNA ·

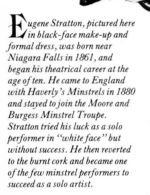

The negro character was usually portrayed in music hall as either a knockabout figure of fun or a lovesick romantic, and the sentimental lover is the character Eugene Stratton assumed in this chorus song by Leslie Stuart. The partnership between Stratton and Stuart brought together a Yankee singer from Buffalo, New York State, and a Lancastrian songwriter who had been fascinated by the Deep South and the Wild West from an early age.

Stuart's songs for Stratton included *I Lub A Lubly Gal, I Do, The Dandy Coloured Coon* and *The Idler*, but *Lily Of Laguna* was their greatest success. The songs were performed in the halls as big production numbers, with special effects, stagesets and lighting, like little plays, and they were such effective theatre that they received serious reviews in *The Times*. Stuart did not attend the première of *Lily Of Laguna* because he was in New Orleans, conducting his musical comedy *Floradora*. Although he was only a hundred miles away from Laguna, he never visited the place – perhaps as well, because despite its romantic name, Laguna was a mosquito-infested swamp.

Eugene Stratton, pictured here in black-face make-up and formal dress, was born near Niagara Falls in 1861, and began his theatrical career at the age of ten. He came to England with Haverly's Minstrels in 1880 and stayed to join the Moore and Burgess Minstrel Troupe. Stratton tried his luck as a solo performer in "white face" but without success. He then reverted to the burnt cork and became one of the few minstrel performers to succeed as a solo artist.

WRITTEN & COMPOSED BY LESLIE STUART

1898

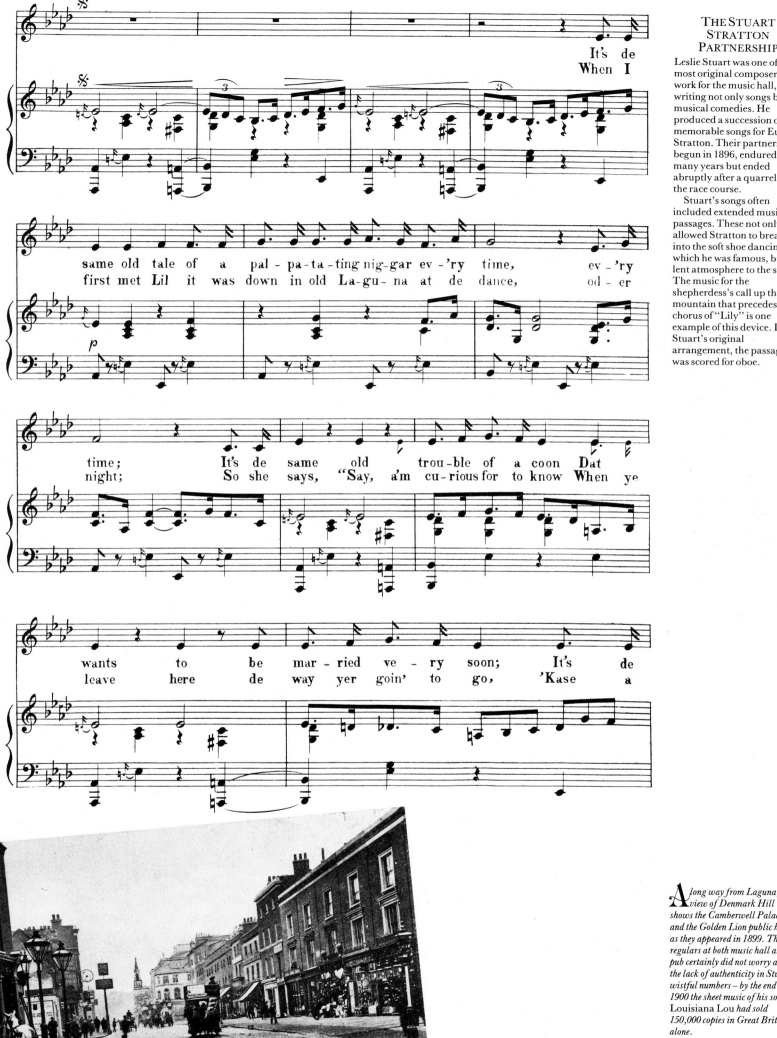

same old tale of a pal‑pa‑ta‑ting nig‑gar ev‑'ry time, ev‑'ry
first met Lil it was down in old La‑gu‑na at de dance, od‑er

time; It's de same old trou‑ble of a coon Dat
night; So she says, "Say, a'm cu‑rious for to know When ye

wants to be mar‑ried ve‑ry soon; It's de
leave here de way yer goin' to go, 'Kase a

It's de
When I

THE STUART STRATTON PARTNERSHIP

Leslie Stuart was one of the most original composers to work for the music hall, writing not only songs but musical comedies. He produced a succession of memorable songs for Eugene Stratton. Their partnership, begun in 1896, endured for many years but ended abruptly after a quarrel at the race course.

Stuart's songs often included extended musical passages. These not only allowed Stratton to break into the soft shoe dancing for which he was famous, but lent atmosphere to the song. The music for the shepherdess's call up the mountain that precedes the chorus of "Lily" is one example of this device. In Stuart's original arrangement, the passage was scored for oboe.

A long way from Laguna, this view of Denmark Hill shows the Camberwell Palace and the Golden Lion public house as they appeared in 1899. The regulars at both music hall and pub certainly did not worry about the lack of authenticity in Stuart's wistful numbers – by the end of 1900 the sheet music of his song Louisiana Lou *had sold 150,000 copies in Great Britain alone.*

Denmark Hill

erwell

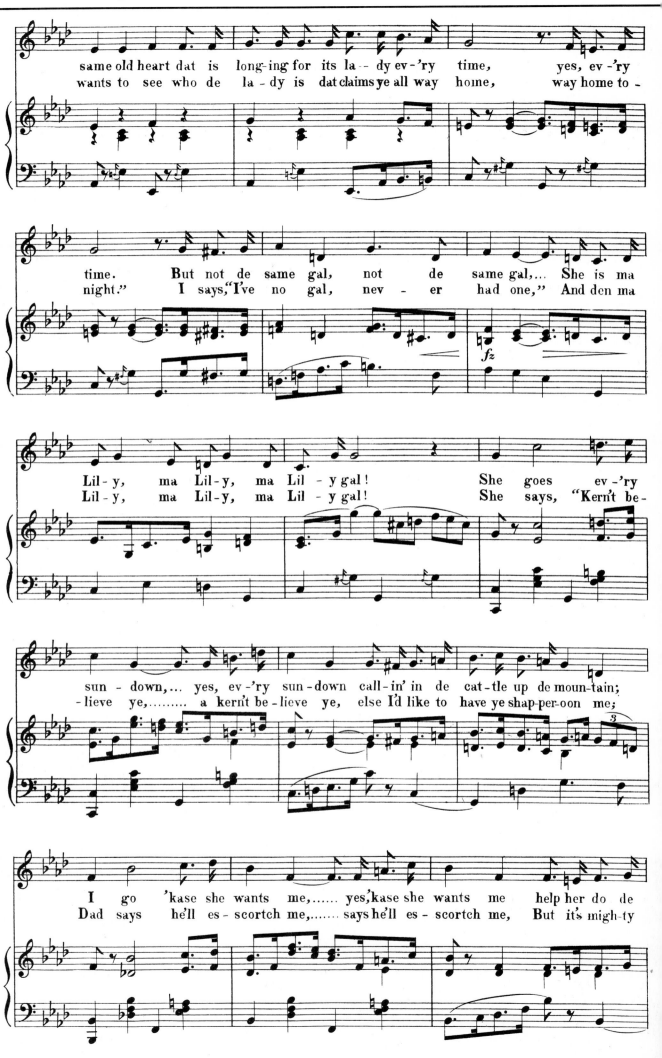

call-in' and de count-in'. She plays her mu - sic......... to call de
ea - sy for to lose him." Since then each sun - down...... I wan-der

lone lambs.... dat roam a - bove, ...But I'm de black sheep and I'm
down here........ and roam a - round ....Un - til I know ma la - dy

wait - in' For de sig - nal of ma lit - tle la - dy love.
wants me, Till I hear de mu - sic ob de sig - nal sound.

Two stereotypes of minstrelsy decorate the music covers on this page. On the left, Eugene Stratton is portrayed as the negro song character wandering far from home. On the right is a dance arrangement by Karl Kaps featuring the anxiously waiting lady of romantic dreams. The Cake Walk billed on the cover was part of the black-face minstrels' traditional three-part act in which the entire cast, dressed supposedly in their masters' and mistresses' cast-off finery, competed for a prize cake awarded to the performer who got the most shouts from the audience.

(SHEPHERDESS'S CALL UP THE MOUNTAIN.) (Optional.)

The pensive lady waiting at the gate was typical of the romantic heroines created by the partnership of Leslie Stuart and Eugene Stratton. This one comes from the song cover of Little Dolly Daydream. *Many Victorian writers, from Arthur Clough to Thomas Hardy, felt the attraction of the rustic lass, so honest and straightforward compared with the painted ladies of the town.*

COMPOSER'S FOOTNOTE
*The first eight bars may be omitted.

She's ma la-dy love,..... she is ma dove, ma ba-by love,

She's no gal for sit-tin' down to dream, She's de on-ly queen La-

-gu-na knows; I know she likes me, I know she

likes me Be-kase she says so; She is de Lil-y of La-

-gu-na, she is ma Lil-y and ma Rose.
1°
Rose.
2°

Just as they appreciated the pastoral themes in Lily of Laguna, *Victorians* would have been quick to perceive the biblical allusions in this engraving of an old cottager and his lamb. Nurturing young or abandoned creatures was thought to bring out the best in human nature and there was widespread affection for animals. This was pandered to by many artists of the period. Ford Madox Brown commented on the hazards of transporting live animal models from Clapham Common to his house in Stockwell for his painting The Pretty Baa Lambs; once there, they made themselves ill eating plants growing in his garden.

D.C.

ON·THE·HALLS
CHARACTER SONGS

If chorus songs were the life blood of the music hall, then character songs were the guts. In each of these items we can find a piece of Victorian social history distilled into a few lines of verse. The songs in this section are, if you like, miniature novels, and in their various ways they are as sharp and as observed as any by Dickens or Thackeray.

The actor sings in the first person, tells a story, and in order to do so, puts on a character. The verses are no less important than the chorus and they serve to illustrate the extraordinary acting ability of some of the great music-hall performers.

Gus Elen – the man of the people – in *It's A Great Big Shame* demonstrates the agonies of an ill matched marriage. Albert Chevalier – the Coster Laureate – is as much at home playing an old codger rhapsodizing about married bliss as he is putting over the sharp cockney who inherits a donkey shay.

The world of entertainment is represented by George Leybourne who loses his girl to the man on *The Flying Trapeze* and George Beauchamp with his disastrous love for a pantomime chorus girl, while Charles Coborn expresses all our dreams of coming up on the pools with *The Man That Broke The Bank At Monte Carlo*.

These artists had only a short time in which to make their impact; their characters had to be instantly recognizable. Alone on stage, without supporting actors, they faced the most stringent of theatrical tests. They succeeded – not once, but a thousand times and more.

A view of Covent Garden, painted in 1864 by Phoebus Levin, captures all the raw vitality of London's main fruit and vegetable market, set in the midst of the West End theatres.

· THE · FLYING · TRAPEZE ·

This studio portrait of Léotard taken during one of his two seasons at the Alhambra, Leicester Square, in the 1860s, was found in an album containing photographs of stage celebrities. At that time the art of screen printing had not evolved sufficiently for photographs to be reproduced on the printed page. Instead they were inserted into theatre magazines as give-aways or sold in theatre foyers to collectors and admirers.

In 1860, the Alhambra, Leicester Square, was converted from an exhibition centre and circus into a splendid music hall, and to bring in the crowds, the new management introduced a brilliant French trapeze artist named Léotard. He performed without a net, flying over the heads of the audience as they sat at their tables. He had charming manners and a modest disposition, and the Victorian ladies went wild over him.

George Leybourne, who had a triumphant success with *Champagne Charlie (page 92)*, saw Léotard as the perfect subject for a character song. He enlisted the help of *Champagne Charlie*'s composer, Alfred Lee, who adapted an old circus melody to fit the words. *The Flying Trapeze* was the result. It has been a consistently popular song.

Léotard himself died young from either smallpox or consumption at the age of 28 or 37, depending which books you read. But his name has survived in the term used for the costume worn by dancers and gymnasts all over the world.

ACTS OF DARING AND SKILL

To bring the crowds flocking into music and variety halls, London managers signed up the best and most sensational novelty acts they could find.

Among the famous names that thrilled the public were two Frenchmen who reigned supreme as the greatest gymnastic stuntmen of the age. The first, known simply as Léotard, attained instant fame in Paris in 1859 when he introduced for the first time his own invention of the flying trapeze. He made two visits to the Alhambra Palace of Varieties in London.

An even greater sensation was the appearance at the Crystal Palace in 1861 of the most renowned tight-rope walker of all time, Jean François Gravelet – alias Blondin. His eight-minute walk across Niagara Falls on a tight hemp cord on 30th June, 1859, was the start of a dazzling career of daredevil exploits on the high wire.

Working as always without a safety net, he made the art of tight-rope walking as complicated and nerve-wracking as possible, performing it blind-folded, while cooking an omelette, with his head in a sack, riding a bicycle, pushing a wheelbarrow, and carrying a man on his back. Sometimes he pretended to fall in order to terrify or thrill his audiences even more.

The "Hero of Niagara" – as a contemporary verse had it – lived in St. John's Wood Road, north London, in a house called Niagara Villa, and was created a Chevalier of the Legion of Honour by Napoleon III.

WRITTEN BY GEORGE LEYBOURNE COMPOSED BY ALFRED LEE 1868

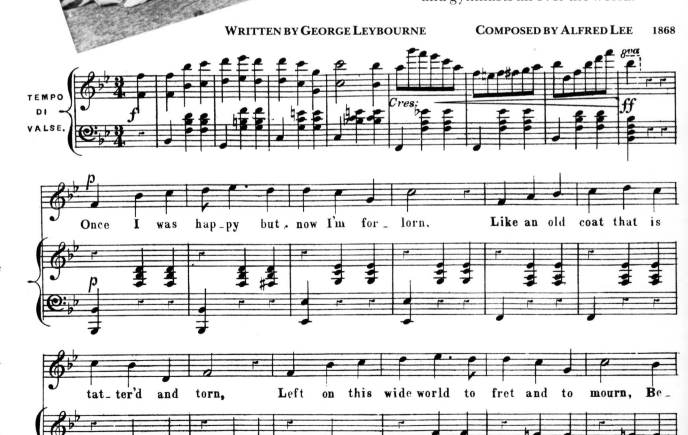

_tray'd by a maid in her teens.......... The girl that I lov'd she was

hand_some........ I tried all I knew her to please......... But

rall: CHORUS.

I could not please her one quarter so well, Like that man up_on the Tra_peze. He'd

Cres:

tempo.

fly through the air with the greatest of ease, A daring young man on the flying Tra_

p

_peze, His movements were graceful All girls he could please, And my love he purloin'd a

Cres:

THE TICHBORNE CLAIMANT

One of the most intriguing figures to appear on the halls in the 1880s was the so-called Tichborne Claimant. Arthur Orton, a butcher from Wagga Wagga in Australia, claimed that he was heir to the noble Tichborne title, precipitating the longest lawsuit in 19th-century Britain.

Orton lost the case and served ten years for fraud. On his release, styling himself as Sir Roger Tichborne, he took to the halls with a one-man celebrity act. He advertised his appearances in music hall publications such as *The Entr'acte* and promised, according to a playbill of the time, to "Address the Audience upon the Tichborne Case, upon the Trials, upon Juries, and upon various incidents of His Prison Life".

The halls were not solely the domain of the singer, and special turns, many of them transplanted from the circus, like this group of acrobats, featured on the bills. Ventriloquists, magicians, trick cyclists, tumblers and animal acts were also popular, as were assorted oddities such as Sacco the Fasting Man, the Peckham Fat Boy, and Zazel the human cannon ball, whom Leybourne celebrated in a song called simply Zazel.

The young man kneeling at the feet of the object of his desire was a stock figure of Victorian times, in popular imagination if not in reality. In The Cigar Girl, from which this picture comes, the hero falls for a shop girl. In She Was One Of The Early Birds (page 141), the attentions were lavished on Sweet Mabel, the show girl.

WALKING IN THE ZOO

THE GREAT VANCE

Not content to vie with each other in the champagne, wine and beer stakes (see page 92), George Leybourne and Alfred Vance rivalled each other with songs on London pastimes. This song, Walking In The Zoo, was a hit for Vance – a comment on the Victorian habit of taking a stroll dressed to the nines. Leybourne responded with Lounging In The Aq, a reference to the Royal Aquarium which then stood in Tothill Street, Westminster.

A cartoon from an 1891 issue of Pick-Me-Up comments on the craze for trapeze artists which followed Léotard's success at the Alhambra. The caption recorded a conversation from the pit: "Masculine Voice: 'It's her benefit to-night. She takes the nett profits.' Feminine Voice: 'Oh, I see; and there is the net.'"

GEORGE LEYBOURNE.
ALFRED LEE.

George Leybourne is illustrated here in the characteristic style of the artist Alfred Bryan – a large head atop a midget body – as the "daring young man on the flying Trapeze".

As this Canterbury Theatre programme proclaims, for sixpence in the gods or two shillings in the balcony, patrons could enjoy not only the bill, but the joys of open air entertainment when the patent sliding roof was winched open. Frederic Villiers, the designer, had already installed a similar device at the Pavilion, Piccadilly Circus. The Performer, commenting on its success, described how in the event of a sudden shower, it took such a long time for the attendant to climb the 85 steps to operate the winch, that people would raise their umbrellas, blocking the view of the stage and causing the rest of the audience to bellow: "Put yer umberellers dahn".

4.

One night I as usual went to her dear home,
Found there her father and mother alone,
I ask'd for my love and soon they made known
To my horror, that she'd run away!
She'd pack'd up her box and elop'd in the night,
With him with the greatest of ease,
From two storeys high, he had lower'd her down
To the ground on his flying Trapeze!

Chorus

He'd fly thro' the air with the greatest of ease,
A daring young man on the flying Trapeze,
His movements were graceful All girls he could please,
And my love he purloin'd away.

5

Some months after this I went to a Hall
Was greatly surprised to see on the wall
A bill in red letters which did my heart gall,
That she was appearing with him.
He taught her gymnastics and dress'd her in tights
To help him to live at his ease,
And made her assume a masculine name
And now she goes on the Trapeze!

Chorus

She floats thro' the air with the greatest of ease,
You'd think her a man on the flying Trapeze,
She does all the work while he takes his ease,
And that's what's become of my love.

THE · MAN · THAT · BROKE · THE · BANK · AT · MONTE · CARLO ·

CHARLES COBORN

Coborn's real name was Colin Whitton McCallum. When he first went on the halls he used the stage name Charles Laurie, but decided on Coborn when talking over the question with a friend at the corner of Coborn Road in Bow.

Until his late twenties Coborn played in the East End of London and the provinces, initially earning only 1/3 a night. But by the time he sang *The Man That Broke The Bank* he was top of the bill at the Oxford Music Hall, and clearly good on the business side.

Having bought the singing rights of *The Man That Broke The Bank* from Fred Gilbert, he opened negotiations with Francis, Day & Hunter for the sale of the publication rights. The standard publisher's fee at the time was £20, shared equally between writer and performer. Coborn demanded £30, but failed to get it. In the event Fred Gilbert accepted £10 as his share, and Coborn settled for a down payment of £5 plus a royalty. This arrangement, which was unusual at the time, eventually earned him the princely sum of £600.

This song was inspired by the exploits of a certain Charles de Ville Wells, who achieved every gambler's dream: he broke the bank at the Monte Carlo casino. Fred Gilbert, the writer of the song, submitted it to Charles Coborn who at first turned it down. It would involve him in adopting the character of a swell and he was afraid that some of the words were a trifle highbrow. Later he had a change of heart and bought the singing rights for a guinea. The song was not an instant success, but it grew in popularity and in 1891 it was put into the Gaiety burlesque *Cinder-Ellen Up Too Late*. Coborn made a lot of money from it, but he still preferred to sing *Two Lovely Black Eyes (page 99)* which he felt bridged the gap between the Mile End Road and the Trocadero.

WRITTEN & COMPOSED BY FRED GILBERT

1892

Two song covers present Charles Coborn playing the part of a swell, the character he had to adopt for the song. He was initially not entirely at ease in this number, and had to work it very hard before it took the public's fancy. "I believe that the first time I produced the song at the Oxford Music Hall, I sang the chorus of the last verse ten times, introducing all sorts of would-be funny remarks to work the audience up. I have it on newspaper record from one present that 'it made him sick and the audience disgusted'."

By 1891, the year Charles Morton was portrayed in this cartoon by Alfred Bryan, he had become the grand old man of music hall. "A veteran, certainly," commented the caption writer, "but he doesn't look played out, does he!" One of the halls Morton managed was the Oxford, where Charles Coborn performed, but it is as founder of the Canterbury Hall that he is perhaps best remembered (see pages 92 and 93). To a remarkable degree Morton brought culture to the people. He premièred Gounod's opera Faust at the Canterbury, and even built an art gallery there, described by the journalist G. A. Sala as "the Royal Academy over the water".

The theatre magazine Pick-Me-Up commented on The Man That Broke The Bank At Monte Carlo in this front page cartoon of 1892, entitled Heard it in her Sleep. Wife: "I've been dosing, and have had a strange dream Charlie. I thought I was winning at Monte Carlo and broke the bank! What could have made me dream that?" Husband: "The servant has just fallen down stairs, I think, and broken the dinner service!"

I've just got here, through Pa — ris, from the sun — ny south — ern shore; I to Mon — te Car — lo went, just to raise my win — ter's rent; Dame For — tune smiled up — — — on me as she'd ne — ver done be — fore, And I've now such lots of mon — ey, I'm a

This answer to Coborn's song was performed by Harry Pleon, one of the leading parodists of his day. He was as talented a writer as he was a performer, and wrote plays, burlesques and comic songs for himself and others, producing seven parodies of Ta-ra-ra-Boom-de-ay alone. Another parody of The Man That Broke The Bank was written for Walter Munroe. Charles de Ville Wells, the man who did break the bank, was a swindler who spent most of his life in prison, hence Munroe's lines: "All alone, upon his own, At Portland he'll be breaking stone, Instead of breaking banks at Monte Carlo."

gent .... Yes, I've now such lots of

mon - ey, I'm a gent ....

The Palace, claimed in this programme as "the handsomest music hall in Europe", had been intended for higher things. It was erected in 1891 for Richard D'Oyly Carte as the Royal English Opera House, but did not flourish. In 1893 it reopened as a Theatre of Varieties, a grand version of music hall with elegantly appointed smoking saloons, magnificent smoking lounge and "Grand Illuminated Foyer". It was the venue for the first Royal Variety Performance in 1912, and is still very much alive as the Palace Theatre in Cambridge Circus. Its very sumptuousness was symptomatic of the growing respectability of variety theatres and the subsequent decline of music hall.

2.

I stay indoors till after lunch, and then my daily walk
    To the great Triumphal Arch is one grand triumphal march.
Observed by each observer with the keenness of a hawk,
    I'm a mass of money, linen, silk, and starch—
    I'm a mass of money, linen, silk, and starch.

        CHORUS.—As I walk along, &c.

3.

I patronized the tables at the Monte Carlo hell
    Till they hadn't got a sou for a Christian or a Jew;
So I quickly went to Paris for the charms of mad'moiselle,
    Who's the loadstone of my heart—what can I do,
    When with twenty tongues she swears that she'll be true?

        CHORUS.—As I walk along, &c.

Windswept trees cling to a cliff top overlooking the coast near Monaco in an engraving from Nouveau Voyages en Zig Zag by R. Töpffer, published in Paris in 1870. Since the 19th century the 350-acre principality of Monaco has attracted the rich and famous to its casino in Monte Carlo and its beautiful coastline with its dramatic corniche roads and picturesque hillside villages.

The Oxford Music Hall, reproduced here from Harper's New Monthly Magazine, was opened by Charles Morton in 1861. It stood on the site of the Boar and Castle public house at the junction of Tottenham Court Road and Oxford Street, the terminus of the coach route from Oxford. It was twice burnt down – once in 1868 and again in 1872. A few years later, in 1878, stricter fire regulations became law and many music halls which could not afford the necessary alterations were forced to close. The Oxford survived. It was completely rebuilt in 1892, and finally demolished in 1928, to be replaced by a Lyons' Corner House.

·IF·IT·WASN'T·FOR·THE· ·'OUSES·IN·BETWEEN·

If the cockneys had a genius for making comedy out of tragedy, they could also reverse the process and create pathos out of comedy. Gus Elen, who sang this song, created the character of a costermonger living in the claustrophobic atmosphere of a terraced house with a tiny back yard and longing for the wide open spaces. In his imagination he can see across the little terraced houses – rows and rows of them – as far as Hackney Marshes and Wembley. He tries to reproduce a Kent garden in his back yard with left-over fruit and vegetables from the market and even, in a wild flight of fancy, tries to teach his donkey to moo like a cow.

Gus Elen, born in 1862, had a long apprenticeship as a busker, singing in pubs and performing with a black-face troupe at the seaside on the sands before he decided to follow Albert Chevalier's example and produce coster songs. He made enough money from music hall to buy a cottage by the sea after the First World War. He returned to the halls briefly in 1931 and appeared in the Royal Variety Performance in 1935, but resisted all suggestions that he should make a full come-back. He had found his "very pretty garding" and did not intend to leave it, having had enough of the houses in between.

WRITTEN BY EDGAR BATEMAN   COMPOSED BY GEORGE LE BRUNN

1894

MODERATO.

PIANO.

Gus Elen relaxes with a beer in the garden, probably at the house he bought in Thurleigh Avenue, Balham, in south London, when he became established as a music-hall performer. The house is marked with a commemorative blue plaque, as are the birthplaces of Albert Chevalier in Notting Hill Gate and Marie Lloyd in Hoxton.

If you saw my lit-tle back-yard, "Wot a pret-ty spot!" you'd cry— It's a

pic-ture on a sun-ny sum-mer day; Wiv the

tur-nip-tops and cab-ba-ges wot peo-ple does-n't buy, I....

makes it on a Sun-day look all gay. The...

"An' when the dust cart comes arahnd it's jest like 'arvest 'ome,'' says Elen on his song cover, dreaming of country cornfields in autumn but equipped only with a watering can and wilting pot plant. In his coster numbers he created down-to-earth, believable characters. The Echo of 3rd March, 1894, compared his "stern realism" with Albert Chevalier's "sentimental coster wooing his 'donah' like a 19th-century Romeo", and concluded: "We cannot be sure we do not prefer Mr Elen's truthful sketches".

A MUSICAL CANTERBURY TALE

The Canterbury Music Hall, the first purpose-built music hall, arose from the musical evenings held at a public house called the *Canterbury Arms*.

In 1849, its landlord, Charles Morton (1819-1905), built a hall over a skittle alley at the back of the pub where entertainment was provided for 700 people at sixpence a head. Under his ownership, this Canterbury Hall had high aspirations, being the venue for the English première of Gounod's *Faust* and for the popularization of Offenbach's light orchestral music. It also presented comic singers such as Sam Cowell, Morton's chief attraction.

When the first hall grew too cramped, it was replaced in 1854 by a larger building seating 1,500.

In 1867, William Holland succeeded Morton as manager and slowly replaced the classical emphasis with more variety and comic items, presenting a line-up of big names that included Nelly Power, the Great Vance and – the star turn – George Leybourne.

2

We're as countrified as can be wiv a clothes-prop for a tree,
 The tub-stool makes a rustic little stile;
Every time the blooming clock strikes there's a cuckoo sings to me,
 And I've painted up "To Leather Lane, a mile."
Wiv tom-ar-toes and wiv radishes wot 'adn't any sale,
 The backyard looks a puffick mass o' bloom;
And I've made a little beehive wiv some beetles in a pail,
 And a pitchfork wiv the 'andle o' the broom.

neigh_bours fink I grows 'em, and you'd fan_cy you're in Kent, Or at

Ep_som, if you gaze in_to the mews; It's a

won_der as the land_lord does_n't want to raise the rent, Be __

_cause we've got such nob_by dis_tant views.

3

There's the bunny shares 'is egg-box wiv the cross-eyed cock and hen,
    Though they 'as got the pip, and 'im the morf;
In a dog's-'ouse on the line-post there was pigeons nine or ten,
    Till some one took'd a brick and knocked it off.
The dust-cart, though it seldom comes, is just like 'arvest 'ome
    And we mean to rig a dairy up some'ow;
Put the donkey in the wash'ouse wiv some imitation 'orns,
    For we're teaching 'im to moo just like a kah (cow).

A programme from the Oxford Music Hall illustrates the building as it looked after reconstruction in 1893. The Sketch, in a piece generally critical of theatre programmes, gave credit to the music halls when it wrote in 1895: "At a time when theatrical souvenirs of the most charming description are all the vogue, it is an extraordinary thing that theatrical programmes are, as a rule, so inadequate, so expensive, and such miserable specimens of the printer's art. A programme should be a record more or less complete of the play and the players. Some of the music halls have shown the way with some really artistic play-bills."

Gas holders stand in for mountains in this view of the costermonger's back yard. This song was dedicated to G. R. Sims, who wrote that celebrated classic of Victorian sentiment, It Was Christmas Day In The Workhouse.

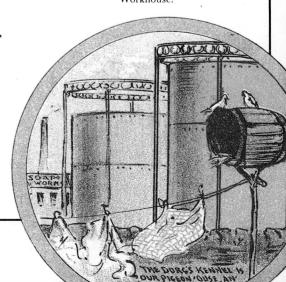

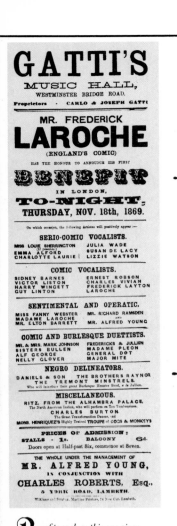

Benefits such as this one given at Gatti's Music Hall were a relatively common occurrence in the 1860s. The night's proceeds or part of them would go to a selected and usually long-serving performer or manager, while the artistes on the bill would give their services free. The result was usually a fine bill of fare for the audience and a good purse for the evening's beneficiary – in this case, Fred Laroche, the comic singer.

CHORUS.

Oh! it real-ly is a wer-ry pret-ty gar-den, And Ching-ford to the east-ward could be seen; Wiv a lad-der and some glasses, You could see to 'Ack-ney Marshes, If it was-n't for the 'ous-es in be-tween.

CHORUS 2	CHORUS 3
Oh! it really is a werry pretty garden,	Oh! it really is a werry pretty garden,
And the soap works from the 'ouse-tops could be seen;	And 'Endon to the westward could be seen;
If I got a rope and pulley,	And by clinging to the chimbley,
I'd enjoy the breeze more fully,	You could see across to Wembley,
If it wasn't for the 'ouses in between.	If it wasn't for the 'ouses in between.

IT'S·A·GREAT·BIG·SHAME!

Written and composed by the same team that produced *If It Wasn't For The 'Ouses In Between*, this song was a perfect fit for Elen. He portrayed characters who were down-to-earth, lugubrious, people you might meet in the streets – not gay, tender and romantic like Chevalier's heroes. He made no obvious attempt to charm, but when he smiled the world smiled with him.

Singing *It's A Great Big Shame* he convinced his audiences that he meant every word. People were genuinely moved by this sad little cockney, his voice going falsetto with emotion, as he lamented the unhappy lot of his pal married to a nagging wife. At the same time the ludicrous disparity in height between the two protagonists – he six foot three and she four foot two – created a hilarious comic picture in the mind. Gus Elen was a small man himself and his diminutiveness added to the comedy of the number as he protected his invisible giant friend.

In his brief return to the halls in the 1930s Elen was filmed singing *It's A Great Big Shame* and two other songs from his repertoire: *'Arf A Pint Of Ale* and *The Postman's Holiday*. In these short snippets, although obviously uncomfortable with the new medium, a glimmer of his sincerity and humour comes over still.

WRITTEN BY EDGAR BATEMAN   **COMPOSED BY GEORGE LE BRUNN**   1895

From the cover of this song, H. G. Banks's Gus Elen extends his hands to compare the heights of the great big drayman and his nagging midget wife. Elen knew how to use props. Here he carries a hammer, to let the nagging wife "know who's who". In If It Wasn't For The 'Ouses In Between *he has a watering can, and in* Catch 'Em Alive 'O *a strip of fly paper.*

A NIGHT AT THE CANTERBURY

The second Canterbury Hall, or Concert Room, built in 1854, was packed nightly. The following account details a visit made to the hall by a Mr Ritchie in the 1850s and comes from his book entitled *The Night Side of London*.

"We proceed up a few stairs, along a passage lined with handsome engravings to a bar, where we pay sixpence if we take a seat in the body of the hall, and ninepence if we ascend into the gallery.

"We make our way leisurely along the floor of the hall. At the opposite end to that at which we enter is the platform, on which are placed a grand piano and a harmonium on which the performers play in the intervals when the previous singers have left the stage.

"The chairman sits just beneath them. It is dull work to him; but there he must sit drinking and smoking cigars from seven to twelve o'clock.

"The room is crowded, and almost every gentleman has a pipe or a cigar in his mouth. Evidently the majority present are respectable mechanics or small tradesmen with their wives and daughters and sweethearts. Now and then you see a midshipman, or a few fast clerks and warehousemen."

In a scene from Verse 2, Gus Elen discovers his pal is not allowed out. To "go out mashing donahs . . . and drink and smoke and sometimes fight inside the nearest pub", as Elen sang in another number, were bachelor joys and not popular with East End wives.

I've lost my pal, 'e's the best in all the tahn, But don't you fink 'im dead, be-cos 'e ain't— But since 'e's wed 'e as 'ad ter 'nuc-kle dahn— It's e--nuf ter wex the tem-per of a saint! 'E's a

2.

Now, Jim was class—'e could sing a decent song,
  And at scrappin' 'e 'ad won some great renown;
It took two coppers for ter make 'im move along,
  An annuver six to 'old the feller dahn.
But to-day when I axes would 'e come an' 'ave some beer,
  To the door-step on tip-toe 'e arrives;
"I daresn't," says 'e—"Don't shout, cos she'll 'ear—
  I've got ter clean the windows an' the knives."

CHORUS.—It's a great big shame, &c.

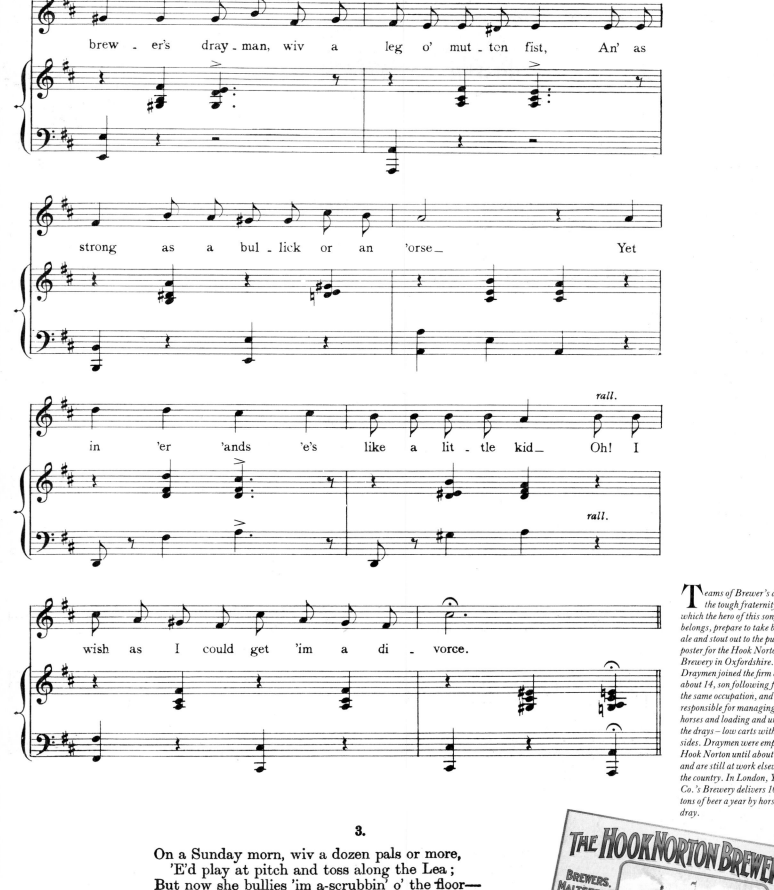

brew-er's dray-man, wiv a leg o' mut-ton fist, An' as

strong as a bul-lick or an 'orse___ Yet

rall.
in 'er 'ands 'e's like a lit-tle kid___ Oh! I

wish as I could get 'im a di-vorce.

Teams of Brewer's draymen, the tough fraternity to which the hero of this song belongs, prepare to take barrels of ale and stout out to the pubs in a poster for the Hook Norton Brewery in Oxfordshire. Draymen joined the firm aged about 14, son following father in the same occupation, and were responsible for managing the horses and loading and unloading the drays – low carts without sides. Draymen were employed by Hook Norton until about 1950, and are still at work elsewhere in the country. In London, Young & Co.'s Brewery delivers 10,000 tons of beer a year by horse-drawn dray.

3.

On a Sunday morn, wiv a dozen pals or more,
 'E'd play at pitch and toss along the Lea;
But now she bullies 'im a-scrubbin' o' the floor—
 Such a change, well, I never did see.
Wiv a apron on 'im, I twigged 'im on 'is knees
 A-rubbin' up the old 'arf-stone;
Wot wiv emptyin' the ashes and a-shellin' o' the peas,
 I'm blowed if 'e can call 'isself 'is own!

CHORUS.—It's a great big shame, &c.

THE GREAT COVER ILLUSTRATORS

The development of colour lithography in the first half of the 19th century had a dramatic impact on the look of sheet music covers, for the new medium provided an opening for a number of highly talented artists.

The leading figures in England were Alfred Concanen, Alfred Bryan and H. G. Banks.

Concanen, born in 1835, was the most senior of the trio. From 1858 he worked freelance, producing thousands of spirited illustrations for books, posters and sheet music.

Although Alfred Bryan produced some sheet music covers, he mostly contributed his sketches to journals, becoming especially known for his large-headed caricatures of music-hall and theatrical celebrities which were a feature of *The Entr'acte* magazine.

When Alfred Concanen died in 1886, two years after his favourite subject, George Leybourne, he was replaced as number one illustrator by Harry G. Banks who drew countless memorable covers during the period 1880 to 1905.

Out for a walk (below), the put-upon husband of the song takes his wife's arm in an altogether respectable style. Self-improvers were a strong force in the working class. Teetotal, thrifty and moralistic, they attended chapel not music hall. But for most working-class couples a trip to a pub like The Crown in Vine Street, Whitechapel (below right), was considered quite acceptable. Towards the end of the century a vogue for partitioning produced small bars and snugs which were popular with women, both with and without their husbands.

CHORUS.

It's a great big shame, an' if she belong'd ter me I'd let 'er know who's who—

Naggin' at a fel_ler wot is six foot free, And 'er not four foot two! Oh! they

'ad_n't been married not a month nor more, When underneath her fumb goes Jim—

Is_n't it a pi_ty as the likes ov 'er Should put up_on the likes ov 'im?

Fine.

D.C.

140

SHE·WAS·ONE·OF·THE· EARLY·BIRDS·

The stage-door Johnny, immortalised in the pages of *Punch* and adopted by T. W. Connor as the subject of George Beauchamp's song, was a familiar character of the 1890s. The lure of the ladies of the stage for young and not-so-young men-about-town has a long history. It is no wild flight of fancy to suggest that the tradition began with Charles II and Sweet Nell of Old Drury. The arrival of such companies as George Edwardes's Gaiety Girls and his Daly's Young Ladies in the 1890s provided a new focus of interest for the Victorian rake.

Girls were the magic ingredient in musical comedy, which Edwardes invented as the successor to burlesque. He put on scintillating shows full of pretty girls in pretty dresses, and managed to fill both the Gaiety Theatre and Daly's Theatre with enchanted audiences. *She Was One Of The Early Birds* was included in the musical comedy *An Artist's Model* at Daly's.

Beauchamp had started his working life in the printing trade, and after an unexceptional career in straight theatre and variety, he came to the fore in music hall with songs like *Git Yer 'Air Cut* and *Phew Dem Golden Kippers*, a parody on Stephen Foster's *Oh! Dem Golden Slippers (page 87)*. After his success with *She Was One Of The Early Birds* he continued to draw big audiences for the rest of his career. He died in 1901 at the age of 38.

WRITTEN & COMPOSED BY T. W. CONNOR

1895

Loud, broad-checked trousers, a silk waistcoat and a badly furled umbrella provide George Beauchamp with the rakish look he required for this song. This kind of costume enabled an artiste to project a strong impression of the character to the back of the hall.

A stage-door Johnny waits at the stage door laden with gifts and flowers. Some admirers were definitely top-drawer. Two Gaiety Girls, Gertie Miller and Rosie Boote, married into the peerage, as did one of the Bilton Sisters, Belle, who became Lady Dunlo.

It was at the Pan — to — mine Sweet Ma — bel and I did meet........................ She was in the bal — let (front row) And I in a five — shil — ling seat:........................

2.

At the stage door ev'ry night
   I waited with my bouquet,
Till my bird had moulted, and then
   We'd drive in a hansom away.
Oyster suppers and sparkling cham—
   Couldn't she go it !—What ho !—
Fivers I spent—tenners I lent,
   For to her I couldn't say " No."

CHORUS.—She was a dear little dickey bird, &c.

3.

Eel-skin coats and diamond rings
   Knocked holes in my purse alone ;
She would have 'em, and in the end
   I got hers by pawning my own.
When at last I was fairly broke,
   'Twixt us a quarrel arose—
Mabel the fair pulled out my hair,
   And clawed all the skin off my nose.

CHORUS.—She was a dear little dickey bird, &c.

She was dress'd like a dick — — ey bird—

Beau — ti — ful wings she had on....................................

Fig — ure di — vine, wish'd she was mine— On

her I was to — tal — ly gone....................................

His fortune spent, the discarded admirer is sent packing by the irate husband while the young lady of his passion calmly gazes on. "This was the last time we met", observed the caption on the song cover.

4.

Full of love and poverty,
    And armed with a carving knife,
One dark night I knelt in the mud
    And asked her if she'd be my wife.
Something struck me behind the ear—
    Some one said, " Now go and get
Wife of your own—leave mine alone !"
    And that was the last time we met.

CHORUS.—She was a dear little dickey bird, &c.

The pawnbroker's sign frequently marked the end of infatuations with pretty show girls. After too many oyster suppers with "sparkling cham", the impoverished victim was left "to fall back on a relative for financial assistance". The relative, in this case, would be Uncle, the common slang for pawnbroker.

· WOT · CHER! ·
KNOCK'D 'EM IN THE OLD KENT ROAD

The creators of this song were Albert Chevalier and his brother, known professionally as Charles Ingle. "One day," Ingle recalled years later, "I was footling on the piano and my brother, who was upstairs, shouted: 'What's that?' So I played it again and he came down – still holding his razor, I remember – and listened, and wrote down some words. And that was The Old Kent Road."

It tells the story of a South Londoner whose rich uncle dies and leaves him a little donkey shay but – to the amusement and taunts of his neighbours in the Old Kent Road – no money. This was one of the songs which made Chevalier's name. Probably the most stylish performer of his day, he had a flair for reproducing cockney expressions and sentiments in a way that could be understood by everybody, and his character impersonations of street sellers earned him the title of the Coster Laureate.

By training and inclination he was a straight actor, and he began writing and performing coster songs among his friends and in burlesque on the legitimate stage. Only after Charles Coborn successfully sang one of the songs in music hall was Chevalier persuaded to show his talent on the halls himself.

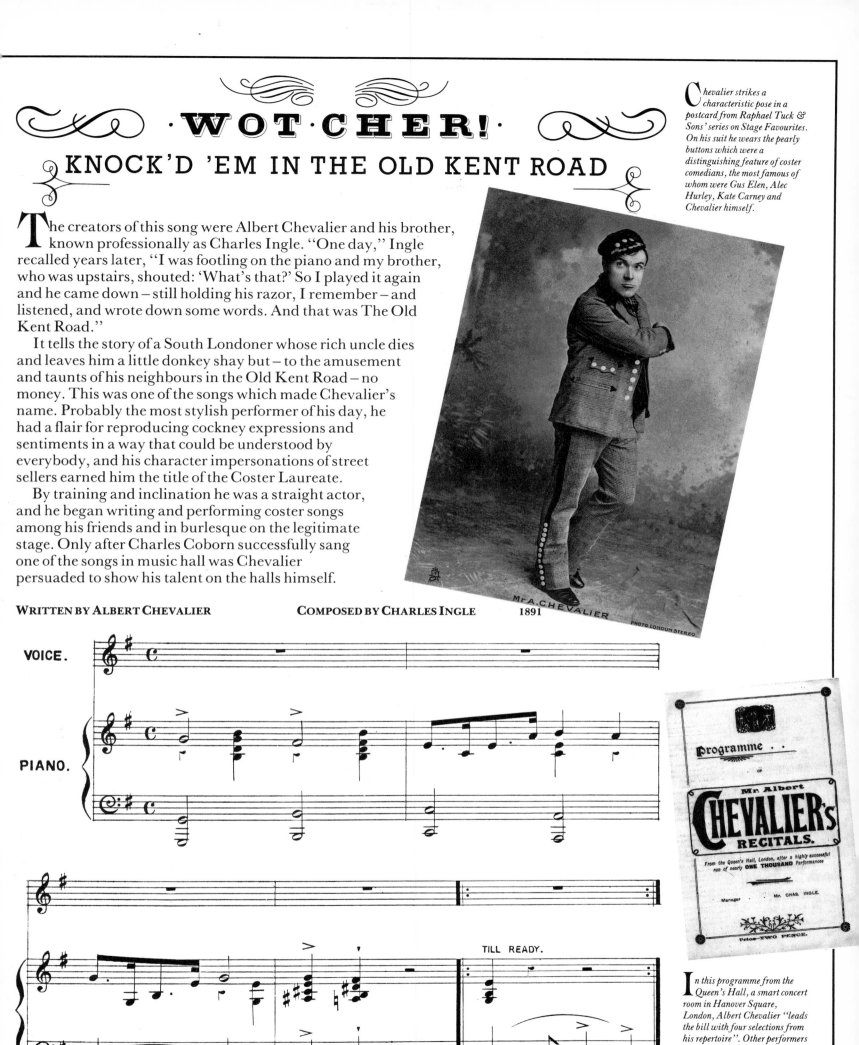

Chevalier strikes a characteristic pose in a postcard from Raphael Tuck & Sons' series on Stage Favourites. On his suit he wears the pearly buttons which were a distinguishing feature of coster comedians, the most famous of whom were Gus Elen, Alec Hurley, Kate Carney and Chevalier himself.

Mr A. CHEVALIER
1891
PHOTO LONDON STEREO

WRITTEN BY ALBERT CHEVALIER   **COMPOSED BY CHARLES INGLE**

VOICE.

PIANO.

TILL READY.

In this programme from the Queen's Hall, a smart concert room in Hanover Square, London, Albert Chevalier "leads the bill with four selections from his repertoire". Other performers filled out the bill with solos on the piano and cello, a "Mimicry" act and a song "with whistling obligato".

THE COSTER STORY

Originally a coster or coster-monger was someone who sold costard apples, a large ribbed variety common in Shakespeare's time. The word came to mean a street seller of fruit, fish and vegetables generally – in London parlance, a barrow boy.

Though many barrow boys were cockneys, born within the sound of Bow Bells, fewer and fewer could claim this distinction as London grew and street markets spread out into the suburbs. They spoke cockney, but were called costers. Especially in Lambeth and around the Old Kent Road, they became a powerful fraternity with their own brand of street wisdom, backchat and flash clothes with mother-of-pearl buttons.

In 1875 a street sweeper named Henry Croft started collecting the pearly buttons the so-called flash boys dropped in the gutter, sewed them all over his suit as a gimmick to raise money for charity, and so founded the Pearly Kings and Queens, a charitable association that now ranks as a folk tradition alongside Bobbies and Beefeaters.

Last week down our alley come a toff,

Nice old geezer with a nasty cough,

Sees my Missus, takes 'is topper off,

In a very gentlemanly way!

The donkey shay, nicely turned out and often daintily painted, was both the pride and butt of the coster fraternity, doubling as delivery cart and holiday chaise.

2

Some says nasty things about the moke,
One cove thinks 'is leg is really broke,
That's 'is envy, cos we're carriage folk,
　　Like the toffs as rides in Rotten Row!
Straight! it woke the alley up a bit,
Thought our lodger would 'ave 'ad a fit,
When my missus, who's a real wit,
　　Says "I 'ates a Bus because it's low!"
　　　　　　　　(CHORUS.)

3

When we starts the blessed donkey stops,
He won't move, so out I quickly 'ops,
Pals start whackin' him, when down he drops,
　　Someone says he wasn't made to go.
Lor it might 'ave been a four in 'and,
My old Dutch knows 'ow to do the grand,
First she bows, and then she waves 'er 'and,
　　Calling out we're goin' for a blow!
　　　　　　　　(CHORUS.)

"Ma'am," says he, "I have some news to tell,

Your rich un_cle Tom of Cam_ber_well,

Popped off re_cent, which it ain't a sell,

Leav_ing you 'is lit_tle don_key shay."

DREAMS OF AN INHERITANCE

A recurring theme in coster and cockney songs is the sudden acquisition of wealth, bringing with it escape from poor living conditions and the drudgery of work. The fortune could come from unexpected sources – Gus Elen's *Golden Dustman* finds the hoard of wealth while clearing a miser's house – but usually comes as a legacy from a rich relative. Elen's Covent Garden porter who comes into a "bit of coin" adopts new habits, such as reading *The Telegraph* instead of *The Star*, which disgust his former colleagues. Their conclusion is that *'E Dunno Where 'E Are*.

The legacy can be disappointing, however, as in *Wot Cher!* and in Harry Champion's *Any Old Iron* where the rich uncle's gold watch turns out to be of baser metal – any old iron, in fact.

A riverside idyll, with Cupid and Psyche making music among the summer grasses, decorates this programme from the London Pavilion. It was here in Piccadilly Circus that Chevalier made his first music hall appearance in 1891.

4

Ev'ry evenin' on the stroke of five,
Me and missus takes a little drive,
You'd say, "Wonderful they're still alive,"
If you saw that little donkey go.
I soon showed him that 'e'd have to do,
Just whatever he was wanted to,
Still I shan't forget that rowdy crew,
'Ollerin' "Woa! steady! Neddy Woa!"
(CHORUS.)

Opposite:

Purchasers of the cheapest seats fill the gallery of the Middlesex Music Hall in 1872. Known until 1851 as the Mogul Saloon, it was one of the first London pubs to be converted into a music hall. When this engraving was published, the building (at 167 Drury Lane) had just been reconstructed in a typically extravagant Baroque style, and could hold an audience of 1,200.

"Wot cheer!" all the neigh-bours cried,

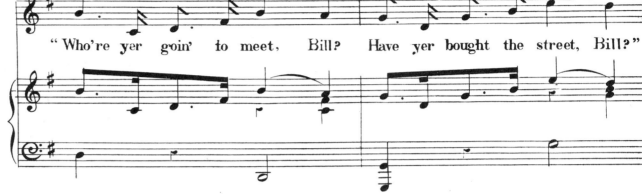

"Who're yer goin' to meet, Bill? Have yer bought the street, Bill?"

This songsheet with its decorative typographical cover cost four shillings, a high price which was standard in the 1890s. Song pirates illegally selling cheap copies on street corners forced the big music publishers in the early 1900s to simplify their cover designs and introduce shilling and later sixpenny songsheets.

Laugh! I thought I should 'ave died,

Knock'd 'em in the Old Kent Road! Road!

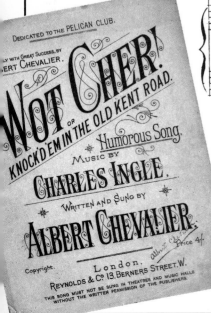

·MY·OLD·DUTCH·

Plenty of dramatic possibilities lie waiting in these lyrics about an old man who, after 40 years of marriage, can still fill four verses with praises of his dear old Dutch. (Old Dutch is cockney rhyming slang for wife: Duchess of Fife – Wife. It is always abbreviated to Dutch.) Nowadays the song is a favourite with music hall performers who play the role of the sentimental old buffer. Chevalier sometimes sang it with a picture of a workhouse as the backdrop. Old couples who went into the workhouse were generally segregated, and by introducing the idea of a forced parting, he was able to heighten the emotional impact of the song.

WRITTEN BY ALBERT CHEVALIER   **COMPOSED BY CHARLES INGLE**   1892

An outing to Chingford was a popular pastime for Londoners with money to spend in the 1890s. Then a country village, Chingford had a hotel and pleasure garden with swings and coconut shies, and evidently provided many couples with happy memories, in the words of My Old Dutch, *of "them young days of courtin' ".*

I've got a pal, A reg'lar out an' out_er. She's a dear good old gal, I'll tell yer all a_bout 'er; It's

ma_ny years since fust we met, 'Er 'air was then as black as jet, It's

whiter now, - but she don't fret, Not my old gal..........

In a scene daily repeated in Great Britain until well into the 20th century, men and women queue for admission to the casual ward of a workhouse where they would be given a wooden sleeping platform or perhaps a straw-covered floor for the night. Others less fortunate went in permanently, especially the old and infirm who often formed the largest group of inmates.

2

I calls 'er Sal,
'Er proper name is Sairer,
An' yer may find a gal
As you'd consider fairer.
She ain't a angel — she can start
A jawin' till it makes yer smart,
She's just a *woman*, bless 'er eart,
    Is my old gal! *Chorus.*

3

Sweet fine old gal,
For worlds I wouldn't lose 'er,
She's a dear good old gal,
An' that's what made me choose 'er.
She's stuck to me through thick and thin,
When luck was out, when luck was in,
Ah! wot a wife to me she's been,
    An wot a *pal! Chorus.*

4

I sees yer Sal —
Yer pretty ribbons sportin'!
Many years now, old gal,
Since them young days of courtin'
I ain't a coward, still I trust
When we've to part, as part we must,
That Death may come and take me fust
    To wait . . . . . my pal! *Chorus.*

151

CHORUS.

We've been · to _ ge _ ther now for for _ ty years, An' it

don't seem a day too much,.................... There

ain't a la _ dy liv _ in' in the land, As I'd swop for my dear old

*N*ew Cut, Lambeth, seen here in 1893, was the most important retail market south of the Thames and the centre of the coster fraternity. At that time most of London's food was sold through the markets, providing a tough living for 30,000 traders of whom 15,000 were reckoned to be regular costers and the rest interlopers or "underminers".

Dutch, ... There ain't a la_dy liv_in'
strepitoso. *decres:*

in the land, As I'd swop for my dear old Dutch.
Tempo Primo. *f*

f *poco rit:*
f

Outside the Caledonian Market in about 1900, some of the London poor loiter in hopes of gleaning leftovers. General Booth, founder of the Salvation Army, estimated in 1890 that 993,000 Londoners were very poor, starving, homeless or on public relief, a dark social abyss that formed the background to so much of contemporary songwriting.

THE·HEIGHT·OF·SENTIMENT·

The last flowering of the Victorian ballad occurred as the century neared its close. Ballads had traditionally been written either for the working-class audiences of the music halls or for the polite society of the drawing room, but by the 1880s many English songwriters and their counterparts in New York's Tin Pan Alley were churning out thousands of ballads designed to be popular in both worlds. Enormous sheet music sales testified to the success of the genre.

Under the American influence ballads became more comfortable and acceptable in their sentiments, relating simple tales that were far removed from the harsh realities of life. *Sweet Rosie O'Grady*, written by a 19-year-old New York girl, tells us nothing except that Rosie lives in a charming cottage and is "the sweetest flower that ever grew". The American style was often lachrymose, and some songwriters were even cynical in their tear-jerking approach. But Charles K. Harris truly believed in his songs, and is said to have cried whenever he sang his big success, *After the Ball*.

A number of coster songs were written in the ballad style, particularly *The Coster's Serenade*, *Are We to Part Like This?* and *When the Summer Comes Again*. The last two, belted out by Kate Carney in true music-hall style, are unlikely to have found their way into the society drawing room, but some middle ground was occupied by Albert Chevalier, who courted both audiences and had to sentimentalize his subject in order to do so.

All these songs have one thing in common: they are eminently singable.

In The Village Wedding, *painted in 1883, Sir Samuel Luke Fildes portrays a sentimental view of love and marriage which also lay behind many contemporary ballads.*

·AFTER·THE·BALL·

The American Charles K. Harris became a millionaire on the strength of *After the Ball*, the first song to have sheet music sales of more than five million. It owed its success to its lilting and evocative chorus, and was performed by both Charles Godfrey and Vesta Tilley.

WRITTEN & COMPOSED BY CHARLES K. HARRIS

1892

Charles Godfrey, a thoroughly Bohemian character and a most versatile performer, had a wide repertoire of comic and descriptive songs and good-time numbers such as Hi-Tiddley-hi-ti. He is credited with the invention of the military scena, a song and monologue enacted in an elaborate stage set. One of his most powerful, On Guard, depicted the fate of a veteran from the Crimea no longer wanted by his country, dying outside a workhouse.

With his cry "Two under fifty for a fardy!", this "Long-Song Seller" engraved from an early daguerreotype personifies the tradition of peddling cheap songsheets, or broadsides, in the streets. Later there was a vogue for the songster, a four- or eight-page booklet of song lyrics sold in the music halls. By the end of the century popular music publishing had become big business on an international scale.

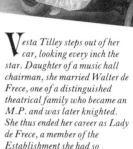

Vesta Tilley steps out of her car, looking every inch the star. Daughter of a music hall chairman, she married Walter de Frece, one of a distinguished theatrical family who became an M.P. and was later knighted. She thus ended her career as Lady de Frece, a member of the Establishment she had so brilliantly portrayed on stage.

THE LONDON IDOL

Vesta Tilley had many popular songs to her credit, including *Burlington Bertie* (not to be confused with the later *Burlington Bertie from Bow* sung by Ella Shields), *Following in Father's Footsteps* and *The Midnight Son*. Her one regret was that *Daisy Bell*, which she described as the best music hall chorus ever written, was the property of another artist, Katie Lawrence.

She adopted the name Vesta Tilley soon after her London music hall debut in 1878. Tilley, or Matilda, was in fact her first name (she was known as the Great Little Tilley when she first went on stage at the age of four) and she chose Vesta after the Vesta match, because it was "a striking name". Surely one of the most appealing of all music hall stars, she perfected the art of male impersonation, a tradition that goes back beyond the days of Charles II when, according to Samuel Pepys, "Mistress Gwynn excelled in breeches parts". Vesta was especially memorable for her elaborate characterizations of immaculate men about town. With her trim figure, clear voice and beautiful male attire, she entranced her audiences and won numerous adoring admirers. She was fittingly called the London Idol and enjoyed a big success in America.

(Key G.)

CHORUS.

After the ball is o _ ver, after the break of morn,........ After the dancers'

leav _ ing, after the stars are gone,............ Many a heart is ach _ ing

if you could read them all,........... Many the hopes that have van _ ished, af _ ter the

ball............

In a display of music-hall memorabilia, pride of place goes to one of Vesta Tilley's dinner jackets complete with white silk scarf, white waistcoat and white topper. Tilley's costumes were so well designed and chosen that she even became a setter of male fashions in the 1890s.

A stylish cartoon commemorates Vesta Tilley's classic costume act as a swell, mimicking upper-class or would-be upper-class young men. Male attire allowed her to sing male songs, among them Come into the Garden Maud, and at one time she was nicknamed the Pocket Sims Reeves, after the leading tenor for whom Michael Balfe composed the song. Later writers retrospectively dubbed her the Pocket Astaire.

THE · BOY · IN · THE · GALLERY ·

The theatrical agent George Ware wrote this very simple, sweet and wistful song for his client Nelly Power. He gave her the rights as a gift, and she later sold them for five pounds. The song was "borrowed" by Marie Lloyd who sang it without permission in 1885 when she was 15 and just starting her career. Marie planted her young sister in the gallery of the theatre with instructions to wave her handkerchief at the right moment in the chorus. Afterwards the waving of the handkerchief became a feature of the song whenever Marie performed it.

NELLY POWER

This versatile music-hall artiste started her career as a child singer in the 1860s and made her name as a male impersonator. She was thus the forerunner of Vesta Tilley, Hetty King and Ella Shields, but in the style then prevalent usually wore tights and spangles rather than full masculine dress. Two of her most popular songs were *Tiddy-fol-fol* and *La-di-da*.

She died in poverty and obscurity aged 34 in 1887, two years after Marie Lloyd pirated *The Boy in the Gallery*. George Ware, her agent, was sued by the undertaker for the funeral expenses of £7 19s. 6d. He paid up. He could afford to. He was now Marie Lloyd's agent!

The gallery is crowded in this painting by Walter Sickert entitled Noctes Ambrosianae (Divine Nights), *set in the Middlesex Music Hall. One of the most important British Impressionists, Sickert as a young man was a great devotee of the music hall and a friend of Bessie Bellwood who became famous as one of the first female singers of cockney songs.*

WRITTEN & COMPOSED BY GEORGE WARE   1885

PIANO. Moderato.

I'm a young girl and have just come over, O_ver from the Country where they do things big; And amongst the boys I've got a lover, And since I've got a lov__er, why I don't care a fig!

I'm a young girl and have just come o-ver. O-ver from the Country where they do things big; And amongst the boys I've got a lo-ver, And since I've got a lo-ver, why I don't care a fig! The boy I love is up in the gal-le-ry. The boy I love is looking now at me; There he is, can't you see, wa-ving his handkerchief, As merry as a Ro-bin that sings on the tree.

A FAMILIAR VARIATION

Since its first publication *The Boy In The Gallery* has changed in subtle ways, no doubt under the influence of Marie Lloyd who enhanced the song's reputation and her own in numerous performances. On these three pages we have printed the original version of the music, but the tune which appears on the right is nowadays more familiar. Without too much adjustment this tune may be sung to the earlier accompaniment.

The lights of the Empire Theatre, Leicester Square, illuminate the Saturday night crowds in this sketch from an 1891 issue of Harper's New Monthly Magazine. *The site had been a place of entertainment since 1849, when it was known as Savile House, a former royal residence which served variously as an exhibition gallery and saloon theatre. It became the Empire Theatre in 1884. Rebuilt as a cinema in 1928, and again in 1963, it is still emblazoned with the title The Empire (see also page 247).*

The boy I love is up in the galle_ry. The boy I love is looking now at me;

There he is can't you see waving his handkerchief, As merry as a Robin that sings on the tree.

DANCE.

Overleaf:

On the day of the 1862 Oxford and Cambridge Boat Race, Hammersmith Bridge presents a scene of amazing bustle in this painting by Walter Greaves. Two horse buses carrying advertisements for the Oxford Music Hall and the Cremorne pleasure gardens provide grandstand views for their passengers, while a troupe of black-face minstrels entertains the crowd with banjos and popular songs.

2
The boy that I love they call him a cobbler,
　But he's not a cobbler, allow me to state;
For Johnny is a tradesman, and he works in the Boro',
　Where they sole and heel them whilst you wait.
　(Chorus.) The boy I love, &c.

3
Now if I were a Duchess and had a lot of money,
　I'd give it to the boy that's going to marry me;
But I hav'nt got a penny so we'll live on love and kisses,
　And be just as happy as the birds on the tree.
　(Chorus.) The boy I love, &c.

The Marie Lloyd, one of several London pubs named after music hall artistes, is in Marie's native Hoxton, a neighbourhood in East London once noted for its many small music halls and "free-and-easy" taverns. A few streets away is the house where she was born, marked by a blue plaque. Other singers remembered in pub names are George Robey and Gertie Gitana, while Florrie Forde gave her name to a bar "down at the old Bull and Bush" near Hampstead Heath.

Kate Carney's robust good humour shines through in a portrait from one of her song covers. She married the comedian George Barclay, who became her manager, and they celebrated their golden wedding anniversary in 1935. She died in 1949.

·ARE·WE·TO·PART· LIKE·THIS?·

The coster singer Kate Carney made this song one of her big successes. Born Catharine Mary Pattinson in 1869, she came from a theatrical family. Her father belonged to a singing duo known variously as the Peterson Brothers and The Brothers Raynard, but she ignored both these names. She made her first appearance under her own surname in 1885 singing Irish songs in minor music halls, and adopted the Irish-sounding Kate Carney as her stage name in 1889. As the vogue for coster songs grew, Kate abandoned the Emerald Isle for ballads nearer home – so successfully that she was still performing to enthusiastic audiences at the age of 70. She has been likened to the late Ethel Merman for her ability to belt out songs in a sort of heart-shattering roar.

Are We To Part Like This? has a lovely singable melody by Harry Castling and Charles Collins, who also wrote the words. The very gaucheness of the lyrics adds pathos to the story of unrequited love, and saves it from becoming over-sentimental.

WRITTEN & COMPOSED BY   **HARRY CASTLING & CHARLES COLLINS 1903**

The illustration (above right), entitled A Lion Comique at the Oxford, is from a drawing made by John Pennell in 1890. In that year Kate Carney, billed as The Irish Brilliante, started to appear regularly in London halls such as the Royal Albert, Canning Town, and the Temple, Hammersmith. It was only after she established herself as a coster singer that she began appearing at the famous West End music halls.

1. Three weeks a-go, no lon-ger, I was as gay as a bird on the wing, But since me and Bill have been part-ed, you know, Life is a blank, and it's chang'd ev'ry-thing;

I saw him out with an-oth-er that night, None can guess how I felt at the sight, With tears in my eyes, that I tried to keep back, I crept to his side and said:........ Are we to part like this, Bill, Are we to part this way?........... Who's it to be, 'er or me, Don't be a-fright-en'd to say;........... If ev-'ry-thing's o-ver be-tween us, Don't nev-er pass me by,............... 'Cos you and me still friends can be, For the sake of the days gone by............. by...............

The foundation stone of John Wilton's Music Hall in Wellclose Square, Stepney, was laid in 1858 and the hall opened the following March. Soon billed as "the Handsomest Room in London" the hall was particularly successful in the 1870s, when it was managed for a time by the comic singer George Fredericks, with George Leybourne appearing frequently on the bill. Damaged by fire in 1877, the building had a chequered history over the next century, but in 1976 it was taken over by the London Music Hall Protection Society for restoration and use once more for its original purpose.

The image of childhood sweethearts has always appealed to ballad writers, but in many songs the early dream is shattered, often because one introduced the light of one's life to a close friend. The theme of Are We To Part Like This? is echoed in Alice Lloyd's Never Introduce Your Bloke To Your Lady Friend, and Gus Elen warned, Never Introduce Your Donah To A Pal. (The cockney word for girlfriend, "donah", is a corruption of the Italian donna – woman.)

2

We went to school together,
Lived side by side, me and Bill, in the mews;
When 'e was ill, too, I stayed up for nights,
Nursed him — to do it I'd never refuse;
'E used to tell me his wife I should be —
I never thought that he'd turn against me,
Sleeping or waking, at work or at home,
I find myself murmuring this — CHORUS.

3

Down in a little laundry,
Me and 'er work side by side every day;
She was my pal, and I looked to 'er well,
Trusted and helped 'er in every way;
Still, if my Bill cares for 'er more than me,
I wish 'em no harm — no, but prosperetee;
I try to forget him, but each day I find
These words running through my mind — CHORUS.

WHEN THE SUMMER COMES AGAIN
THREE POTS A SHILLING

This haunting and evocative little song beautifully expresses the hopes and dreams of the costermongers. The winters were hard for street vendors, but they could always look forward to the summertime ahead, when there would be flowers to sell, and the cry ''three pots a shilling'' would be heard in the environs of London town.

The coster sings this song to his girlfriend Nell, ''the girl who's ever willing'', and it can be sung as a duet. However, it was written by Harry Bedford, a prolific composer of music hall songs, as a solo number for Kate Carney, and it is remembered for her rough yet touching performance.

WRITTEN & COMPOSED BY HARRY BEDFORD

1895

*T*he Bedford in Camden Town re-opened in 1899 after a fire had destroyed the first music hall built on the site in 1861. Both old and new halls had a convivial atmosphere and they were often portrayed by the artist Walter Sickert, who lived just round the corner from the Bedford in Mornington Crescent. His paintings of Little Dot Hetherington At The Old Bedford and The Boy I Love Is Up In The Gallery are two of the finest evocations of the lost world of music hall.

KATE CARNEY'S DONKEY

Several of Kate Carney's coster sketches included real animals, and *Three Pots A Shilling* featured a donkey. In this interview, she recounts some of the ensuing mishaps: "One night the donkey trained for the part got lost somehow, but I sent a man with a brougham to get another, and in due course he reached the hall with a young ass standing broadside on in the carriage, his head out at one window, his tail through the other, and the inside like a stable!

"On another occasion to get the donkey in at a certain stage door we had to fix up a little gangway over the narrow passage leading to it, the approach being flanked by a couple of rather high walls. One night the donkey made a misstep and rolled off the gangway over the wall, and before we recovered him it was necessary to go and ask the owner of the plot of ground on the other side, 'Please can I get my donkey; it's gone over your garden wall!'"
Nottingham Football News, 24th March, 1906

The association of a young girl with flowers is rendered in a very romantic light in this illustration from the magazine Black and White, after a painting by John Temple. Flower sellers were a favourite subject of artists depicting London street scenes, and they were often idealized by the painter. Three Pots A Shilling strikes a more realistic note. Of course the most famous flower seller is George Bernard Shaw's Eliza Doolittle, heroine of Pygmalion. With her appearance on the stage in 1912, the coster flower girl moved triumphantly from the East End music halls to the West End theatre.

2

Sweet window flow'rs then you'll cry, Nell,
  When the summer comes again;
Toffs from us will buy 'em, gell,
  When the summer comes again;
For I knows the best of houses,
  Where lots of profit we can gain —
Splendid clothes they'll give for flow'rs,
  When the summer comes again. — *Chorus.*

3

Oh! won't we turn out dashing, Nell,
  When the summer comes again;
Folks will talk about it, gell,
  When the summer comes again;
You shall dress in "broshey" velvet,
  And me a silver watch and chain —
Let coves see we knows our book, Nell,
  When the summer comes again. — *Chorus.*

· THE · COSTER'S · SERENADE ·

Albert Chevalier made his music hall debut with this song at the London Pavilion in 1891, after 14 years on the legitimate stage. He was billed to follow Bessie Bellwood, a loud cockney performer who specialized in banter with the audience, and he was afraid they would not listen to a plaintive serenade. Instead, he got an ovation: the charm and originality of *The Coster's Serenade* were appreciated at once.

Chevalier was no cockney: he was born in Notting Hill, came from a modest middle-class background, and had toyed with the idea of becoming a Roman Catholic priest. But he was fascinated by the coster scene, and his songs evolved from a professional study of the street life of the East End. Some of the cadences used by John Crook in this song are reminiscent of the gypsy fiddlers who were a popular feature of the London streets.

Albert Chevalier sings at a fashionable private function in 1895, watched by ladies with lorgnettes and distinguished-looking gentlemen in evening dress. Despite his fame as a coster comedian, Chevalier was not really happy with this role. His years in the legitimate theatre had led him to expect an attentive audience, and he found the music-hall public noisy and unruly. Whenever he had the opportunity he would present his own concert recitals or appear at drawing room soirées.

WRITTEN BY ALBERT CHEVALIER   **COMPOSED BY JOHN CROOK**   1891

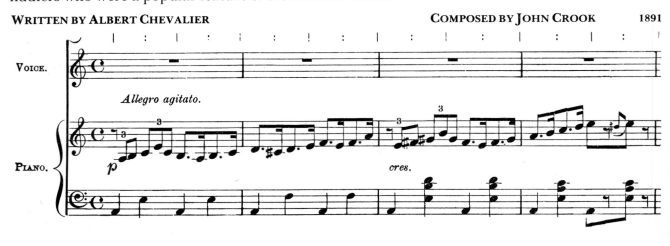

Tom Tinsley, portrayed in a drawing of 1890 by John Pennell, was Chairman of Gatti's Music Hall off the Strand. By the 1890s the gavel-wielding chairman, who introduced the acts and kept order when the audience got out of hand, was already becoming outmoded. Tinsley was one of the last in a line that had included Harry Fox of the Middlesex Theatre and the unceremonious "Old Paul" of Paul's Varieties, Leicester, who used to interrupt the acts to announce the arrival of hot pies.

You ain't for-got-ten yet   that night in May,

Down at the Welsh 'Arp, which is 'En-don way; You fan-cied win-kles, and a
pot of tea, "Four-'alf" I mur-mured's "good e-nough for me." "Give me a word of 'ope that
I may win," You prods me gent-ly with the win-kle pin,
We was as 'ap-py as could be that day, Down at the Welsh 'Arp, which is 'En-don way.

An advertisement from The Entr'acte bills the Bank Holiday attractions at the Welsh Harp public house in Hendon, north London, in 1885. The pub takes its name from the D-shaped reservoir close by, and its leafy surroundings encouraged East Enders to spend a day out in the London suburbs.

A sketch from a song entitled Dancing In The Streets recalls the days when open-air dancing was a popular entertainment. The young man's rakish bowler reflects a popular cockney style; today, the bowler hat is associated with formality, but when it was first designed by the Victorian hatter John Bowler it was intended for casual wear, and marked the City clerks and shopkeepers from their silk-hatted superiors.

2.

You ain't forgotten 'ow we drove that day,
Down to the Welsh 'Arp, in my donkey shay,
Folks with a "chy-ike" shouted "ain't they smart?"
You looked a queen, me every inch a Bart.
Seemed that the moke was saying "do me proud"
Mine is the nobbiest turn-out in the crowd;
Me in my "pearlies" felt a toff that day,
Down at the Welsh 'Arp, which is 'Endon way.

Oh Arriet, &c.

3.

Eight months ago and things is still the same,
You're known about 'ere by your maiden name,
I'm getting chivied by my pals cos why?
Nightly I warbles 'ere for your reply.
Summer 'as gone, and it's a freezin' now,
Still love's a burnin' in my 'eart I vow;
Just as it did that 'appy night in May,
Down at the Welsh 'Arp, which is 'Endon way

Oh 'Arriet, &c.

Albert Chevalier.

Semplice con moto.

Oh! 'Ar - ri - et, I'm wait - ing, wait-ing for you my dear,........ Oh!

'Ar - ri - et, I'm wait - ing, wait-ing a - lone out here,........

accelerando.

When that moon shall cease to shine, False will be this 'eart of mine; I'm

Albert Chevalier is depicted as ringmaster in this drawing by G. F. Scotson-Clarke, published in 1899 in an illustrated volume of well-known songs collected by George Gamble and entitled The Halls. Scotson-Clarke's witty caricatures included sketches of Marie Lloyd, Dan Leno, George Robey, Vesta Tilley and other leading music-hall artistes.

St George's Hall, Langham Place, was opened in 1867. The imposing building, with its raked stage and organ, was first used as a concert hall, but from 1904 until 1933 it was taken over by the Maskelyne and Dwant management, who used it for popular magic shows combining conjuring tricks, illusion and comedy. The building was badly damaged in the Blitz, and subsequently demolished.

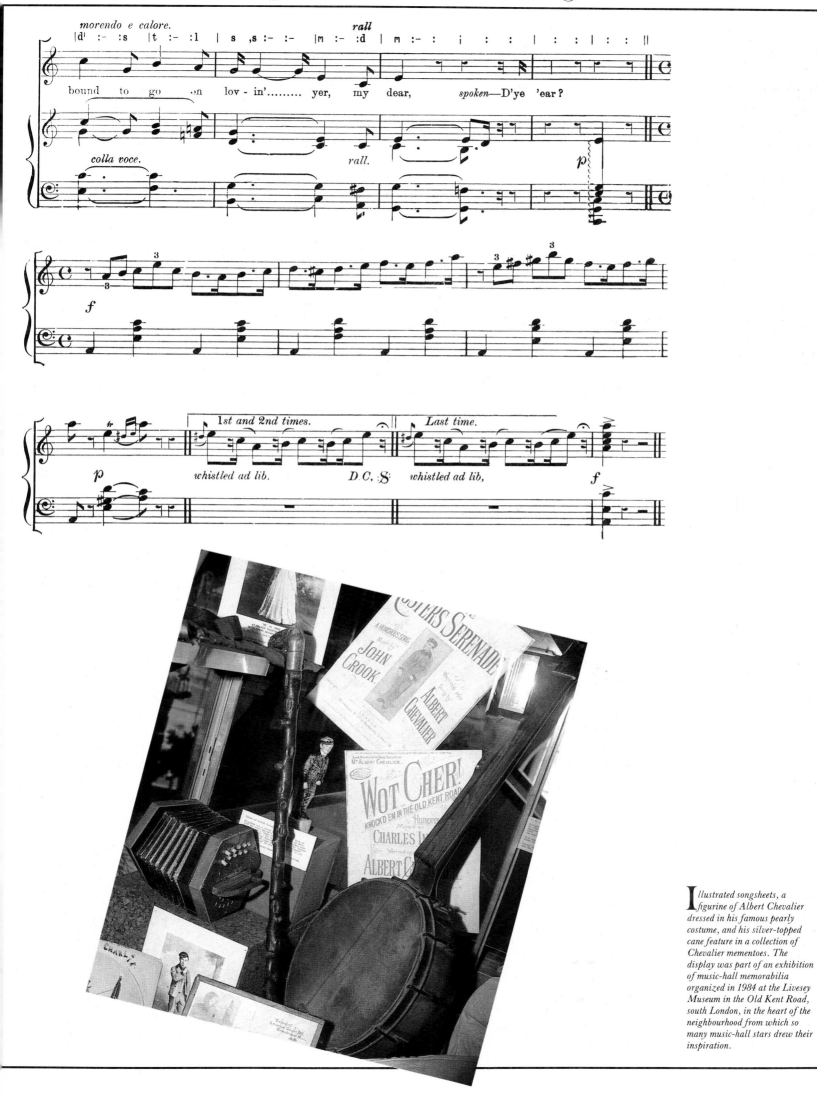

Illustrated songsheets, a figurine of Albert Chevalier dressed in his famous pearly costume, and his silver-topped cane feature in a collection of Chevalier mementoes. The display was part of an exhibition of music-hall memorabilia organized in 1984 at the Livesey Museum in the Old Kent Road, south London, in the heart of the neighbourhood from which so many music-hall stars drew their inspiration.

·A·BIRD·IN·A·GILDED·CAGE·

Harry Von Tilzer's song about riches not buying happiness is a typical morality ballad. It tells the story of a young girl "sold for an old man's gold" and doomed to pay for her luxurious surroundings with a life of regret, "for youth cannot mate with age".

Harry Von Tilzer was a circus performer before he went on the New York vaudeville stage in 1892, and he wrote this lilting waltz when he was 28. He also sang a number of sentimental but jaunty songs including *Wait Till The Sun Shines, Nellie* and *I Want A Girl Just Like The Girl That Married Dear Old Dad*. He founded the Von Tilzer Music Company, leading publishers of popular songs. He is also said to have been one of the first pianists to stuff paper between the strings to create a "honky-tonk" effect; a journalist, Munroe Rosenfeld, dubbed this "tin pan" and the nickname Tin Pan Alley came to apply to the New York popular music industry as a whole.

WRITTEN BY ARTHUR J. LAMB   **COMPOSED BY HARRY VON TILZER**   1900

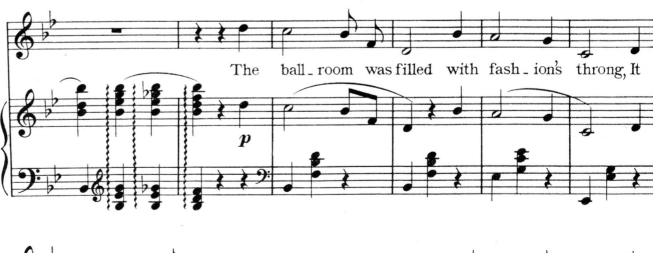

The handsome young man in this drawing is the prototype of the ardent admirer whom the bird in the cage might have chosen had she not married for money. This is a portrait of Arthur Lennard, a successful music hall artist who sang comic numbers as well as tear-jerking ballads.

passed a _ long, The fair _ est of all the sights, ___ A

girl to her lov_er then soft _ ly sighed, "There's rich_es at

her com _ mand;" ___ "But she married for wealth, not for

love" he cried, Though she lives in a mans _ ion grand. ___

rit:

Allarg:

An early vaudeville routine photographed at the Fifth Avenue Theatre features two tramps and a dog. It is a comment on American life at the turn of the century that the tramp was such a popular comic figure; in Charlie Chaplin's hand, the stock comedy turn was later transformed into a universal emblem of pathos.

Florrie Forde, who launched A Bird In A Gilded Cage in London, poses in a wasp-waisted gown, lavish jewellery and plumed hat, a grand lady of music hall. Born in Australia, she made her London debut in 1897. Her popular successes included Down At The Old Bull And Bush, Antonio, Flanagan and Has Anybody Here Seen Kelly? She also appeared in pantomime as a robust principal boy, and for many years she had her own summer show at Douglas on the Isle of Man.

2
The beautiful woman surveyed the scene,
Her flatterers by the score;
Her gems were the purest, her gown divine,
So what could a woman want more.
But memory brings back the face of a lad,
Whose love she had turned aside,
But happiness cannot be bought with gold,
Although she's a rich man's bride.

CHORUS.

3
I stood in a church-yard just at eve,
When sunset adorned the west;
And looked at the people who'd come to grieve,
For loved ones now laid at rest.
A tall marble monument marked the grave,
Of one who'd been fashion's queen,
And I thought she is happier here at rest,
Than to have people say, when seen.

CHORUS.

CHORUS.

She's on-ly a bird in a gild-ed cage, A beau-ti-ful sight to see,_____ You may think she's hap-py and free from care, She's not, though she seems to be,_____ 'Tis sad when you think of her wast-ed life, For youth cannot mate with age,_____ And her beau-ty was sold, For an old man's gold, She's a bird in a gild-ed cage._____

Allarg:

rit:

sost:

D.C.

This suggestive postcard illustrates the other side of Victorian morality, the girl of easy virtue. The cheerful dissipation of champagne drinking could only have been paid for by a wealthy admirer: whether respectably married or living in the twilight of the demi-monde, women were almost inevitably "kept".

The caged bird imagery is echoed in graphic form on the song cover of The Linnet Polka. The girl at the window is surrounded by convolvulus, a binding plant symbolizing captive emotions. The same images were employed by the Pre-Raphaelite artist Holman Hunt in a painting entitled The Awakened Conscience. It shows a young woman sitting on her lover's knee at the piano, clearly contemplating leaving him for a more virtuous life. Next to her is a vase of convolvulus, while her imminent escape from sin is signified by a bird flying free of the predatory domestic cat.

SWEET·ROSIE·O'GRADY·

Maude Nugent, a New York vaudeville singer, composed this ballad when she was only 19. Having hawked it around the music publishers for months without success, she eventually took matters into her own hands and sang it herself at Tony Pastor's theatre on 14th Street. The song was soon taken up by other singers, and *Sweet Rosie O'Grady* became part of the repertoire of singers in the league of Walter Munroe and Pat Rafferty, who specialized in songs about romantic Irish ladies.

WRITTEN & COMPOSED BY MAUDE NUGENT   1896

Flower names for girls, such as Lily, May, Violet and Primrose, were popular at the turn of the century, and the language of flowers enjoyed a vogue: lovers would express their feelings through bouquets of carefully chosen blossoms, each with a symbolic meaning. Bluebells, for example, stood for constancy, and violets for modesty. But in the words of this song, "Rose, my Rose, is just the sweetest little flow'r of all".

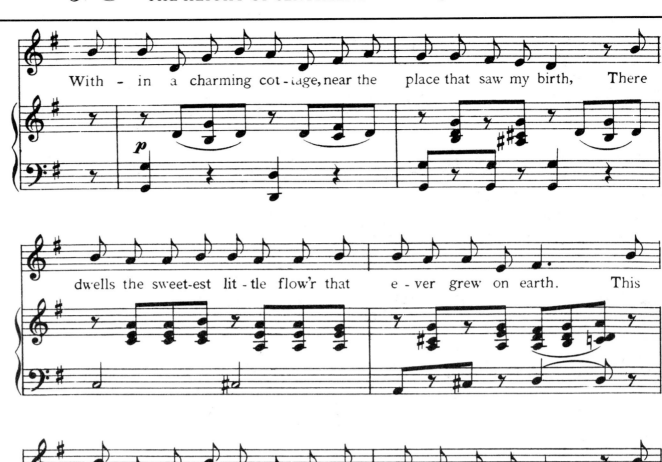

With - in a charming cot - tage, near the place that saw my birth, There

dwells the sweet-est lit - tle flow'r that e - ver grew on earth. This

flow'r is known as Ro - sie — 'tis her love - ly Christ - ian name, But

had she a - ny o - ther name, I'd love her just the same.

rall:

In a drawing of 1891, a mistress and maid sit sewing at the parlour table, typifying peaceful domesticity. Needlework, like music, was thought to be a suitable occupation for the gentle sex. Fancy needlework was especially popular, with the result that most middle-class homes boasted an amazing array of hand-embroidered articles ranging from curtains and bedspreads to pin cushions and watch-pockets. Some of the less desirable products of this home industry found their way to charity bazaars, and in The Long Vacation the novelist Charlotte M. Yonge described one such "fat red cushion" as "just like brick-dust enlivened by half-boiled cauliflowers".

2.
I never shall forget the day she promised to be mine,
As we sat telling love tales with a happiness divine.
Upon her finger then I plac'd a small engagement ring,
While in the trees the little birds this love song seem'd to sing.
Chorus

3.
I've been in love with Pansy, and I've spoon'd with Ivy Green,
With Mignonette and Violet I've now and then been seen.
Both Olive and Camelia are graceful, dark and tall,
But Rose, my Rose, is just the sweetest little flow'r of all.
Chorus

CHORUS.

Tempo di Valse

Sweet Ro-sie O' Gra — dy, My beau-ti-ful Rose,............

She's my lit-tle la — dy, That ev'-ry-one knows,............

And when we are mar — ried, How happy we'll be;........................ I love sweet

Ro-sie O' Gra — dy, And Ro-sie O' Gra-dy, loves me. me............

D. C. %

The rustic cottage, with its steeply pitched roof and rose-covered trelliswork, was an ideal many urban Victorians dreamed of. Garden suburbs were designed to provide a semi-rural environment within reach of the town. When the Bedford Park estate at Turnham Green, west London, was built in the 1870s it was advertised as a place where the inhabitants could "hear the nightingale sing and yet live within the sound of Bow Bells". In an age before the Trade Descriptions Act, estate agents' fantasies knew no bounds.

RAMPANT PATRIOTISM

I *Want To Be A Military Man:* so went a popular chorus of the day. The Victorians were intensely proud of their Army and their Sons of the Sea, and paid tribute to them in many fine patriotic songs. The first great military venture of Victoria's reign was the Crimean War of 1854-56, and the images of that conflict – particularly the doomed heroism of the Noble Six Hundred, immortalized in Alfred Tennyson's *Charge Of The Light Brigade* – were imprinted on the consciousness of a whole generation.

By the end of the century, the romantic view of war had given way to a more realistic approach, and Rudyard Kipling's Tommy Atkins personified a new kind of soldier-hero: tough, resilient, and mocking his superiors with the ironic humour that also found its place among the coster comedians of the music hall.

During Victoria's reign, national pride was identified in the popular mind with pride of empire – the belief in Britain's civilizing mission to govern subject peoples. It is difficult for us to identify with such sentiments, but our collection ranges beyond mere chauvinism. The belligerence of *Macdermott's War Song* and *Soldiers Of The Queen* is balanced by *Comrades* – an appealing tribute to the loyalty of brothers-in-arms – and *Good-Bye Dolly Gray*, a nostalgic song of farewell. Both prove that, by the end of the era people were becoming more aware of the sadness and tragedy of war.

In a print of the Battle of Balaclava in 1854, published by the German-born engraver Rudolph Ackermann, the Scots Greys and Enniskillings force their way through Russian troops to reach cavalry regiments trapped by enemy advance.

· MACDERMOTT'S · WAR · SONG ·

Resplendent in their tasselled bearskins and bristling with gold braid, the Light Brigade charge towards the enemy guns in an illustration from a late Victorian song cover for Will Atkins's The Last Roll Call (The Survivor's Story).

"We don't want to fight but by jingo if we do . . . We've got the ships, we've got the men, and got the money too!" With this chorus, the Great Macdermott brought the audience of the London Pavilion to its feet in 1878, and the word jingoism entered the English language. The song captured the mood of the moment: Russia was threatening to advance into Turkey and capture Constantinople, thus challenging Britain's naval supremacy in the Mediterranean. Popular opinion was inflamed to fever pitch and the "jingo song" was quoted by statesmen, shouted in the streets, and could hardly be printed fast enough to meet public demand. As *The Era* commented in 1901, "It was not an ordinary political song but a manifesto".

G. H. Macdermott was already well known for *Dear Old Pals (page 95);* this song made him a household name.

G. W. Hunt had previously used the phrase "by Jingo" in a song for George Leybourne in 1868, but now the term became his sobriquet, and he was nicknamed "Jingo" Hunt.

Both Hunt and Macdermott took the song very seriously as a contribution to British foreign policy, though it was diplomatic pressure, not public opinion in Britain, that led to the Russian withdrawal and paved the way for the Congress of Berlin in 1878, from which Disraeli returned bringing "Peace with Honour".

WRITTEN & COMPOSED BY G. W. HUNT

1878

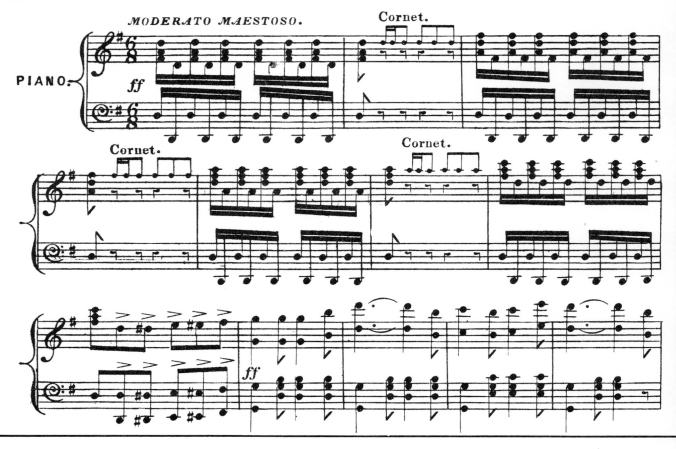

The Russian Bear receives a sharp rebuke from the British Lion in a Punch cartoon of 1885. Russia threatened British interests in the Indian sub-continent, and both powers vied for mastery over the warlike Afghan tribes on India's North-west Frontier. In 1885 a menacing Russian army defeated the Afghans at Penjdeh, but the prompt mobilization of British forces in India led to a diplomatic settlement of the Anglo-Russian dispute. The agreement on the Russo-Afghan border was regarded in Britain as a victory, and the Bear withdrew behind his old frontier.

"We've got the men": a British grenadier, flanked by soldiers from other parts of the Empire, stands guard under the Union Jack in this illustration from a Boer War song entitled So They All Came. *Native Indian troops had fought in the Crimea, and by the end of the century the idea that colonial soldiers as well as British regiments would respond to the call of imperial defence was already strongly established.*

POPULAR PARODIES

Although *Macdermott's War Song* was hugely popular, not everyone took it seriously. Henry Pettit, who had written Macdermott's first success, *The Scamp*, produced a parody of the jingo song which went:

"I don't want to fight
I'll be slaughtered if I do.
I'd let the Russians have
    Constantinople!
Newspapers talk of
    Russian hate,
Of its ambition tell;
Of course they want a war
    because
It makes the papers sell.
Let all the politicians
Who desire to help the
    Turk
Put on the uniforms
    themselves
And go and do the work!"

Politicians, like politics, have always provided rich material for parody. The appointment of W. H. Smith, a member of the newsagent family, as Secretary for War in 1886 moved the radical MP Wilfred Lawson to write this verse:

"A paper fleet they say is
    ours,
If what we hear is true.
Let's hope the fleets of other
    powers
Are stationary too!"

"The Dogs of War" are loose and the rug-ged Russian Bear, Full
bent on blood and rob-be-ry, has crawl'd out of his lair.... It
seems a thrash-ing now and then, will ne-ver help to tame.... That
brute, and so he's out up-on the "same old game".... The
Li-on did his best.... to find him some ex-cuse.... To

crawl back to his den a_gain, all ef_forts were no use.... He

hun_ger'd for his vic_tim, he's pleas'd when blood is shed.... But

let us hope his crimes may all re_coil on his own head...

2

The misdeeds of the Turks have been "spouted" thro' all lands,
But how about the Russians, can they show spotless hands?
They slaughtered well at Khiva, in Siberia icy cold,
How many subjects done to death will never perhaps be told,
They butchered the Circassians, man, woman, yes and child,
With cruelties their Generals their murderous hours beguiled,
And poor unhappy Poland their cruel yoke must bear,
Whilst prayers for "Freedom and Revenge" go up into the air.
CHORUS.

3

May he who 'gan the quarrel soon have to bite the dust,
The Turk should be thrice armed for "he hath his quarrel just,"
'Tis sad that countless thousands should die thro' cruel war,
But let us hope most fervently ere long it will be o'er;
Let them be warned, Old England is brave Old England still,
We've proved our might, we've claimed our right, and ever, ever will,
Should we have to draw the sword our way to victory we'll forge,
With the Battle cry of Britons, "Old England and Saint George!"
CHORUS.

The management of the Elephant and Castle Theatre advertises Harry H. Hamilton's Diorama of Afghanistan and Zululand in 1879. Before the advent of newsreel, this kind of three-dimensional scene with illuminated effects was a way of providing spectators with an exciting reconstruction of the battlefield. Both these imperial adventures had involved military disasters – in Kabul, the Afghan tribesmen fell upon the British forces sent to protect them from Russian control, while at Isandhlwana British troops were decimated by Cetawayo's Zulu legions. This defeat was redeemed by the gallant British defence at Rourke's Drift and the subsequent destruction of the Zulu army, while in Afghanistan the 1880s saw British victories in the "Great Game" for the control of India's North-West Frontier.

CHORUS.

We don't want to fight but by jin-go if we do.... We've got the ships, we've got the men, and got the mon-ey too! We've fought the Bear be-fore... and while we're Britons true!. The Russians shall not have Constanti- no _ _ _ ple...

mf gvas ad lib:

ff

"We've got the ships": the Royal Navy was the nation's first line of defence, and the symbol of the Navy's honour was HMS Victory (above), Nelson's flagship at the Battle of Trafalgar. Launched in 1765, she was regarded as a masterpiece of shipbuilding. She weighed over 2,000 tons and carried 104 guns. Fifty years later, the Victory was dwarfed by ships weighing 15,000 tons, measuring three times her length, and mounting single guns more powerful than her entire broadside.

The Crimean War demonstrated the enormous advantages of steam over sail, and subsequent decades saw the conversion of existing craft into steam vessels such as the ship on the right. Steam power brought radical changes in the dimensions, design and construction of fighting ships, and by the 1880s the Royal Navy boasted a formidable array of iron-clad battleships. New fighting ships were not cheap, but in the words of the jingo song, "We've got the money too."

·COMRADES·

A Tivoli programme advertises "popular prices" ranging from a shilling for the Upper Circle to the five-shilling Reserved Fauteuils and the much more costly boxes, evidence of later music hall's increasingly respectable clientele.

Felix McGlennon's song evokes the comradeship of brothers-in-arms. Typical of Victorian songs extolling the virtues of the military man, it was introduced by Tom Costello in May 1890. He sang it at both the newly opened Tivoli Music Hall in the Strand and at the South London Music Hall in Lambeth: it was quite common for music hall artistes to appear in several halls in one evening – all that was needed was a hansom cab, a few good songs, and inexhaustible energy.

Tom Costello was born in Birmingham in 1863, and made his name in the London halls after a successful appearance in the pantomime *Jack And The Beanstalk* at the Surrey Theatre. He sang in both serious and comic style: *Comrades* was a tearful number (though it has since been parodied) and he sang a similar song, "I'll go down in the angry deep, with the ship I love", with equal solemnity. But in another of his numbers, *At Trinity Church I Met My Doom*, the accent is on comedy, and *His Funeral's Tomorrow* shows that Costello was an early exponent of grim humour. His act included hoaxes like being served with a writ on stage, or threatening to shoot the next man who shouted out and then firing a gun at him – it was loaded with blanks, but the man, who had been planted, promptly expired and was carried out through the audience.

In this and other ways Costello built up a reputation as an innovator. *The Entr'acte*, reviewing his performance of *Comrades* at the South London in July 1890, remarked that he was "again evidencing his creative power. This is the element that is wanted at the music-hall . . . Imitators are as plentiful as blackberries. Mr Costello invests all his essays with an amount of originality that is refreshing."

Costello appeared in the Veterans Variety show in 1923 and died in 1943 at the age of 80.

WRITTEN & COMPOSED BY FELIX McGLENNON   **ARRANGED BY E. JONGHMANS**   1890

Tom Costello is pictured as an off-duty soldier in this drawing from the cover of The Comrade's Waltz. *His simple presentation emphasized the pathos of the song.*

ALLEGRO.

V.1. We from childhood play'd to-gether, My dear comrade Jack and I,......We would fight each o-ther's bat-tles, To each o-ther's aid we'd fly;..... And in boy--ish scrapes and troubles, You would find us ev'-ry where, Where one went the --ther follow'd, Naught could part us for we were—

Two friends pledge their loyalty as they enlist in the Army on the sheet music cover for this song, performed by Tom Costello.

A VOLUNTEER ARMY

Throughout Queen Victoria's reign, Britain's fighting force was an army of volunteers, and though taking the Queen's Colours might mean long years of service in Africa or India there was no shortage of recruits.

The Army was small by standards on the Continent, where conscription was the rule. Numbers of regular soldiers in British regiments varied from 200,000 in 1855 at the height of the Crimean War to 115,000 in 1870 and 150,000 at the end of the century.

During the Boer War and in 1914 volunteers flocked to take the oath, and it was not until 1915 when the First World War was taking its toll of the nation's youth that conscription was introduced.

2

When just budding into manhood,
I yearn'd for a Soldier's life,
Night and day I dream'd of glory,
Longing for the battle's strife;
I said, "Jack I'll be a Soldier,
'Neath the Red the White and Blue,
Good-bye Jack!" said he, "no never!
If you go, then I'll go too."

We were, &c.

3

I enlisted, Jack came with me,
And ups and downs we shared,
For a time our lives were peaceful,
But at length war was declared;
England's Flag had been insulted,
We were ordered to the front,
And the Reg'ment we belong'd to,
Had to bear the battle's brunt.

We were, &c.

CHORUS. TEMPO DI VALSE.

*We were com __ rades, com __ rades e __ ver since we were boys,....

Sharing each o __ ther's sor __ rows, sharing each o __ ther's joys,......

Comrades when manhood was dawn __ ing, Faithful whate'er might be __ tide,.... When danger

threatened __ my dar __ ling old comrade was there by my side.... We were side...

1° 2°

NOTE
*Omit the words "we were" when singing the chorus after the first verse.

PUT THEM IN THE LORD MAYORS S
Sung with Enormous Success by HARRY NICHOLLS

Words & Music By
HARRY NICHOLLS
Sung Nightly with Immense Success

CHARLES COBORN.
London. B. MOCATTA & C° 37 Berners Street. W.

"Put them in the Lord Mayor's Show" exhorted Charles Coborn and Harry Nicholls in this popular song calling for public recognition of aged veterans.

The Union Jack was often adopted as a symbol of freedom from oppression. In the Bishop of Wakefield's hymn for Queen Victoria's Diamond Jubilee in 1897 there is a verse that runs:
"Where England's flag flies wide unfurl'd,
All tyrant wrongs repelling;
God make the world a better world
For man's brief earthly dwelling!"
The hymn was set to music by Arthur Sullivan, and was sung to the Queen on the anniversary of her accession in each of the last three years of her reign.

Last Verse.
agitato.

In the night the sa_vage foemen, Crept a_round us as we lay, To our

arms we leap'd and faced them, Back to back we stood at bay; As I

fought, a sa_vage at me, Aimed his spear like lightning's dart, But my

com_rade sprang to save me, And re_ceiv'd it in his heart......

"*Here comes the Boys'
Brigade
All smovered in marmalade,
A Tup'ny-'apenny pill-box
And 'arf a yard of braid*",
*mocked ribald versifiers when the
Boys' Brigade first paraded in the
1880s. In this illustration a
private in the Brigade stands to
attention, embodying the cause of
"Christian manliness" to which
the Brigade's founder, the
Glasgow Sunday School teacher
William Smith, hoped to win
working-class lads.*

*British troops engage in hand-
to-hand combat with Zulu
warriors in this sketch from the
cover of* Comrades. *Small wars
in far-flung places provided the
public with plenty of examples of
personal heroism against the
savage hordes.*

THE·SOLDIERS·OF· THE·QUEEN·

In 1897 Queen Victoria celebrated her Diamond Jubilee, and her 60 years on the throne were marked by military parades and public rejoicing throughout the Empire. Leslie Stuart's *Soldiers Of The Queen* caught the mood of patriotic sentiment and was adopted as a marching song for the occasion.

Leslie Stuart was born Thomas Augustine Barrett in Southport, Lancashire, in 1864. When he was only 15 he became organist at the Roman Catholic Cathedral in Salford, and he spent seven years in this post and a further seven years at the Church of the Holy Name in Manchester. He composed sacred music during this time, but he also wrote songs for his brother Lester Barrett, a music hall comedian, and items for a concert series at the Hallé Hall in Manchester. The music publishers Francis Day & Hunter persuaded him to come to London and become a professional composer of popular music. He changed his name to Leslie Stuart and was one of the most successful composers of light music in his time: his musical comedies *Floradora*, *The Silver Slipper* and *The Belle Of Mayfair* had long runs in London and New York, and he also composed popular songs, many for Eugene Stratton *(see page 116)*. But despite his versatility, Stuart could not adapt to the new vogue for syncopation: the advent of ragtime after 1912 made his music outdated, and financial difficulties plagued the last years of his life. He died a poor man in 1928.

1895

WRITTEN & COMPOSED BY LESLIE STUART

Leslie Stuart was a quiet man, always immaculately dressed and, according to his friend John Abbott who wrote The Story of Francis Day & Hunter, *generous to a degree: he left a standing order at the Savoy that any friend of his could be served with a meal at his expense.*

VICTORIA'S EMPIRE

Pride of Empire had little meaning in the early years of Queen Victoria's reign, when the Crown followed rather reluctantly in the footsteps of traders and missionaries. Disraeli once described the colonies as "a millstone round our necks".

But by the late 1860s the *Spectator* could define imperialism "in its best sense" as the duty to bring civilization to the backward races of the world, an idea best expressed in Rudyard Kipling's *The White Man's Burden*, written in 1899:
"Take up the White Man's burden –
Send forth the best ye breed –
Go bind your sons to exile
To serve your captives' need".

In 1876 Victoria had become Empress of India, and by the time of her death in 1901 her empire extended over 12 million square miles, one fifth of the world's surface.

Albert Christian specialized in military songs and scored a considerable success when he sang Soldiers Of The Queen *on the halls. The song had first been performed in 1895 by Hayden Coffin in a musical comedy, but it was not suited to that medium and was dropped from the show. Leslie Stuart then offered it to Christian, whose repertoire included two other patriotic songs of Stuart's,* The Dandy Fifth *and* Little Anglo-Saxon Every Time.

1. Britons once did loy-al-ly declaim A-bout the way we rul'd the waves—.. Ev'-ry Bri-ton's song was just the same, When sing-ing of our sol-dier-braves. All the world had heard it— wonder'd why we sang, And some have learn'd the rea-son why— But

Verse 2
War clouds gather over ev'ry land,
Our flag is threaten'd east and west,
Nations that we've shaken by the hand
Our bold resources try to test.
They thought they found us sleeping — thought us unprepar'd,
Because we have our party wars
But English men unite—when they're call'd to fight
The battle for Old England's common cause,
The battle for Old England's common cause.
So when we say that England's master,
Remember who has made her so.   Refrain

we're for-getting it, And we're letting it Fade away and gradu-al-ly die,

Fade a-way and gra-du-al-ly die.

So 'when we say that Eng-land's mas--ter, Re-mem-ber who has made her so—

p marcato.

A young girl dreams of glory for her absent soldier in this late Victorian postcard. The verse is entitled Sweet Jenny Gray and runs:
"Jenny Gray, when I'm away, send sweet words to cheer,
And when danger is near, Jenny, I'll know no fear;
'Tis true love that makes a soldier boy do and dare,
Sweetheart, if you care, just let your lips breathe a prayer.
When the soldier boys play wedding music so grand,
Jenny, you'll understand, I'll claim your heart and hand;
If I win war's glory, my story is true,
The honour, dear, will belong to you."

SWEET JENNY GRAY (3).

Verse 3

Now we're rous'd we've buckled on our swords,
We've done with diplomatic lingo,
We'll do deeds to follow on our words,
We'll show we're something more than "jingo".
And though Old England's laws do not her sons compel
To military duties do
We'll play them at their game—and show them all the same
An Englishman can be a soldier too,
An Englishman can be a soldier too.
So when we say that England's master.
Remember who has made her so.

Refrain

VICTORIA

Her Majesty the Queen stands in full regalia in the Throne Room at Windsor Castle in this painting by Franz Xavier Winterhalter (1805-73), the German-born artist favoured by all the royal courts of Europe. He first visited London in 1841 at the invitation of the Prince Consort, and over the next two decades he provided an elegant and richly decorative record of the Royal Family. When Albert's death in 1861 plunged the British court into mourning, Winterhalter found a new patron in the French Emperor Napoleon III.

REFRAIN.

It's the Soldiers of the Queen, my lads, Who've been my lads, Who're seen my lads, In the fight for Eng-land's glo-ry, lads, When we have to show them what we mean: And when we say we've al-ways won And when they ask us how it's done We'll proudly point to ev'-ry one Of England's soldiers of the Queen! It's the Queen!

Opposite:

Soldiers with fixed bayonets wait in the trenches at Ladysmith, where in the early months of the Boer War the British garrison was besieged by the Boers. This realistic portrayal of war-torn, weary troops was very different from the romanticized versions of cavalry charges published half a century before.

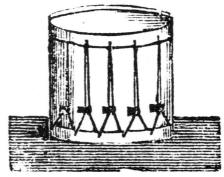

GOOD-BYE · DOLLY · GRAY

Wars entail separation, tragedy and death, and the moment when the departing soldier leaves for the war has inspired a long line of poignant songs. Such tunes have been played by military bands at the point of embarkation, sung by soldiers on the march, and nostalgically echoed by the public waiting for news from the front. In this sense, *Good-bye Dolly Gray* was the theme song of the Boer War.

Surprisingly, the song is American. It was written by the New York songwriter Will D. Cobb to the music of Paul Barnes in 1898, when the United States went to war with Spain to force her to relinquish control over Cuba. The US Navy destroyed the Spanish fleet within the week, and the war was over so quickly that songs of good-bye composed for the event were printed with additional verses welcoming the homecoming troops. Demand for these songs soon slumped, but as war clouds gathered over the Transvaal in 1899, American music publishers found an opportunity to export their pigeon-holed titles.

In 1900, when British music-hall artistes were dressing up in spectacular military uniforms to perform patriotic songs, the Australian-born baritone Hamilton Hill, in ordinary civilian evening dress, captivated London audiences with his rendering of *Good-bye Dolly Gray*. A speedy victory was expected but the Boer War began badly for Britain and the British strongholds of Kimberley, Mafeking and Ladysmith were besieged by the Boers. When the relief of Mafeking was announced in May 1900, the favourite heroine of the cheering crowds was New York's Dolly Gray.

WRITTEN BY WILL D. COBB **COMPOSED BY PAUL BARNES** 1898

"I could not love thee, dear, so much,
Lov'd I not honour more."
The timeless emotion of the soldier leaving his sweetheart, expressed by the Cavalier poet Richard Lovelace in the 17th century, was translated into Victorian music hall terms by Dolly Gray. The soldier in this drawing from sheet music of 1900 wears khaki, the new uniform introduced for the British troops in South Africa because the traditional red jacket was too conspicuous a target for the Boer guerrillas.

"I have come to say good-bye, Dol-ly
Hear the roll-ing of the drums, Dol-ly
Gray ———— It's no use to ask me why, Dol-ly
Gray ———— Back from war the reg'-ment comes, Dol-ly
Gray ———— There's a mur-mur in the air You can
Gray ———— On your love-ly face so fair I can
hear it ev'-ry-where, It is time to do and dare, Dol-ly Gray ———— Don't you
see a look of care For your sol-dier boy's not there, Dol-ly Gray ———— For the

Left in Charge, a painting by James Gow first exhibited at the Royal Society of British Artists in 1869, exemplifies the narrative style so popular with the Victorians. It depicts the faithful family dog standing guard for both mother and child while the master of the house is away.

This postcard of the 1890s would have conjured up home thoughts from abroad for any British soldier serving in South Africa. The peaceful rural setting, with blossoming trees and carefully tended lawns, is an idyllic representation of the home the boys in khaki left behind them; in fact, most recruits came from the city working class, and their stunted physique and poor general health caused such concern that it led to an improvement in the standards of food and medical care in the British Army as well as fuelling the campaigns of social reformers at home.

195

Hamilton Hill made his name on the halls as a singer of patriotic songs and ballads. Born in Australia, he came to London in the 1890s and scored a considerable success with Goodbye Dolly Gray and Bluebell, another American song about a hero who dies with his sweetheart's name on his lips. Hamilton Hill's later career took him on successful tours of the United States, and he made many recordings.

A NOTE ON THE MUSIC

In the third line of the chorus opposite, eight small notes are included in the accompaniment under the words, "See the soldier boys are marching". They serve as an orchestral cue to a phrase intended for another instrument, perhaps a trumpet, and cannot be played as they stand because the pianist does not have enough fingers. The accompanist who attempts to play the cue will therefore have to leave something else out.

Pertinently, this phrase is a quotation from another popular song, Tramp, Tramp, Tramp, The Boys Are Marching.

There is a second witty orchestral comment in the next line (third bar) where two triplets illustrate the bugle call of the lyrics.

Another song liberally supplied with orchestral cues is After The Ball (page 156), where it is well worth while adapting the accompaniment to include them.

KIPLING AND MUSIC HALL

The regular soldier, much put upon by his superior officers and seldom recognized as a hero, found his apotheosis in Rudyard Kipling's *Barrack Room Ballads*, published in 1892. Kipling's verse owes much to music hall. As a 23-year-old journalist, newly arrived from India in 1888, Kipling found rooms in Villiers Street, just off the Strand and opposite Gatti's Music Hall. "It was here", he wrote in *Something of Myself*, "in the company of an elderly but upright barmaid from a pub nearby that I listened to the observed and compelling songs of the Lions and Mammoths Comiques . . . the smoke, the roar and the good fellowship at Gatti's set the scene for a certain sort of song." The music hall influence is explicit in this verse from *Tommy Atkins*:
"I went into the theatre as sober as could be
They gave a drunk civilian room but 'adn't none for me
They sent me to the gallery all round the music 'all—
But when it comes to fighting, Lord!
They shove me in the stalls".

Boy Bugler Taps sounds his final call on a sentimental picture postcard, one of a series of carefully posed war scenes devised during the First World War. The verse is from A Little Boy Called Taps *by Edward Madden, who also wrote Hamilton Hill's song* Bluebell *and runs:*
"'Midst the battle's strife, Fighting, life for life, One by one the soldiers fall. From the ranks of death, With his parting breath, Taps is sounding his final call." When this postcard was published, such sentimentality already smacked of the bygone Victorian age; the ravages of modern warfare had rendered the romanticization of the battlefield out of date.

197

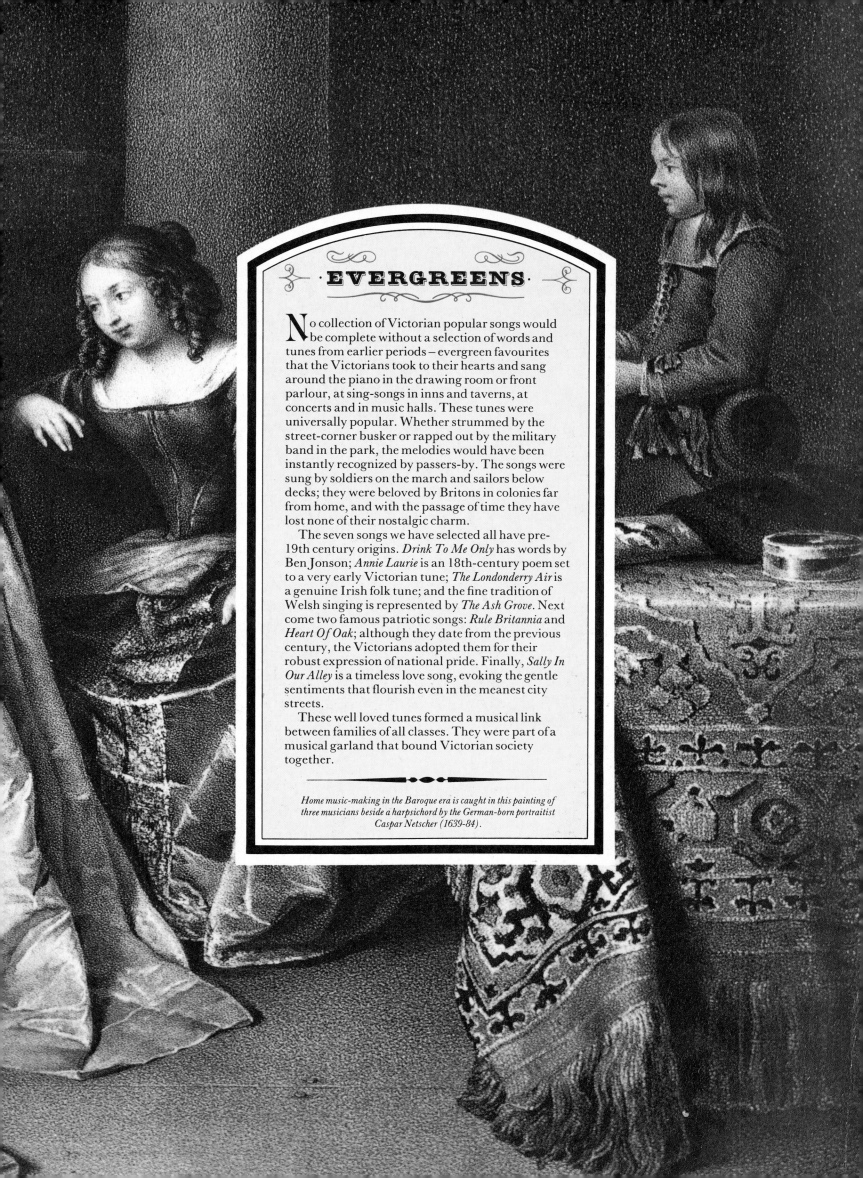

· EVERGREENS ·

No collection of Victorian popular songs would
be complete without a selection of words and
tunes from earlier periods – evergreen favourites
that the Victorians took to their hearts and sang
around the piano in the drawing room or front
parlour, at sing-songs in inns and taverns, at
concerts and in music halls. These tunes were
universally popular. Whether strummed by the
street-corner busker or rapped out by the military
band in the park, the melodies would have been
instantly recognized by passers-by. The songs were
sung by soldiers on the march and sailors below
decks; they were beloved by Britons in colonies far
from home, and with the passage of time they have
lost none of their nostalgic charm.

The seven songs we have selected all have pre-
19th century origins. *Drink To Me Only* has words by
Ben Jonson; *Annie Laurie* is an 18th-century poem set
to a very early Victorian tune; *The Londonderry Air* is
a genuine Irish folk tune; and the fine tradition of
Welsh singing is represented by *The Ash Grove*. Next
come two famous patriotic songs: *Rule Britannia* and
Heart Of Oak; although they date from the previous
century, the Victorians adopted them for their
robust expression of national pride. Finally, *Sally In
Our Alley* is a timeless love song, evoking the gentle
sentiments that flourish even in the meanest city
streets.

These well loved tunes formed a musical link
between families of all classes. They were part of a
musical garland that bound Victorian society
together.

*Home music-making in the Baroque era is caught in this painting of
three musicians beside a harpsichord by the German-born portraitist
Caspar Netscher (1639-84).*

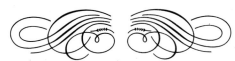

THE · LONDONDERRY · AIR ·

A genuine folk tune, *The Londonderry Air* was written down by Jane Ross of Limavady as she heard it from peasants coming to town on market day. Her version of the tune was published in 1855 by George Petrie, a collector of Irish folk songs. In 1880 the poet Alfred Graves (father of the more famous Robert Graves) published words to the tune, beginning "Would I Were Erin's Apple Blossom O'er You". Later he tried again with *Emer's Farewell*, the lines used here.

Versions by other authors followed: "Emer's Lament For Cuchillin" by Mrs Granville Bantock; "Would God I Were The Apple Blossom" by Katharine Tynan Hinkson; "Acushla Mine" from Terry Sullivan, and, most famous of all, "Oh Danny Boy" by Frederic Weatherly. It is not surprising that so many people have tried to find the right words for this air, described by Hubert Parry – composer of Blake's *Jerusalem* – as "the most beautiful tune in the world".

·EMER'S · FAREWELL·

WRITTEN BY ALFRED PERCEVAL GRAVES   **TRADITIONAL, ARRANGED BY CHARLES V. STANFORD**

Described as "A Very Sunbeam", this cheerful example of clear-eyed innocence serves as a model of Victorian girlhood. She is wreathed with apple blossom, the flower symbolizing the gentleness and constancy of the lover in Alfred Grave's first verses for The Londonderry Air. The sentiments he ascribes to Emer as she longs for her departing hero Cucullain were equally appropriate to later patriotic warriors and the girls they left behind.

A passionate pair from the 1890s prove that determined young lovers could evade chaperones. Queen Victoria's own home life had been a model for strict middle-class morality; but by the Naughty Nineties the pleasure-loving Prince of Wales and his set were leaders of society. While Marie Lloyd delighted music-hall audiences, worldly theatre-goers enjoyed the urbane and witty comedies of Oscar Wilde. His trial, on charges of homosexuality, not only broke him personally but destroyed the spell of other rebel influences. Decadence went out; respectability and fine emotions resumed their former sway.

THE ORIGINS OF THE AIR

The tune of this song is surrounded in mystery, for it has a rhythm unlike that of any other native Irish folk tune. Perhaps Miss Ross misheard what was sung when she wrote it down, or perhaps there is some stranger explanation.

The great Irish tenor John McCormack, one of the most famous singers of the air, had a story to account for its mysterious beauty, which he was fond of recounting. An Irish fiddler had been playing at a wedding, and after a drink or two to toast the bride and groom, set off for home.

Overcome by tiredness, he lay down in the moonlight and fell asleep. Suddenly he awoke to the most heavenly melody, and saw a leprechaun orchestra playing the most beautiful tune he had ever heard. He took some paper, jotted down the notes and went back to sleep. In the morning he took his fiddle and played the notes he had written down and – would you believe it – it was *The Londonderry Air!*

ORIGINAL PUBLISHER'S FOOTNOTE

✳ Cucullain was one of the most famous of the Irish legendary heroes, and is said to have withstood all Queen Meave of Connaught's champions at the great battle of the Ford.

had not hid-den to thy wrong-ing A bleed-ing heart be-neath a smil-ing cheek; I had not stemmed my bit-ter tears from start-ing, And thou hadst learned my bo-som's dear dis-tress, And half the pain, the cru-el pain of part-ing, Had passed, Cu-cul-lain,✳ in thy fond ca-ress.

In the days before wireless and gramophone, parties and family gatherings relied heavily on home-grown talent. Shy performers may have found such occasions an ordeal. Bolder spirits with the "pair of sparkling eyes" and "dainty fingerettes" beloved by W. S. Gilbert – like the devastatingly pretty pianist in this engraving of 1866 – doubtless relished the chance to show off the results of long hours of practice.

But go! Con _ na _ cia's hos_tile trumpets call thee, Thy char_iot

JOHN BULL'S OTHER ISLAND

The story of Victorian Anglo-Irish relations is a sad tale of mutual hostility and misunderstanding. In the Great Hunger of the 1840s, potato blight brought famine, disease and death to one million Irish people and caused another million to emigrate, yet England offered little sympathy or assistance.

Against a background of mounting violence, the veteran Liberal Prime Minister W. E. Gladstone, convinced that his mission was to pacify Ireland, later tried to secure Home Rule for Ireland; he failed and the problem remained unsolved.

Queen Victoria tried to encourage her Irish subjects' loyalty by making four visits to Ireland, the last of them in 1900 when she was over 80. The most successful was the first, in 1849, when she dazzled the people of Cork with a carefully chosen wardrobe including two dresses made of Irish poplin – one emerald green, the other pink and elaborately figured with gold shamrocks.

mount   and ride the ridge of war,   And prove what e _ ver feat of arms be _

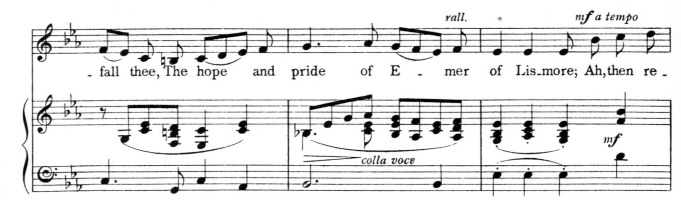

_ fall thee, The hope   and   pride   of E _ mer of Lis_more; Ah, then re _

turn,   my he_ro, girt with   glo_ry,   To knit my vir _ gin heart so near to

ORIGINAL
PUBLISHER'S
FOOTNOTE
❋ Connaught's

thine, That all who seek thy name in E_rin's sto_ry Shall find its

lov_ing let_ters linked with mine.

A NOTE ON THE MUSIC

* This otherwise impeccable setting by Stanford contains a curious departure from the well-known original. At the end of each eight-bar phrase, after the *rallentando*, Stanford uses three repeated E flats for the words "smiling cheek", "fond caress" and so on. The effect of the plonking crotchets is somewhat heavy, but the lilting quality of the traditional air is easily restored by singing the words to the quaver melody in the previous bar, ending with one sustained E flat on the last syllable; most singers follow this practice.

· LOVE'S · WISHES ·

WOULD I were Erin's apple-blossom o'er you,
   Or Erin's rose in all its beauty blown,
To drop my richest petals down before you,
   Within the garden where you walk alone ;
In hope you'd turn and pluck a little posy,
   With loving fingers through my foliage pressed,
And kiss it close and set it blushing rosy
   To sigh out all its sweetness on your breast.

Would I might take the pigeon's flight towards you,
   And perch beside your window-pane above,
And murmur how my heart of hearts it hoards you,
   O hundred thousand treasures of my love ;
In hope you'd stretch your slender hand and take me,
   And smooth my wildly-fluttering wings to rest,
And lift me to your loving lips and make me
   My bower of blisses in your loving breast.

DRINK·TO·ME·ONLY· WITH·THINE·EYES·

A courting couple from the 1880s celebrate with music-hall brashness the same tender, imploring sentiment which could be found in the passionate arias of 19th-century grand opera and the eloquent simplicity of the traditional love song.

Ben Jonson's verses, properly entitled *To Celia*, were based on a passage in the letters of Philostratus, the 3rd-century Greek writer and teacher. The poem was written in 1616, but the tune cannot be traced back beyond 1770, when it was published in a collection of Glee Songs. It has been attributed to Thomas Arne, to a Colonel Mellish, and even to Mozart. There is no authority for any of these.

The glee is a purely English form of song for unaccompanied male solo voices (the word "glee" derives from the Old English *gleo*, meaning "music"). The songs are associated with the tradition of barbershop singing, which goes back to the 1500s, when the barber would provide a cittern or lute so that customers could amuse themselves playing and singing while waiting for shaving, haircutting, blood-letting and tooth-drawing, the multifarious services provided by the barber-surgeon. Barbershop singing declined in the 18th century, but the glee tradition was carried on in gentlemen's clubs, notably the Glee Club itself, which flourished in London from 1783 until 1857.

A NOTE ON THE MUSIC
The rare example of fingering at the end of this song uses the old "English" system (originally German), with + for the thumb and 1-4 for the fingers, now completely displaced by the "Continental" system (originally English), starting with 1 for the thumb.

WRITTEN BY BEN JONSON, 1616

COMPOSED, c. 1777

Customers in an 18th-century barber's shop smoke, sing or catch up with the newspapers as they await the attentions of an operatic-looking barber. Until the abolition of the Paper Duties in Gladstone's budgets of 1853 and 1860, the tax on newspapers encouraged a public hungry for news to share copies of the papers in taverns, coffee houses and barbershops.

wine;...... The thirst that from the soul doth rise, Doth
he; But thou there on didst on ly breathe, And

ask a drink di vine, But of Love's nec tar
sent it back to me, Since when it grows, and

might I sip, I would not change for thine........
smells, I swear, Not of it self but thee........

D.%

Ben Jonson (1572-1637) prided himself on his classical learning, and criticized his contemporary, Shakespeare, for his lack of Latin and Greek. In his own tragedies he tried to observe the rules of ancient drama, and in Volpone, The Alchemist and Bartholemew Fair he developed a new kind of satirical comedy. Jonson also collaborated with the architect and designer Inigo Jones to produce spectacular masques for the court of James I.

This etching was made in 1635 by Wenceslas Hollar, a Bohemian artist who spent some years in England. The lady is playing a virginal, a portable keyboard instrument popular in the 16th, 17th and early 18th centuries. The quiet refinement of the instrument was well-suited to the lyricism of love poems such as Jonson's.

NOTE
*The familiar quaver (eighth note) appogiatura on C before this B♭ can easily be added.

"I sent thee late a rosy wreath", runs the second verse of Jonson's poem. This charming engraving of cherubs and garlands from the Black and White Magazine of 1899 plays upon the same theme, also providing an example of the high quality of lithography found in late Victorian periodicals.

· ANNIE · LAURIE ·

William Douglas of Fingland in Dumfriesshire, Scotland, wrote this poem in praise of his beloved Annie Laurie, who was born at Maxwelton in 1682. Unhappily for William she married another, but she lived to the age of 83 and was buried in Glencairn churchyard, close to the bonnie braes – or, in more prosaic standard English, the beautiful banks – of Maxwelton.

The air was written by Lady John Douglas Scott (1810-1900), who did not hesitate to change the words to fit her tune; it was published in 1838 in an arrangement by Edward James Loder, composer of the lugubrious Victorian favourite, *The Diver*. The arrangement we know is thus the work of many hands; indeed, Donald Francis Tovey, the founder of modern musical scholarship, was fond of remarking that the first seven notes of the tune, with their complete reliance for effect on the accompanying harmony, were enough to show that this could not be a genuine folk melody. Nevertheless it soon became popular, and was one of the favourite songs of both English and Scottish regiments during the Crimean War.

Travellers take their journey gently on a road with a magnificent view across Loch Ness. Scottish scenery had inspired and enchanted English visitors at least since Dr Johnson made his famous tour of the Hebrides. Wordsworth's idea of the spiritual power of nature and Sir Walter Scott's Border romances further influenced Victorian appreciation of Scotland, which was given the royal seal of approval when Queen Victoria and her family took to spending regular holidays at Balmoral. The Queen herself published Leaves from the Journal of Our Life in the Highlands, *and many artists and musicians left records of their Scottish expeditions.*

WRITTEN BY WILLIAM DOUGLAS

COMPOSED BY LADY JOHN DOUGLAS SCOTT, 1835

Maxwellton braes are bonnie, Where early fa's the dew, And it's there that Annie Laurie Gie'd me her promise true; Gie'd me her promise true, Which

ne'er for-got will be, And for bonnie Annie Laurie, I'd lay me doune and dee.

Her brow is like the snaw-drift, Her throat is like the swan; Her face it is the fairest That e'er the sun shone on, That e'er the sun shone on, And dark blue is her e'e; And for bonnie An-nie Laurie, I'd lay me doune and dee.

In a sheet music illustration from a selection of Scotch Quadrilles, *a Highland lassie is graced by a most becoming costume. Scottish fashions were much popularized during the 19th century by Queen Victoria, who liked to see all her family in "Highland things". She herself often sported a tartan satin crinoline, and her journal records dinner being late "owing to Albert's struggles to dress in his kilt".*

SIR WALTER SCOTT AND HIS PUBLIC

Sir Walter Scott (1771-1832) inspired the Victorian passion for Scottish history and folklore. His readers doted on narrative poems such as *The Lay of the Last Minstrel* and the Waverley novels, including *Rob Roy* and *Redgauntlet*, which vividly recounted the Border legends.

He was Queen Victoria's most admired novelist, and no well-found home was without a bound set of his works. Indeed, Herbert Gladstone, son of the Prime Minister, acknowledging a wedding present of a leather-bound set of Scott's novels, expressed his gratitude by explaining that though of course he had a set in his London home, he did not yet have one for his country residence.

Sir Walter had numerous inferior imitators – writers of historical fiction afflicted with what Robert Louis Stevenson called "tushery" – but the wide appeal of his books contributed to a genuine appreciation of history and legend.

As Victorians crowded into the growing industrial towns and cities, their image of the countryside became increasingly sentimental. Many city-dwellers would have sighed at this image of a Scottish shepherd boy, envisaging a life of rural innocence spent amidst the ennobling influence of beautiful scenery. The illustration comes from The Casquet of Literature, published by Blackie & Son in 1881, and accompanies a poem on just such a theme: "He wearies not while o'er him the hours of summer glide; His fleecy flock before him, His faithful dog beside, And thoughts that wander wide."

Sir Walter Scott's tomb at Dryburgh is the subject of this splendid example of early 19th-century photography. Scott's tomb was a place of pilgrimage for Victorian tourists, who doted on souvenir pictures, portraits and commemorative plates depicting the novelist.

·THE·ASH·GROVE·

Our version of this traditional Welsh air includes the Welsh text by Talhaiarn and the well known English words by T. Oliphant. The early 19th century saw Romantic nationalist movements all over Europe reviving ancient cultural traditions, and Wales was no exception: the eisteddfod was revived after 130 years, and the so-called National Welsh costume of tall hat and long gown was introduced in 1834. It is therefore appropriate that our collection includes an example reflecting the Welsh literary revival. Like all well known songs, this one has often been parodied, as anyone who has travelled with a group of Welsh rugby supporters will know.

The Welsh harp or telyn – here played by Evan Jones of Waen Oer, a leading performer of his day – is an ancient instrument. In the middle ages every noble family in Wales boasted its own fine harp, handed down through generations of domestic bards. Up to the end of the 19th century many villages in Wales had their own harp-maker and a new generation of Victorian musicians kept the ancient bardic traditions alive. The Welsh harp requires considerable skill to play, since it has three rows of strings, the inner one for the semitones, so that the player has to insert his fingers inside the outer rows to realize the instrument's full harmonic capacity.

WELSH WORDS WRITTEN BY TALHAIARN
ENGLISH WORDS WRITTEN BY T. OLIPHANT

ARRANGED BY JOHN THOMAS

JOHN THOMAS, BARD

John Thomas, who produced this arrangement of *The Ash Grove*, was born in 1826 and had a distinguished musical career. He won a harp at an eisteddfod at the age of 11 and was sent to the Royal Academy of Music in London, where he became a professor. His bardic name was Pencerdd Gwalia.

Thomas toured Europe as a harpist and adjudicated at the Chicago Eisteddfod in 1893. He was a prolific composer and a dedicated collector of Welsh folk music, as well as official harpist to Queen Victoria. He died in 1913.

tryd...ar man ad....ar a miw...sig a.......wel...on, Mae
at the bright noon...tide, in so......li...tude wan...der, A...
ad...ar yn tryd...ar i lon...i y gwyrddlwyn, A
trembles the moon-beam on stream-let and foun-tain, But

gof.....id a thrist...yd yn lleth...u fy mron:
...mid the dark shades of the lone....ly Ash Grove.
min......nau mewn breuddwyd heb sylwedd na sail,
what are the beau...ties of na...ture to me?

Fan ym......a mi wel....ais y fein......wen an....
'Twas there, while the black...bird was cheer......ful......ly
Yn gof.....yn i'r blod...au, y coed, a'r a....
With sor......row, deep sor.....row my bo.....som is

...wyl.....af, A phleth......iad o flod....au'n co......
sing......ing, I first met that dear one ___ the
wel...on Yn is......el, ac ofn...us, ac
la.....den, All day I go mourn...ing in

All good little upper- and middle-class girls learned to play the piano and sing. This particular young lady with ringlets was portrayed by Daniel Maclise, an artist much admired by the Prince Consort. Maclise was a friend of Charles Dickens, whom he frequently sketched. His larger portraits expressed the prevalent nostalgia for the Middle Ages, showing Victorian families masquerading as medieval knights and ladies (see also page 22).

Like many folk songs and hymn tunes, *The Ash Grove* has a simple melody that lends itself well to harmonization. This quality has been explored to the full by generations of Welsh choirs, who have performed the song with striking contrapuntal effects.

Although our version is for one voice only, any small group of experienced singers – and there were many such groups in Victorian times, especially west of the Marches – would have added the other vocal lines that can transform this gentle tune into a dazzling display of harmonic colour.

The reputation of the Welsh as a great nation of choral singers was recorded by Giraldus Cambrensis (Gerald of Wales) in 1188. He observed that "In their musical concerts they do not sing in unison, like the inhabitants of other countries, but in many different parts, so that in a company of singers, which one very frequently meets with in Wales, you will hear as many different parts as there are performers".

211

The cover of the Victorian sheet music reproduced here describes Heart Of Oak as a National Song of the reign of George II. It was published as part of a collection "with Historical Introductions, Remarks & Anecdotes by Wm Chappell, F.S.A." which filled two imperial octavo volumes priced at two guineas.

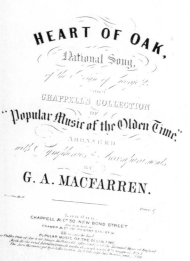

Heart Of Oak – not Hearts of Oak – comes from a pantomime, Harlequin's Invasion, which was written by the great actor-manager David Garrick, set to music by William Boyce and staged at the Drury Lane theatre. It was a topical song intended to mark the victories of 1759, the wonderful year when British forces prevailed on land and sea and the battles of Minden, Quiberon and Quebec were won. A triumphal song of celebration fitted the mood of the day.

David Garrick, who was manager of Drury Lane from 1747 until 1776, was not only the leading actor of his age, but an innovative theatrical director. His management at the Lane brought many changes in both dramatic technique and stagecraft. He put an end to the declamatory style of delivery so popular at the time, pioneered developments in stage lighting and, following the example set by Voltaire in Paris, turned the public off the stage. He also began to dress plays in the costume of their own period.

William Boyce, the composer of *Heart Of Oak*, became Master of the King's Musick in 1775 and organist of the Chapel Royal. Boyce composed music for both Church and stage. Increasingly deaf in his later years, he devoted himself to editing a collection of English cathedral music which remained in use for 150 years.

The power of this tune as a rallying cry was soon recognized across the Atlantic, where resentment of British rule was producing a new variety of patriotism among the American colonists. By a historical irony, the tune was adapted as a song of the American Revolution and reappeared in 1768 as *The Massachusetts Liberty Song;* another American version entitled *The Liberty Song* was written by John Dickinson, but its anonymous predecessor is better known.

Our arrangement is by George Alexander MacFarren (1813-87), who composed operas, oratorios and cantatas and was Professor of Music at Cambridge.

SHIPS AND THE SEA

"Break, break, break,
On thy cold grey stones,
O Sea!"

ran the famous ode by the Poet Laureate, Alfred Lord Tennyson. Ships and the sea were potent images in Victorian poetry, and in one of his last verses Tennyson saw death in nautical terms:
"Sunset and evening star,
And one clear call for me!
And may there be no
moaning of the bar,
When I put out to sea."

In the course of the century, the advent of steam step by step transformed the old sailing ships into iron-keeled vessels powered only by engines. Some ships, like Isambard Kingdom Brunel's *Great Eastern*, were ambitious, rather than successful, experiments, but by the late 19th century the new designs had triumphed, giving rise to a new set of poetic images. In 1893 Rudyard Kipling's Scottish ship's engineer MacAndrew hailed the power of the new technology in these striking words:
"Lord, Thou has made this world below the shadow of a dream,
An', taught by time, I tak' it so – exceptin' always Steam.
From Couple-flange to spindle-guide I see Thy Hand, O God –
Predestination in the stride o' yon connectin' rod."

WRITTEN BY DAVID GARRICK　**COMPOSED BY DR WILLIAM BOYCE**　c.1759

sons of the waves? Heart of oak are our ships, Heart of oak are our men, We always are ready,
cannot do more. Heart of oak &c.

Steady, boys, steady! We'll fight and we'll con-quer a-gain and a-gain.

13689

last time

3.

Still Britain shall triumph her Ships plough the sea,
Her standard be Justice, her watchword "Be free";
Then cheer up, my lads, with one heart let us sing
"Our soldiers, our sailors, our statesmen, our King!"
Heart of oak are our ships, Heart of oak are our men,
We always are ready, Steady, boys, steady!
We'll fight and we'll conquer again and again.

Stories of the past are handed down the generations in this oil painting by Edward Thompson Davis (1833-67), a respected painter of domestic scenes. A typical example of his work, the picture is entitled On Grandfather's Knee.

A contemporary view of the capture of Quebec by General James Wolfe in 1759 illustrates the formidable task confronting British forces when they attacked the French citadel. Wolfe led his men to a landing place just over a mile beyond the city, where they ascended the wooded cliffs under cover of darkness, taking the French by storm. Both Wolfe and the French commander, Montcalm, were mortally wounded in the battle.

The cover of the song shows Britannia bearing a trident in one hand and an olive branch in the other, with a shield at her side bearing the arms of England, Ireland, Scotland and Wales.

· RULE · BRITANNIA ·

Rule Britannia came to the Victorians from an earlier century, but they took it to their hearts and seemingly acted upon it. By the turn of the century, they possessed the largest and most powerful navy the world had known. Dr Thomas Arne (1710-1778), celebrated for his settings of Shakespeare songs such as *Under The Greenwood Tree*, composed *Rule Britannia* as the finale to his masque *Alfred*. It was first performed in 1740 in the gardens of Cliveden House before the Prince and Princess of Wales, and was later produced at Drury Lane. The famous tenor Thomas Lowe was the first to sing it, and 250 years on, 2,000 promenaders at the Royal Albert Hall give voice to it as they bring the annual season of Promenade Concerts to its end.

The tune has been admired by many a rival composer. It was quoted by Handel in his *Occasional Oratorio* and by Beethoven in his "Battle" Symphony. Richard Wagner, who based a youthful overture on the theme, said that "the first eight bars express the whole character of the British nation". Nearer home, it has been suggested as the hidden theme in Elgar's *Enigma Variations*.

Our version is not unadulterated Arne, but No. 58 of the *Musical Bouquet*, a series ranging from Schubert to the Monkey Quadrilles. The words were written by James Thomson (1700-1748), a Scots poet remembered for his verse sequence, *The Seasons*. Most people turn the second line of the chorus into a statement – "Britannia rules the Waves" – instead of Thomson's firm command: "Britannia! Rule the Waves!"

CIVIS BRITANNICUS SUM

"He is an Englishman", sang the chorus in Gilbert and Sullivan's *H.M.S. Pinafore* – and in Victorian days that really meant something.

Lord Palmerston's attitude to the Englishman abroad was summed up in his famous speech during the Don Pacifico debate in 1850: "As the Roman, in days of old, held himself free from indignity, when he could say *Civis Romanus Sum*, so also a British subject, in whatever land he may be, shall feel confident that the watchful eye and the strong arm of England will protect him against injustice and wrong."

On the home front, Britons were proud of their traditions of liberty and freedom, boasting that, alone amongst the European powers, they had been left unscathed by 1848, the Year of Revolution. Some would say that the Chartist agitation of the 1840s ran things pretty close, but it remained true that no British government had been overthrown by force since the Glorious Revolution of 1688 – an exceptionally stable record which was upheld by the great reform bills of 1832 and 1867 and their extension of the franchise which led ultimately to the realization of the principle one man one vote.

WRITTEN BY JAMES THOMSON   **COMPOSED BY DR THOMAS ARNE   1740**

1. char..ter of the land, And guar..dian An....gels sang the strain.
2. flou..rish great and free, The dread and en.......vy of them all.

Rule Bri..tannia, Bri..tannia rule the waves, Britons ne...ver shall be slaves

CHORUS.

1st TREBLE.

Rule Bri..tan..nia, Bri..tan..nia rule the waves, Bri..tons ne....ver

2nd TREBLE.

Rule Bri..tan..nia, Bri..tan..nia rule the waves, Bri..tons ne....ver

TENOR.

Rule Bri..tan..nia, Bri..tan..nia rule the waves, Bri..tons ne....ver

BASS.

Rule Bri..tan..nia, Bri..nia rule the waves, Bri..tons ne....ver

PIANO FORTE.

ff

By a pleasant irony, this sumptuously patriotic postcard was printed in Germany! The postcard was in fact a continental invention, originating in Austro-Hungary in 1869. By the 1880s picture postcards of many continental resorts were available to holiday-makers, and the first British picture postcard appeared in 1894. In the following year the Post Office handled an impressive total of 314 million cards.

shall be slaves.

shall be slaves.

shall be slaves.

shall be slaves.

1st time.   2nd time.

ff

215

· SALLY · IN · OUR · ALLEY ·

This charming song about an apprentice and his lady-love has often touched the heart since it was written by Henry Carey (1690-1743). His inspiration came from the sight of a pretty London girl out on holiday with her sweetheart. Carey's friends mocked him for making a song out of such a low-life subject, and dubbed him The Alley Poet, but the song became popular in the composer's own lifetime, and was sung before royalty. In 1790 the words were set to another traditional tune, *What Though I Am A Country Lass*. This was the version favoured by the Victorians, and the one we give here.

Henry Carey wrote mostly for the theatre, but his name has been linked with *God Save The King*. After his death his sons claimed royalties on the grounds that Carey had composed the national anthem to celebrate victory over the Jacobites in 1745. This was patently absurd as the Jacobite rebellion occurred two years after Carey's death. Nevertheless, he was credited as the original composer when in 1831 the anthem was published in the United States with the new words, *My Country 'Tis Of Thee*.

Carey's poem, *Sally In Our Alley*, had seven verses, and is printed in full in *Palgrave's Golden Treasury;* the arrangers of the song reduced the number of verses – partly for typographical reasons – and also bowdlerized the text: Carey's apprentice is first "banged", and later "blamed" for leaving his work to go to Sally; then he sneaks out of a sermon on Sunday to meet her, and the original poem ends not with "And happy ever strive to live" but with:

"O then we'll wed, and then we'll bed . . .

But not in our alley!"

WRITTEN BY HENRY CAREY, 1729

TRADITIONAL

An open gutter runs down the middle of an alley where tenement buildings block out light and air. In the summer of 1902 the American writer Jack London lived in the slums of the East End, which were full of alleys of this kind, and described his experiences in his book, People of the Abyss, *the model for George Orwell's* Road to Wigan Pier. *London described "an abomination called a house", where 28 people of both sexes ate, cooked, slept and worked in six tiny rooms.*

1. Of all the girls that are so smart There's none like pret-ty Sal-ly, She is the dar-ling of my dear
2. Of all the days that's in the week I dear-ly love but one day, And that's the day that comes be-
3. When Christ-mas comes a-bout a-gain O then I shall have mon-ey; I'll hoard it up with box and
4. My mas-ter and the neigh-bours all Make game of me and Sal-ly, And but for her I'd bet-ter

a tempo.

heart,   And   lives   in   our   al - ley;   There   is   no
twixt   A   Sat   ur - day   and   Mon - day: For   then   I'm
all   And   give   it   to   my   hon - ey: Would   it   were
be   A   slave   and   row   a   gal - ley;   But   when   my

a tempo.

ia - dy   in   the   land   That's   half   so   sweet   as
drest   all   in   my   best,   To   walk   a - broad   with
twice   ten   thou - sand   pounds,   I'd   give   it   all   to
seven   long   years   are   out   I   then   will   mar - ry

The pretty young girl in this late Victorian illustration wears simple finery, including a wide-brimmed hat. Fashions in millinery underwent a complete change in the course of the century. Mid-Victorian women plaited their hair and coiled the plait in a knob; they wore bonnets tied under their chin or held on from behind by elastic. From the 1880s it became fashionable to brush hair forward, and elastic gave way to the hat pin which reigned for the next 30 years, until women adopted the cloche.

Sal - ly,   She   is   the   dar - ling   of   my   heart,   And
Sal - ly,   She   is   the   dar - ling   of   my   heart,   And
Sal - ly,   She   is   the   dar - ling   of   my   heart,   And
Sal - ly,   And   hap - py   ev - er   strive   to   live,   But

lives   in   our   al - ley.
lives   in   our   al - ley.
lives   in   our   al - ley.
not   in   our   al - ley.

f

D.S.

SONGS · FROM · THE · SHOWS ·

The world of opera, be it grand, light or comic— or even, in its diminutive form, operetta— provided a wealth of songs for the drawing room. The music hall was a bit naughty, the minstrel show was respectable, but the opera stage was a cut above the rest. It was definitely legitimate.

Elsewhere in this book are songs which were introduced to the public as part of an opera, play or musical comedy, but which, in our view, are better known as songs in their own right. *Home! Sweet Home!*, for example, is no longer remembered as a number from *Clari, Or The Maid Of Milan*. Our choices in this part of the book, however, remain much more closely associated with the operas or plays for which they were written.

An early success was Michael Balfe's opera *The Bohemian Girl*, which set Drury Lane audiences alight in 1843 and provides this section with two famous songs. Balfe's position as the Victorian public's favourite composer was taken in the 1870s by Arthur Sullivan. Although he longed to be respected for his serious work, Sullivan's name lives on with W. S. Gilbert's in the credits of the Savoy comic operas, a long string of dramatic triumphs including *HMS Pinafore* and *The Mikado*, represented here.

The 1890s heralded the arrival of musical comedy. At Daly's and the Gaiety Theatres George Edwardes produced *An Artist's Model*, *The Geisha* and a string of lavish shows with Girl in the title and girls in the cast—beautiful, charming and elegant, his marriageable young ladies were an important part of the late-Victorian and Edwardian scene.

Four representative characters from London's musical comedy stage celebrate a new show, An Artist's Model, *which opened at Daly's Theatre on 2nd February, 1895.*

· I·DREAMT·THAT·I·DWELT· IN·MARBLE·HALLS ·

The Bohemian Girl was the most successful opera to be staged at Drury Lane in the mid-19th century and "the Dream" is one of its best known arias. The libretto was written in 1843 by Alfred Bunn, then manager of the Lane. Bunn was known derisively by his colleagues as "the poet Bunn" and dubbed "Mr Hot Cross" by Jenny Lind. A somewhat pompous figure, he was notorious in the theatrical world for his pandering to popular taste. He courted publicity assiduously and scandalized the purists by introducing popular extravaganzas into Drury Lane in order to compete with the variety shows which drew packed houses at the minor theatres. He put on a wild beast show which so delighted the young Queen Victoria that she saw it six times in one month and was taken backstage to meet the cast and watch them feeding.

Bunn showed his libretto of *The Bohemian Girl* to the prolific Michael Balfe *(page 23)* and asked him to supply the music. Within a matter of weeks the score was finished. The opera tells the story of a child Arline, who is stolen by gypsies from her father, the Count. Arline grows into a beautiful young woman among the gypsies, but remembers in her dreams her past life in the paternal mansion.

The song's lasting popularity was proved in 1963 when a recording was made by Joan Sutherland of the original version.

An engraving entitled The Coquette, *after a painting by Georges Roussin, appeared in the periodical* Black and White *in February 1899. Fifty years after the first production of* The Bohemian Girl, *songs from the opera were still popular, but fashions had changed and bohemian had acquired a new meaning. Flowing, loosely draped garments were adopted by artists, intellectuals and social reformers as well as such hangers-on as the "twenty love-sick maidens" of Gilbert and Sullivan's opera* Patience. *The new styles attracted much comment – not all good-natured, as the title of this engraving suggests.*

WRITTEN BY ALFRED BUNN   **COMPOSED BY MICHAEL WILLIAM BALFE**   1843

ORIGINAL PUBLISHER'S FOOTNOTE
This song may also be had a third lower.

dwelt in mar - ble halls, With vassals and serfs at my side, ...
sui - - tors sought my hand; That knights, up - on ben - ded knee, ...

And of all who as - - sembled with - - - -in those walls That
And with vows no mai - den heart could with - stand, They

I was the hope and the pride. . . . . . I had riches , too
pledged their faith to me. . . . . . And I dreamt that

great to count — could boast Of a high an - ces - - tral
one of that no - - ble host Came forth my hand to

The foremost actor-manager of the Georgian stage was David Garrick (1717-79), painted here by Thomas Gainsborough in about 1770. After achieving rapid success on the London and Dublin stages with his novel style of naturalistic acting – climaxed by a triumphant season at the Theatre Royal, Covent Garden, in 1746 – he became joint manager with James Lacy of the Theatre Royal, Drury Lane from 1747 until his retirement in 1776.

A NOTE ON PERFORMANCE

*These notes should be quavers (eighth notes) in the second verse.

The Theatre Royal, Covent Garden, as it appeared with its neo-classical portico in 1850, was the second of three great London theatres to stand on the same site. Designed by Sir Robert Smirke along the lines of the Parthenon in Athens, it was opened on 18th September, 1809, at a cost of £150,000, a gigantic sum at that time. On 6th April, 1847, after extensive altering of the auditorium, foyer and staircases, the 3,000-seat theatre reopened as the Royal Italian Opera which it remained until the building burnt down in March 1856. Its replacement is the present Royal Opera House, Covent Garden, which was completed two years after the fire.

In Psyche in the Palace of Love, painted in 1882 by Sir Edward John Poynter (1836-1919), Victorian neo-classicism is seen at its finest. Set in a phantasy of Roman architecture, the artist has depicted the maiden, Psyche, holding a sprig of honeysuckle while day-dreaming about her beloved, Cupid, the Roman god of desire, who visits her only by night in order to preserve his anonymity. The cabbage white butterfly on the flowers and the background doves symbolize her purity, while the details of the building reflect Poynter's reputation as the greatest academic draughtsman of his time.

THEN·YOU'LL· REMEMBER·ME·
WHEN OTHER LIPS

We make no apology for introducing two numbers from *The Bohemian Girl* – this and "the Dream" *(page 220)* were among the most widely sung songs of the day.

The words of *Then You'll Remember Me* were written by Alfred Bunn for the part of Arline's gypsy lover, to be played by the tenor William Harrison. Usually Balfe could sit down and write a tune directly he received a lyric, but in this case it just did not happen. He submitted six or seven settings to Harrison, but none were satisfactory. Then one night, as Harrison lay asleep, Balfe rushed into the bedroom, waving a roll of music over his head and shouted, "I've got it!" Having thoroughly woken Harrison, Balfe sat down at the piano and played the tune which later swept the country: his greatest triumph!

Written by an Englishman and composed by an Irishman, *The Bohemian Girl* was one of the few home-grown operas ever to achieve recognition in England. Apart from performances at Drury Lane, it was presented at the Grecian Saloon in Islington and travelled to the United States the year after its first London production. It was revived at Covent Garden in 1950.

The Bohemian girl – Arline – is eventually rescued from the gypsy camp and restored to her father, the Count, who recognizes her from a scar on her body. Her gypsy lover turns out to be an aristocrat in disguise. So all ends satisfactorily. An astute business man Mr Bunn may have been; original he certainly was not!

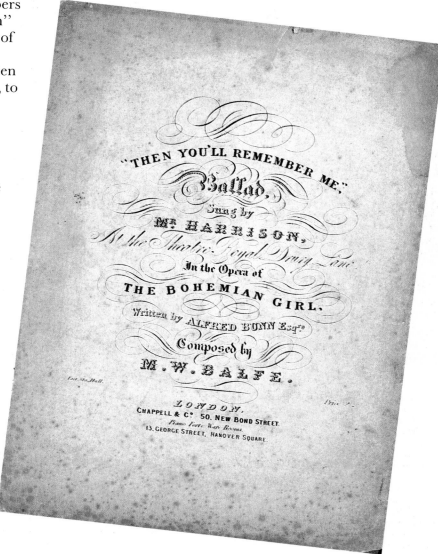

WRITTEN BY ALFRED BUNN   **COMPOSED BY MICHAEL WILLIAM BALFE**   1843

The cover to the sheet music published on these pages comes from one of the earliest editions of the ballad. The first production of Balfe's opera, which was staged in 1843, ran for 100 nights.

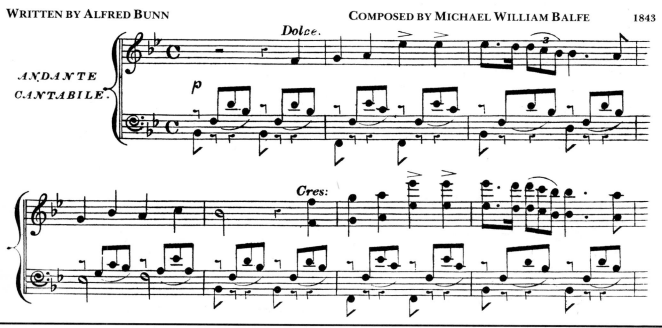

PUBLIC AMUSEMENTS FOR THE WEEK.

THEATRE ROYAL, DRURY-LANE.
Under the Management of Miss L. Pyne and Mr. W. Harrison.
Last week but Two of the Season.
TO-MORROW (Monday), and Thursday, will be produced (first and second times thisseason) THE BOHEMIAN GIRL. Thaddeus (his original character), Mr. W. Harrison—Arline, Miss Louisa Pyne. On Tuesday and Friday, 11TH DIAMONDS, and 28th times, THE SON OF CASTILE. On Wednesday, THE CROWN DIAMONDS. Conductor, Mr. Alfred Mellon. To conclude with, each evening, a BALLET DIVERTISEMENT.
Doors open at 7; commence at half-past.

A classified advertisement which appeared in The Times *of late 1843 or early 1844 announces two performances of* The Bohemian Girl *at the Theatre Royal, Drury Lane. The management of the theatre is given as Miss Louisa Pyne and Mr William Harrison, the two principal singers in the opera, who probably had administrative control during the interregnum before Alfred Bunn took on full managerial responsibility from the previous manager.*

ORIGINAL
PUBLISHER'S
FOOTNOTE
This song may also be had in the original key D flat, a third higher.

hap--py been, And you'll re--mem--ber me,....... and you'll re-

member, you'll remem--ber me.

Cres:

Cres:

When coldness or de--ceit shall slight The

pp

beau--ty now they prize, And deem it but a

fa--ded light Which beams within your eyes, When

The large auditorium of the Theatre Royal, Drury Lane, in 1804, is packed with people in an engraving from Old and New London, *a 19th-century narrative by Edward Walford on the history, people and places of the metropolis. This building, the third on the site to bear the name Theatre Royal, was designed by Henry Holland and was opened on 12th March, 1794 by its owner, the famous playwright, Richard Brinsley Sheridan. It was "a model of elegance and beauty", according to Walford, but it had a short life for it burnt down in February 1809. It was almost four years before a new Theatre Royal – the present one – rose in its place.*

225

Throughout the ages the rose has been the symbol of romance and the advent of summer. These roses, luring a squadron of butterflies with their powerful scent, decorate a lyrical article from The Girl's Own Paper called Hope: As A Tonic For Body And Mind. In it the author, writing under the pseudonym Medicus, enthuses about nature and human hope reborn after the "long dreary winter". Even the roses of hope have thorns, however; in the midst of the perfumed prose comes the sharp reminder "laziness is contrary to the rules of health".

hol _ _ low hearts shall wear a mask, 'Twill break your own to

see, In such a moment I but ask That you'll re _ mem _ ber

me,....... that you'll re _ mem _ ber, you'll re _ mem _ ber me.

A coach and horses pulls up in front of the Theatre Royal, Drury Lane, where a knot of play-goers has already gathered for a performance. The handsome Georgian façade with its Ionic pilasters and pediment crowned with heraldic beasts identify the building as the second Theatre Royal which had opened on 26th March, 1674. The design was by Sir Christopher Wren, an architect more renowned for his churches, but major reconstructions were carried out in 1775 by Robert Adam who added this façade and made internal improvements. The theatre eventually became too cramped for comfort, and was demolished in 1791, to make way for Henry Holland's building (page 225).

·THE·MOON·HAS·RAISED· HER·LAMP·ABOVE·

This duet for two male voices comes from the opera *Lily of Killarney*, first produced in Germany in 1862 under the title *Rose of Erin*, and based on the record breaking melodrama by Dion Boucicault, *The Colleen Bawn*, which was staged at the Adelphi in the 1850s. Julius Benedict, the composer, was born in Stuttgart in 1804 and conducted in Vienna, Naples and Paris before arriving in Britain in 1835. He was knighted in 1871. In the opera this tender love duet is sung by a murderous boatman, Danny Mann, and a would-be bigamist, Hardress Creegan.

WRITTEN BY JOHN OXENFORD

COMPOSED BY JULIUS BENEDICT 1862

Jenny Lind (1820-87), the most famous soprano of her day, poses for a studio photograph in the 1850s with an unknown child – perhaps one of the orphans who benefited from her charity donations. She made her English début in 1847, attracting praise from Queen Victoria herself who jotted in her journal: "Jenny Lind's acting and singing exceeded all I have ever heard". Almost immediately Lind left the operatic stage to sing in oratorios and concerts. On her American tours her musical director and accompanist was Sir Julius Benedict, composer of The Moon Has Raised Her Lamp Above.

tell me eyes more bright than they Are watching thro' the night,— Are watching thro' the night! I come, I come, my heart's de-light, I come,— I come, my heart's de-light,— I come, I come, I come my heart's de-light! I come, I come, my heart's de- -light! I come, I come my heart's de-light!

In an engraving from a mid-19th-century sheet music cover for a song entitled The Moon Has Risen!, *a woman is serenaded by a minstrel under the moonlight. Perhaps no other image has been so identified with romantic love as the moon, celebrated in song, prose, poem and picture through the ages. This song, composed by E. Solis to words by R. Ryan, is described on the cover as "An Answer" to another ballad of the day called* Rise, Gentle Moon *and as such provides a gently mocking antidote to the lunar cult in songwriting.*

AN IRISH PLOT

In order to pay off the mortgage on his mansion, the squire Hardress Creegan plans to marry Anne Chute, an heiress. The only problem is that he is already secretly married to Eily O'Connor (the Colleen Bawn), whom he tries to cast aside. She refuses to be discarded. (She has a big number in the second act.)

Hardress has a devoted servant called Danny Mann, a vulgar boatman, who tries to drown Eily. The attempt is thwarted by the arrival of Myles, a smuggler who is in love with Eily. Unknown to Squire Hardress, Danny is shot in the struggle and Eily survives.

As Hardress is just about to tie the knot with Anne Chute, a policeman arrives on the scene and arrests Hardress for the murder of Danny. Eily and Myles come to his rescue by telling the story of the struggle in the boat. Hardress is released, forgiven by Eily and they stay married.

Anne Chute, no doubt grateful for her narrow escape, pays off the debts.

*S*ir Julius Benedict was the conductor of the Monday Popular Concerts (the "Monday Pops") at St. James's Hall in London. For more than 40 years he promoted his own yearly fund-raising concert in London with such determination that he was tagged with the nickname "Sir Jubilee Benefit".

A full moon over the Cape Fear River, Wilmington, North Carolina, provides a hauntingly attractive scene for a postcard sent by an English visitor on the east coast of the United States to a relative in England in the 1870s.

The piano was well suited to industrial methods of production, and consequently less expensive than its predecessors, the harpsichord, the spinet or the organ. In the 18th century a typical harpsichord workshop could produce only about 20 instruments a year, but John Broadwood, who began manufacturing pianos in England in 1782, averaged 400 a year up to 1802, and 2,000 a year up to 1824.

In 1850 Britain as a whole produced 25,000 instruments. France, the first country to promote the upright piano as a space saver for smaller rooms, made 10,000, and America in 1851 built 9,000.

After the 1850s pianos were being mass-produced in factories rather than workshops and their price halved, relative to the cost of living, between then and 1914. By the end of the 19th century, more than 300,000 pianos a year were being manufactured in America alone, and the two-piano family had arrived.

It would seem, however, that many of the instruments were simply used to ornament the drawing room. In 1887 the American Music Teachers' National Association estimated that although the USA had by then produced something like one million pianos, there were only half a million piano pupils.

By 1919, American production had fallen from its peak, despite an increase in population, and the supremacy of the piano was over.

I·AM·THE·RULER·OF·THE QUEEN'S·NAVEE·

A perfect patter song with witty words and a jolly tune, this evergreen favourite comes from *HMS Pinafore*, one of Gilbert and Sullivan's most popular comic operas. In the song Sir Joseph Porter, First Lord of the Admiralty, is welcomed aboard the *Pinafore* by a chorus of sailors. Sir Joseph loses no time in disclosing to them the secret of his success in life.

HMS Pinafore's success, however, took some time coming. It was produced at the Opera Comique, which, being in a rather slimy alley near the Strand, was not a popular theatre. Shortly after the opening on 25th May, 1878, there came a tremendous heat wave, guaranteed then as now to keep the customers away.

It was suspected that the character of the admiral was based on W. H. Smith, founder of the newsagency, who really was First Lord of the Admiralty. Although Gilbert strenuously denied using him for a model, the similarities were so great that Disraeli dubbed him Pinafore Smith, and the nickname stuck. But this little political stir did nothing for the box office receipts, which by the end of July had dwindled to £40 a week.

By a happy chance, Arthur Sullivan was conducting the Promenade Concerts that year at Covent Garden, and he introduced into the programme a selection from Pinafore. The reaction was ecstatic, and by the end of August the Opera Comique was full every performance.

Pinafore fever had started. Pirated copies of the work appeared in America and five theatres in New York were soon running their own versions. A rival version even started in London at the Royal Aquarium, transferring to the Olympic almost next door to the Opera Comique. But it was eventually killed by the authentic version with the great George Grossmith (page 42), who starred in many of the D'Oyly Carte operas, playing the role of Sir Joseph Porter.

For the Christmas season of 1879-80 and 1880-81, the matinée performances of HMS Pinafore *at the Opera Comique were played entirely by a cast of children. This montage of pen and ink drawings by George Cruikshank from 1880 illustrates five scenes from the production. To suit the young voices, the vocal score was re-orchestrated and the opera re-arranged into shorter tableaux.*

WRITTEN BY WILLIAM SCHWENCK GILBERT　　　　**COMPOSED BY ARTHUR SULLIVAN**　　1878

1. When I was a lad I serv'd a term As of-fice boy to an At-
2. As of-fice boy I made such a mark That they gave me the post of a

-tor-ney's firm. I clean'd the windows and I swept the floor, And I
ju-nior clerk. I serv'd the writs with a smile so bland, And I

po-lish'd up the han-dle of the big front door. He
co-pied all the let-ters in a big round hand. He

CHORUS

po-lish'd up the han-dle of the
copied all the let-ters in a

SIR JOSEPH PORTER

big front door. I po-lish'd up that han-dle so care-ful-lee, That
big round hand. I co-pied all the let-ters in a hand so free, And

CHORUS

now I am the ru-ler of the Queen's Na-vee. He po-lish'd up that han-dle so
now I am the ru-ler of the Queen's Na-vee. He co-pied all the let-ters in a

CHORUS *in unison*

care-ful-lee That now he is the ru-ler of the Queen's Na-vee.
hand so free And

Three members of the D'Oyly Carte Opera Company, standing on the quarterdeck of HMS Pinafore, perform in an 1899 production of the comic opera. On the left, Henry Lytton plays Captain Corcoran; in the centre, Walter Passmore is Sir Joseph Porter, First Lord of the Admiralty; and on the right the character of Able Seaman Ralph Rackstraw is played, most probably, by Robert Evett, principal tenor of the company.

3.

In serving writs I made such a name,
That an articled clerk I soon became;
I wore clean collars and a bran' new suit
  For the pass examination at the Institute,
  For the pass examination at the Institute.
That pass examination did so well for me
That now I am the ruler of the Queen's Navee.
  That pass examination did so well for he
  That now he is the ruler of the Queen's Navee.

SIR JOSEPH PORTER

5. I grew so rich that I was sent By a
6. Now lands-men all, who-ev-er you may be, If you

pock-et borough in-to Par-lia-ment. I al-ways vo-ted at my
want to rise to the top of the tree, If your soul is-n't fettered to an

CHORUS

par-ty's call, And I ne-ver thought of thinking for my-self at all, He
of-fice stool, Be care-ful to be guided by this gold-en rule, Be

SIR JOSEPH PORTER

ne-ver thought of thinking for him-self at all, I thought so lit-tle they re-
care-ful to be guid-ed by this gold-en rule, Stick close to your desks and

A lithograph from a song cover of 1897 portrays an able seaman of the Royal Navy. The sailor's lot had changed out of all recognition since the days of sail earlier in the century when life on a man-of-war had been more threatened by peacetime accidents, disease and flogging than by battle. Sailors had been provided with uniforms since 1857, and were no longer press-ganged into service.

4.

Of legal knowledge I acquired such a grip,
That they took me into the partnership,
And that junior partnership I ween
    Was the only ship that I ever had seen,
    Was the only ship he ever had seen.
That kind of ship so suited me
That now I am the ruler of the Queen's Navee.
    That kind of ship so suited he
    That now he is the ruler of the Queen's Navee.

The music-hall singer Arthur Reece appears as a Royal Navy commander in this illustration from the cover of his song Sons Of The Sea. Britain in the 1890s had a fleet both vast and ungainly, with too many types of ships, machinery, guns and ammunition. But from 1901 when Admiral "Scrap the lot" Fisher became Second Sea Lord, a new navy was designed and built with the famous dreadnoughts as its capital ships.

235

· A · WAND'RING · MINSTREL · I ·

The Mikado, by Gilbert and Sullivan, opened at the Savoy Theatre in the Strand on 14th March, 1885, and ran for two years. In all 672 performances of the production were given. It was the third Gilbert and Sullivan comic opera to be presented at the new theatre built especially for the purpose by Richard D'Oyly Carte in 1882. From that date Gilbert and Sullivan's productions were known as the Savoy Operas and the performers as the Savoyards.

A Wand'ring Minstrel I is performed by Nanki-Poo, son of the Mikado, or Emperor, of Japan. The young man is in love with Yum-Yum, ward of the Lord High Executioner. Searching for her, he appears in the Lord High Executioner's garden disguised as a threadbare minstrel, and acts out the part by presenting a miniature compendium of Victorian ballads – lullabyes, patriotic songs, love songs, sea shanties – which provide any singer with a perfect chance to show off his versatility.

W. S. Gilbert got his inspiration for this play from a Japanese exhibition in Knightsbridge, where the streets were uncharacteristically enlivened by Japanese men and women out walking in their oriental costumes. Japan itself was being westernized, and England and France were hungrily seizing on Japanese art and culture. The moment was ripe for a Japanese comic opera.

The Mikado is Gilbert's usual blend of satire and comment on English public life wittily transposed to the land of the rising sun. Much effort went into ensuring authenticity, and one of the girls from the Knightsbridge exhibition acted as adviser; she was known as Miss Sixpence Please, after the only words of English she was said to know. This new opera immediately became one of the most valuable theatrical properties in the world.

It was also a coup for Liberty's, the Regent Street store which specialized in exotic materials. Although the principal artists in The Mikado received costumes direct from Japan, Liberty's supplied the costumes for other members of the cast.

The success of The Mikado inspired a string of shows with an oriental flavour, including The Geisha which opened at Daly's in 1896 and Puccini's Madame Butterfly in 1904. In New York there was even a show called Wang.

An English actor on tour in New York in August 1885 with D'Oyly Carte's production of The Mikado poses for a publicity photograph in the guise of Nanki-Poo, the "wand'ring minstrel" of the song. He is plucking a samisen, the Japanese guitar which he carries on his entrance in Act One.

WRITTEN BY WILLIAM SCHWENCK GILBERT   **COMPOSED BY ARTHUR SULLIVAN**   1885

pas___sion rang_ing, And to your hum_ours changing I

tune my sup_ple song!_____ I tune my sup_____ple

Andante espressivo.

song! Are you in sen_ti_men_tal mood? I'll sigh with you,

Oh,_____ sor___row! On maid_en's cold_ness do you brood? I'll

A JAPANESE VILLAGE AT TH...

MR. RUTLAND BARRINGTON.
A SAVOYARD.

A cartoon (top) by Alfred Bryan from The Entr'acte of 21st March, 1885, depicts W. S. Gilbert – his arms angled like semaphores while doing a Japanese dance – and a monocled, mutton-chopped Arthur Sullivan. Around them swirl various characters from The Mikado. The part of Poo-Bah was first played by Rutland Barrington (above), also caricatured by Alfred Bryan. Barrington had a reputation for singing slightly off key. After one performance, Richard D'Oyly Carte is said to have approached him with the question, "Barrington, what's the matter? Someone has just come out of the stalls and says you are singing in tune. It will never do".

THE SAVOY.
MR. GEORGE GROSSMITH, TO MR. D'OYLY CARTE:—"WHAT DO YOU SAY, D'OYLY?
SHALL I COME AND GIVE YOU A LEG-UP AGAIN!"

In an Alfred Bryan sketch of 1894, a bespectacled George Grossmith asks whether D'Oyly Carte wants him to take a part in the next Gilbert and Sullivan operetta, which was to be The Grand Duke. Grossmith had left the company in 1889 after many successful performances, and contrary to rumour he never did return.

237

THE BATTLE FOR AMERICA

The first American performance of *The Mikado* was presented by a British cast assembled and shipped across the Atlantic in the greatest secrecy. Copyright law in the United States at that time offered no protection to British composers and librettists. D'Oyly Carte, having seen American producers pirate other Gilbert and Sullivan operas, was determined this time to steal the show back by putting on his own.

Hearing that a pirated version of *The Mikado* was being prepared in New York, he rehearsed an entire cast in London on the pretext that they were to tour the provinces, booked them on board a Cunard liner under assumed names – he himself travelled as Mr Henry Chapman – and triumphantly opened his own Mikado just a few days before the rival American version was ready.

The authentic production ran for 430 performances, fully realizing D'Oyly Carte's hopes, but probably a hundred "butchered, botched, mauled and mangled" productions, to use the words of the *New York Herald*, were put on across the States, prompting D'Oyly Carte to send another five genuine companies to tour the United States and Canada in 1886.

"It seemed to be their opinion," said Arthur Sullivan bitterly of the pirates, "that a free and independent American citizen ought not to be robbed of his right of robbing somebody else."

The Copyright Act of 1911 established statutory controls over the ownership of copyrighted works in Britain, but it was not until the United States joined the Universal Copyright Convention in 1955 that composers and librettists could finally consign to the past the kind of extreme tactics adopted by D'Oyly Carte.

Two famous caricatures from Vanity Fair show (far left) W. S. Gilbert by Spy (alias Leslie Ward), published on 21st May, 1881 under the title Patience; and (left) Arthur Sullivan in a cartoon entitled English Music by Ape (Carlo Pellegrini), published on 14th March, 1894.

George Grossmith appears as
Ko-Ko, the Lord High
Executioner of Titipu, in the first
production of The Mikado at
the Savoy in 1885.

Gilbert and Sullivan pose in Japanese costume in a Punch *cartoon of 1885 captioned "Two Very Fanny Japs at the Savoy", referring to the large fans they are carrying. A portrait of D'Oyly Carte appears on the fan held by Gilbert. Fans were extremely popular in London at this time – possibly more as a result of* The Mikado *than of the 1884 Japanese Exhibition in Knightsbridge.*

The Two Very Fanny Japs at the Savoy.

Opposite:

An illustration from an 1896 sheet music cover shows the actress Marie Tempest in the sort of Japanese kimono she wore for The Geisha, *London's latest musical comedy, in which she took the title role (see overleaf). The craze for things Japanese resurfaced with the success of this play, recalling a similar phenomenon when* The Mikado *took London by storm in 1885.*

A programme of 1897 advertises The Geisha *which opened at the opulent Daly's Theatre in Leicester Square on 25th April, 1896 and ran for 760 performances. The theatre, designed by Spencer Chadwick, had been built between 1891 and 1893 by George Edwardes (see overleaf) for the American impresario, Augustin Daly, to house productions of the classics. These were not a success, and Edwardes started to use the theatre for musical comedies, finally taking back the lease in 1898.*

· THE · AMOROUS · GOLDFISH ·

The Geisha, starring Marie Tempest in the leading role as O Mimosa San, is the story of a Japanese girl who falls in love with a British officer. In *The Amorous Goldfish* the geisha parallels the plot of the play with the hopeless story of a goldfish who falls in love with a sailor. The producer was George Edwardes, who introduced at Daly's the glittering age of musical comedy. He was a stickler for discipline and good taste and is said to have been heartbroken by the advent of ragtime, which threw all his elegant values out of the window.

WRITTEN BY HARRY GREENBANK   COMPOSED BY SIDNEY JONES   1896

A gold-fish swam in a big glass bowl, As dear lit_tle gold-fish

George Edwardes (c.1854-1915) was familiarly known in the theatrical profession as "the Guv'nor". He learnt much about the theatre during his years as box-office manager for D'Oyly Carte at the Opera Comique and as acting manager at the Savoy Theatre. He later went on to manage the Empire, Gaiety and Daly's Theatres, specializing in light-hearted and colourful musicals that emphasized feminine charms and grace, with romance thrown in. Many of his productions featured the word "girl" in their titles: The Shop Girl, The Circus Girl, A Gaiety Girl and The Runaway Girl.

A courtier with prancing cupids whimsically illustrates the programme for the burlesque Monte Cristo, Junior which opened at the Gaiety Theatre on 23rd December, 1886. As was usual in burlesque, the male lead was played by a woman, in this case Nellie Farren. A minor role was given to Lottie Collins, the music-hall star later famed for her song Ta-ra-ra-Boom-de-ay, but she found the three lines she had to speak and the bit of dancing she had to do too minor, and she left after only a short stint. The Gaiety had been opened in 1868 by John Hollingshead who produced 40 musical burlesques over 18 years until the theatre was taken over by George Edwardes in 1886. Monte Cristo, Junior was his first production there.

_fit_ter He should love my glit_glit_glit_ter, Than his heart give a_way To the

but_ter_flies gay, Or the birds that twit_twit_twit_ter.

She flash'd her frock in the sun-shine bright, That
That charm_ing girl for a time up_set The

of_fi_cer brave to charm, And he vowed she was quite a de_light_ful sight, So her
of_fi_cer brave and gay, And his sad lit_tle pet he con_trived to for_get, For with

spirits were gay till he came one day With a girl on his stal_wart arm. In
ne_ver a crumb did he chance to come, So the gold fish pined a_way. Un_

246

whis - pers low they talked of love; He begged for a rose and a
-til one day some care-less soul With a smash knock'd o - ver the

worn out glove; But when they kissed a fond good-bye, The poor lit_tle gold-fish
big glass-bowl, And there onthecar_pet dead and cold Laythe poor lit_tle fish in her

longed to die. .... And she sobbed, "Its bit - bit -
frock of gold. .... And her fate so bit - bit -

- bit _ ter He should love this crit_crit_crit_ter, When I thought he would wish For a
- bit _ ter Is a sto_ry fit_fit_fit_ter For a sad lit_tle sigh And a

nice lit_tle fish, With a frock all glit_glit_glit_ter."
tear in the eye, Than a thought_less tit_tit_tit_ter.

Fine.

D.C.

A programme cover of about 1887 for the Empire Theatre of Varieties, Leicester Square, features a representative dancer from the corps de ballet which regularly appeared there during the 1880s and 1890s with assorted variety acts. Designed by the English architect, Thomas Verity, the Empire had been completed in 1884 with such architectural novelties as a spacious foyer and two promenades at the back of the dress-circle tiers where ladies of the town plied their trade. The joint managing directors of the theatre were George Edwardes and Augustus Harris.

·THE·HONEYSUCKLE· AND·THE·BEE·

Ellaline Terriss married the comic actor, Seymour Hicks, in the early 1890s. She had a happy private life, though it was marred in 1897 when she lost three members of her close family: her first baby; her father, who was stabbed to death outside his theatre; and her mother, who died soon afterwards. Ellaline was very lucky not to lose her husband as well. In 1900 he was locked in the old Islington Grand all night just 24 hours before the theatre was burnt down, thus narrowly escaping an unpleasant death. In the event the couple celebrated 56 years of marriage.

We end our collection with a song written in the year of Victoria's death. It combines most of the elements of this book, being suitable for music hall, drawing room, theatre, and also the nursery. *The Honeysuckle And The Bee* featured in *Bluebell In Fairyland*, a musical entertainment for children about a London flower girl who is taken by fairies on a series of wonderful adventures. The show, which is chiefly famous for this song, was presented at the Vaudeville Theatre by Seymour Hicks, starring his beautiful wife Ellaline Terriss as Bluebell. *The Honeysuckle And The Bee* became almost her signature tune.

Ellaline Terriss was born in the Falkland Islands in 1871 at a time when her father, William Terriss, was unable to find work as an actor and had temporarily taken up sheep farming in the South Atlantic. She died in 1971 at the age of 100.

William Terriss was a remarkable and tragic figure in Victorian theatre. Not only did he star as the hero of most of the Adelphi melodramas, but he was also the victim of a real-life melodrama played out in the alley which led to the stage door. On 16th December, 1897, as he entered the theatre for the evening's performance, he was stabbed to death by a deranged small-part player, William Arthur Prince. And to this day a tall distinguished gentleman in grey is said to walk through Covent Garden at dusk, disappearing as he reaches the stage door: the ghost of Covent Garden. We have not seen Mr Terriss, but we know people who say they have.

We hope that the ghosts of all the stars, composers, impresarios and librettists we have mentioned will continue to haunt you – in the nicest possible way – and keep you company on your Victorian musical evenings.

MISS ELLALINE TERRISS.

WRITTEN BY ALBERT H. FITZ

COMPOSED BY WILLIAM H. PENN 1901

Weary passengers ride home in a horse-drawn omnibus, some probably coming from an evening at the theatre. The sketch is taken from a January 1892 issue of Pick-Me-Up, *a weekly magazine containing a wide assortment of stories, poems, cartoons and articles on subjects such as the arts and theatre and publicizing itself as "A Literary and Artistic Tonic for the Mind".*

best............ As they sang the songs of love, From the
kiss;............ For her heart had yield ed soon, 'Neath the

ar _ bour just a _ bove, Came a bee which lit up _ on the
hon _ ey _ suck _ le's bloom, And thro' life they'd wan _ der day by

In a late 19th-century poster advertising the Alhambra Theatre in Brighton, a drawing of the building with its twin cupolas, minarets and horseshoe-arched windows, reveals the extent to which it was influenced by the Moorish-style Alhambra Palace in London. The decoration of the original Alhambra – the palace of the 14th-century Moorish kings in Granada, Spain – as well as Islamic architecture in general, was much admired by Victorian architects.

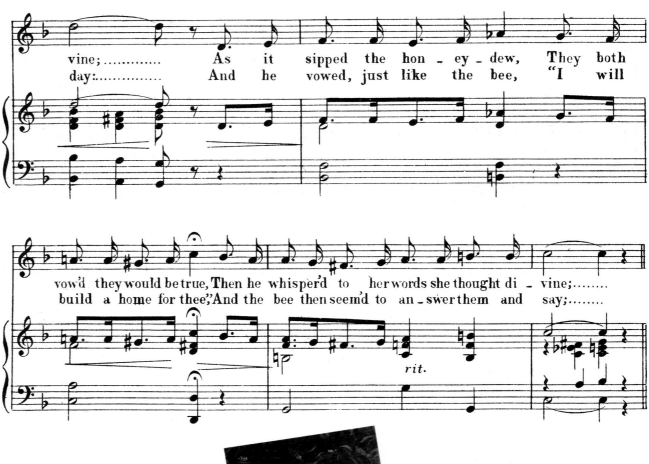

vine; .... As it sipped the hon _ ey _ dew, They both
day:............ And he vowed, just like the bee, "I will

vow'd they would be true, Then he whisper'd to her words she thought di _ vine;........
build a home for thee,'' And the bee then seem'd to an _ swer them and say;........

rit.

The calm and classical beauty of the Fair Student, painted in 1878 by the Italian-born Charles Edward Perugini, is set off by the pleasant background of a leafy arbour, so beloved of Victorian artists and poets. Perugini, who followed the Hellenistic style of painters such as Lord Leighton and Albert Moore, came to London in 1863 at the age of 23 and remained in this country until his death in 1918.

CHORUS.
Daintily.

You are my hon_ey, hon_ey_suck_le, I am the bee, ...

I'd like to sip the hon_ey sweet from those red lips, you see; ....

I love you dear_ly, dear_ly, and I want you to love me, ...

You are my hon_ey, hon_ey_suck_le, I am the bee."

Fine.

*I*n a delightful scene from a show called My Daughter-In-Law, *performed at the Criterion in 1899, Ellaline Terriss and Seymour Hicks fill their wine glasses after dinner. The two appeared in many musical comedies together at the Gaiety Theatre under George Edwardes and at the Vaudeville Theatre under the management of the American impresario Charles Frohman. Seymour Hicks was knighted in 1935.*

*D*aly's Theatre, on the north side of Leicester Square, served as London's premier showcase for musical comedies and operettas for many years. It closed in 1937 and was rebuilt as the Warner Cinema. Among the many shows staged there was the first London performance of Franz Lehar's The Merry Widow *which opened on 17th June, 1907. The composer himself came over from Vienna to conduct the last few rehearsals of the orchestra. The operetta was a triumph, running for two years; King Edward VII saw it four times.*

251

BIBLIOGRAPHY

ABBOTT, JOHN, *The Story of Francis, Day & Hunter*. Francis, Day & Hunter, Ltd, London, 1952.

ATKINSON, BROOKS, *Broadway*. Cassell, London, 1970.

BAILEY, LESLIE, *Gilbert & Sullivan and their World*. Thames and Hudson, London, 1973.

BAILEY, VICTOR, *Bibles and Dummy Rifles*. Article in *History Today*, Vol. 33, 1983.

BARKER, TONY, *Music Hall* magazine. Tony Barker, London, 1978 to present date.

BEHRMAN, S. N., *Conversations with Max*. Hamish Hamilton, London, 1960.

BLAKE, ROBERT, *Disraeli*. Eyre & Spottiswoode, London, 1966.

BRIGGS, ASA, *A Social History of England*. Weidenfeld & Nicholson, London, 1983.

BRIGGS, ASA, *The Power of Steam*. Michael Joseph, London, 1982.

CHANCE NEWTON, H., *Idols of the Halls*. Heath Cranton, London, 1928.

CHESNEY, KELLOW, *The Victorian Underworld*. Purnell Book Services, London, 1970.

CHEVALIER, ALBERT, *A Record by Himself*. MacQueen, London, 1895.

COBORN, CHARLES, *The Man who Broke the Bank*. Hutchinson, London, 1928.

CURTIS, ANTHONY (Ed.), *The Rise and Fall of the Matinee Idol*. Weidenfeld & Nicholson Ltd, London, 1974.

DAVIES, H. WALFORD, *The Fellowship Song Book*. J. Curwen & Sons Ltd and Headly Brothers, London, 1915.

DAVISON, PETER, *The British Music Hall*. Oak Publications, New York, 1971.

DE FRECE, LADY, *Recollections of Vesta Tilley*. Hutchinson, London, 1934.

DISHER, MAURICE WILLSON, *Victorian Songs*. Phoenix House, London, 1955.

DISHER, MAURICE WILLSON, *Winkles and Champagne*. Batsford, London, 1938.

DORE, GUSTAVE, *London*. Arno Press, New York, 1978.

DOBBS, BRIAN, *Drury Lane*. Cassell, London, 1972.

DUNSTAN, R., *A Manual of Music*. J. Curwen & Sons Ltd, London, 1912.

ENSOR, SIR ROBERT, *England 1870-1914*. Oxford University Press, 1936.

Entr'acte, The, various issues, W. H. Combes, London, 1869-1907.

Era, The, various issues, The Era, London, 1838-1939.

FABIAN, MONROE, *On Stage*. Mayflower Books, USA, 1980.

FARSON, DANIEL, *Marie Lloyd and the Music Hall*. Tom Stacey, London, 1972.

FELSTEAD, S. THEODORE, *Stars who Made the Halls*. P. W. Laurie, London, 1946.

GAMMOND, PETER, *Your Own, Your Very Own*. Ian Allan, London, 1971.

GARRETT, JOHN, *Sixty Years of British Music Hall*. Chappell, London, 1976.

GIROUARD, MARK, *Victorian Pubs*. Studio Vista, London, 1975.

GIROUARD, MARK, *The Return to Camelot: Chivalry and the English Gentleman*. Yale University Press, London, 1981.

GLASSTONE, VICTOR, *Victorian and Edwardian Theatres*. Thames & Hudson, London, 1975.

GRAVES, ALFRED PERCEVAL, *Irish Songs and Ballads*. Alexander Ireland and Co., Manchester, 1880.

GROVE, SIR GEORGE, *A Dictionary of Music and Musicians*. Macmillan, London, various editions.

HARTNOLL, PHYLLIS (Ed.), *The Oxford Companion to the Theatre*. Oxford University Press, 1983.

HETHERINGTON, JOHN, *Melba*. Faber, London, 1967.

HILL, C. W., *Edwardian Entertainments, a Picture Post Card View*. M.A.B. Publishing, London, no date.

HINDLEY, GEOFFREY, (Ed.), *The Larousse Encyclopaedia of Music*. Hamlyn, London, 1971.

HOWARD, DIANA, *London Theatres and Music Halls 1850-1950*. The Library Association, London, 1970.

HUDD, ROY, *Music Hall*. Eyre Methuen Ltd, London, 1976.

HYMAN, ALAN, *The Gaiety Years*. Cassell, London, 1975.

JENKYNS, RICHARD, *The Victorians and Ancient Greece*. Basil Blackwell, London, 1980.

KEITH, ALAN, *Your Hundred Best Tunes*. Dent, London, 1975.

KENNEDY, MICHAEL, (Ed.), *The Concise Oxford Dictionary of Music*. Oxford University Press, 1980.

KIPLING, RUDYARD, *Sixty Poems*. Hodder and Stoughton, London, 1939.

KLAMPKIN, MARIAN, *Old Sheet Music*. Hawthorn Books, Inc., New York, 1975.

LAWSON, ANDREW, *Discover Unexpected London*. Elsevier-Phaidon, Oxford, 1977.

LONGFORD, ELIZABETH, *Victoria R.I.* Weidenfeld and Nicholson, London, 1964.

LOESSER, ARTHUR, *Men, Women & Pianos*. Simon and Schuster, New York, 1954.

MANDER, RAYMOND, and MITCHENSON, JOE, *British Music Hall*. Studio Vista, London, 1965.

MANKOVITZ, WOLF, *Dickens of London*. Macmillan, New York, 1976.

MAYHEW, HENRY, *Mayhew's London*, (Ed. Peter Quennell). Hamlyn, London, 1969.

MAYHEW, HENRY, *London Labour and the London Poor*. Griffin Bohn & Co., London, 1851/1862 (four volumes).

McQUEEN POPE, W., *Carriages at Eleven*. Robert Hale, London, 1947.

McQUEEN POPE, W., *Ghosts and Greasepaint*. Robert Hale, London, 1971.

McQUEEN POPE, W., *An Indiscreet Guide to Theatreland*. Muse Arts Ltd, London, no date.

PALGRAVE, FRANCIS, T., *Golden Treasury of Songs and Lyrics*. Macmillan & Co. Ltd, London, 1946.

Poems By Alfred, Lord Tennyson, Illustrated by E. F. Brickdale, Bell & Hyman, London, 1979.

READ, DONALD, *England 1868-1914*. Longman Group, London, 1979.

REYNOLDS, HARRY, *Minstrel Melodies*. Alston Rivers, London, 1928.

SCHOLES, PERCY A., (Ed.), *The Oxford Companion to Music*. Oxford University Press, various editions.

SCOTT, HAROLD, *The Early Doors*. Nicholson & Watson, London, 1946.

SOUTHERN, RICHARD, *The Victorian Theatre*. David & Charles, Newton Abbot, 1970.

STANFORD, CHARLES VILLIERS, *Musical Composition*. Macmillan & Co. Ltd, London, and Stainer and Bell Limited, London, 1949.

STAVEACRE, TONY, *The Songwriters*. BBC, London, 1980.

STUART, CHARLES DOUGLAS, and PARK, A. J., *The Variety Stage*. T. Fisher Unwin, London, 1895.

TOVEY, DONALD FRANCIS, *Essays in Musical Analysis*. Oxford University Press, London, 1935.

TRAGER, JAMES, (Ed.), *The People's Chronology*. Heinemann, London, 1979.

TURNER, MICHAEL R., *The Parlour Song Book*. Michael Joseph, London, 1972.

TURNER, MICHAEL R., *Just a Song at Twilight*. Michael Joseph, London, 1975.

Who's Who in the Theatre, Sir Isaac Pitman & Sons Ltd, London, various editions.

Who's Who in Variety, (Ed. Guy R. Bullar and Len Evans), The Performer Ltd, London, 1950.

WILSON, A. E., *The Lyceum*. Yates, London, 1952.

WOODHAM-SMITH, CECIL, *The Great Hunger*. Hamish Hamilton, London, 1962.

WOODHAM-SMITH, CECIL, *The Reason Why*. Constable, London, 1953.

WOODWARD, SIR LLEWELLYN, *The Age of Reform, 1815-1870*. Oxford University Press, 1962.

WROTH, WARWICK, *The London Pleasure Gardens*. Macmillan, London, 1896.

SOURCES OF MUSIC IN THIS BOOK

Home! Sweet Home! Arranged by Henry R. Bishop; Published by Goulding & D'Almaine, London (7648); On loan from The Raymond Mander & Joe Mitchenson Theatre Collection.

In The Gloaming. Published by Hutchings & Romer, London (H & R 9718); On loan from The Raymond Mander & Joe Mitchenson Theatre Collection; Reproduced by permission of Leonard Gould & Bolttler.
© Copyright by Leonard Gould & Bolttler

Killarney. Published by W. Paxton, London (1271); On loan from Aba Daba, courtesy Aline Waites. Words of verses 2 and 4 from version published by E. Ascherberg & Co., London (E.A. & Co. 405b).

Come Into The Garden Maud. Published by Boosey & Sons (1856); On loan from The Raymond Mander & Joe Mitchenson Theatre Collection.

Come Home, Father. Originally published as No. 3874 of the Musical Bouquet, reproduced in the St. James's Hall volume of Christy's Minstrels' New Songs; Published by Charles Sheard & Co., London; On loan from EMI Music Publishers Ltd.

Love's Old Sweet Song. Published by Boosey & Co., London; On loan from Aba Daba, courtesy Aline Waites.

The Baby On The Shore. Published by Reynolds & Co., London (R & Co. 800); On loan from John Ince.

Abide With Me from *Hymns Ancient and Modern*; On loan from Florence Wykes.

Eternal Father, Strong To Save from *Hymns Ancient and Modern*; On loan from Florence Wykes.

The Holy City. Published by Boosey & Co., London, 1892 (H.689); On loan from Aba Daba, courtesy Aline Waites.

The Lost Chord. Published by Boosey & Co., London; On loan from The Raymond Mander & Joe Mitchenson Theatre Collection.

She Was Poor, But She Was Honest. Arranged by David Wykes; From the collection of Sheldrake Press Ltd.
© Arrangement by David Wykes, 1984

Sam Hall. Arranged by David Wykes; From the collection of Sheldrake Press Ltd.
© Arrangement by David Wykes, 1984

Villikins And His Dinah. Published by G. H. Davidson, London, in Davidson's Musical Treasury No. 691; On loan from The Raymond Mander & Joe Mitchenson Theatre Collection.

The Ratcatcher's Daughter. Published by G. H. Davidson, London, Musical Treasury Nos. 749-50; On loan from The Raymond Mander & Joe Mitchenson Theatre Collection.

Polly Perkins Of Paddington Green. Arranged by J. Candy; Published by Hopwood & Crew Ltd, London (H & C. 492); On loan from The Raymond Mander & Joe Mitchenson Theatre Collection.

Oh! Susanna. Published by G. H. Davidson, London; On loan from John Stanton.

Beautiful Dreamer. Arranged and Edited by Frank G. Galpin A.L.C.M.; Published by R. Jackson & Co., London; On loan from the Players Theatre Library.

The Gipsy's Warning. Published by W. Paxton, London; On loan from Aba Daba, courtesy Aline Waites.

Ring The Bell Softly. Published by John Guest, London; On loan from Aba Daba, courtesy Aline Waites.

Oh, Dem Golden Slippers! Published by C. Sheard, Musical Bouquet series number 6126; On loan from The Raymond Mander & Joe Mitchenson Theatre Collection.

Dear Old Pals. Published by Ascherberg, Hopwood & Crew Ltd, London (H & C 1878); On loan from The Raymond Mander & Joe Mitchenson Theatre Collection.

Two Lovely Black Eyes! Arranged by Edmund Forman. Published by Francis Brothers & Day, London; On loan from The Raymond Mander & Joe Mitchenson Theatre Collection; Reproduced by permission of EMI Music Publishing Ltd and International Music Publications.
© Copyright 1886 by Francis, Day & Hunter, Ltd

Ta-ra-ra- Boom-de-ay! Arranged by Angelo A. Asher; Published by C. Sheard & Co., London; On loan from The Raymond Mander & Joe Mitchenson Theatre Collection.

Daisy Bell. Published by Francis, Day & Hunter, Ltd, London (F & D 3472); On loan from EMI Music Publishers Ltd.

Oh! Mr Porter. Published by Howard & Co., London (H & Co. 2526); Assigned Ascherberg Hopwood & Crew Ltd; On loan from The Raymond Mander & Joe Mitchenson Theatre Collection; Reproduced by permission of Chappell Music Ltd and International Music Publications.
© Copyright 1893 by Howard & Co.

The Lily Of Laguna. Published by Francis, Day & Hunter, Ltd, London (F & D 5650); On loan from The Raymond Mander & Joe Mitchenson Theatre Collection.

The Flying Trapeze. Arranged by Alfred Lee; Published by Herman Darewski Music Publishing Co., London, Incorporating Charles Sheard & Co.; On loan from EMI Music Publishers Ltd.

The Man That Broke The Bank At Monte Carlo. Arranged by Alfred Leggett; Published by Francis, Day & Hunter, Ltd, London (F & D 3289); On loan from John Stanton.

If It Wasn't For The 'Ouses In Between. Published by Francis, Day & Hunter, Ltd, London (F & D 4160); On loan from John Earle; Reproduced by permission of EMI Music Publishing Ltd and International Music Publications.
© Copyright 1894 by Francis, Day & Hunter, Ltd

It's A Great Big Shame. Published by Francis, Day & Hunter, Ltd, London (F & D 4548); On loan from Tony Barker; Reproduced by permission of EMI Music Publishers Ltd and International Music Publications.
© Copyright 1895 by Francis, Day & Hunter, Ltd

She Was One Of The Early Birds. Published by Francis, Day & Hunter, Ltd, London; On loan from the Players Theatre Library; Reproduced by permission of EMI Music Publishers Ltd and International Music Publications.
© Copyright 1895 by Francis, Day & Hunter, Ltd

Wot Cher! Published by Reynolds & Co., London (R & Co. 159); On loan from The Raymond Mander & Joe Mitchenson Theatre Collection; Reproduced by permission of EMI Music Publishers Ltd and International Music Publications.
© Copyright 1891 by Keith Prowse Music Publishing Co. Ltd

My Old Dutch. Published by Reynolds & Co., London (R & C 237); On loan from The Raymond Mander & Joe Mitchenson Theatre Collection; Reproduced by permission of EMI Music Publishers Ltd and International Music Publications.
© Copyright 1893 by Keith Prowse Music Publishing Co. Ltd

After The Ball. Published by W. Paxton & Co., Ltd, London (908); On loan from The Raymond Mander & Joe Mitchenson Theatre Collection.

The Boy In The Gallery. (H & C 2712); On loan from the Westminster Central Music Library; Melody line courtesy David Wykes.

Are We To Part Like This? Published by the "News of the World" Limited, London; On loan from the Players Theatre Library; Reproduced by permission of EMI Music Publishers Ltd and International Music Publications.
© Copyright 1912 by B. Feldman & Co. Ltd

When The Summer Comes Again. Published by Francis, Day & Hunter, Ltd in the "News of the World", number 1798; On loan from Bill Manley; Reproduced by permission of EMI Music Publishers Ltd and International Music Publications.
© Copyright 1895 by Francis, Day & Hunter, Ltd

The Coster's Serenade. Published by Reynolds & Co., London, in *Albert Chevalier's 2nd Album*; On loan from EMI Music Publishers; Reproduced by permission of EMI Music Publishers Ltd and International Music Publications.

© Copyright 1890 by Keith Prowse Music Publishing Co. Ltd

A Bird In A Gilded Cage. Published by B. Feldman & Co., in *Feldman's 6d Edition*; On loan from EMI Music Publishers Ltd; Reproduced by permission of EMI Music Publishers Ltd and International Music Publications.
© Copyright 1899 by B. Feldman & Co. Ltd

Sweet Rosie O'Grady. Published by Frank Dean & Co., London (F. D. & Co. 433); On loan from The Raymond Mander & Joe Mitchenson Theatre Collection; Reproduced by permission of EMI Music Publishers Ltd and International Music Publications.
© Copyright 1896 by J. W. Stern & Co., now E. B. Marks Music Corp (USA), Sub-published by B. Feldman & Co. Ltd

Macdermott's War Song. Published by Hopwood & Crew, London (H & C 1853); On loan from The Raymond Mander & Joe Mitchenson Theatre Collection.

Comrades. Arranged by E. Jonghmans; Published by Francis, Day & Hunter, Ltd; On loan from The Raymond Mander & Joe Mitchenson Theatre Collection; Reproduced by permission of EMI Music Publishers Ltd and International Music Publications
© Copyright 1890 by Francis, Day & Hunter, Ltd

The Soldiers Of The Queen. Published by Francis, Day & Hunter, Ltd, London (F & D 4390); On loan from the Players Theatre Library.

Good-bye Dolly Gray. Published by Howley, Haviland & Co.; On loan from the Raymond Mander & Joe Mitchenson Theatre Collection; Reproduced by permission of EMI Music Publishers Ltd and International Music Publications.
© Copyright 1900 by Howley Haviland & Co., now Shawnee Press Inc (USA), Sub-published by Herman Darewski Music Publishing Co.

The Londonderry Air/Emer's Farewell. Arranged by Charles Villiers Stanford. Published by Boosey & Co. Ltd, London (H. 3515); By courtesy of Boosey & Hawkes Music Archives; Words of **Love's Wishes** from Alfred P. Graves, *Irish Songs & Ballads*; Published by Alexander Ireland & Co., Manchester, 1880.

Drink To Me Only With Thine Eyes. Published by W. Paxton & Co., Ltd, London (Paxton 351); On loan from the Players Theatre Library.

Annie Laurie. Arranged by Edward J. Loder, 1838; Published by W. Paxton, London (331); On loan from Aba Daba, courtesy David Wykes.

The Ash Grove. Arranged by John Thomas; Published by B. Williams, London; On loan from Aba Daba, courtesy Aline Waites.

Heart Of Oak. Arranged by G. A. MacFarren; Published by Chappell & Co. (3689); On loan from The Raymond Mander & Joe Mitchenson Theatre Collection.

Rule Britannia. Published in the Musical Bouquet series No. 58, London; On loan from Bill Manley.

Sally In Our Alley. From a compilation on loan from Marjorie Butcher.

I Dreamt That I Dwelt In Marble Halls. Published by Chappell (6742); On loan from The Raymond Mander & Joe Mitchenson Theatre Collection.

Then You'll Remember Me. Published by Chappell (6738); On loan from Dominic le Foe.

The Moon Has Raised Her Lamp Above. Published by Cassell & Co. Ltd, London, in Cassell's Operatic Selections No. 3, The Lily of Killarney (Op.3.C.); On loan from Dominic le Foe.

I Am The Ruler Of The Queen's Navee. Published in *The Immortal Gilbert & Sullivan Operas*, Part 7, *HMS Pinafore* by George Newnes, London; On loan from Dominic le Foe.

A Wand'ring Minstrel I. Published by Chappell & Co. Ltd, London in *The Mikado* (18056); On loan from Aba Daba, courtesy David Wykes.

The Amorous Goldfish. Published by Hopwood & Crew, London, from *The Geisha* (H & C 3760); On loan from The Raymond Mander & Joe Mitchenson Theatre Collection; Reproduced by permission of Chappell Music Ltd and International Music Publications.
© Copyright 1896 by Ascherberg Hopwood & Crew Ltd

The Honeysuckle And The Bee. Published by Francis, Day & Hunter, Ltd (F & D 7014); On loan from EMI Music Publishers Ltd; Reproduced by permission of EMI Music Publishing Ltd and International Music Publications.
© Copyright 1901 by Sol Bloom (USA), Sub-published by Francis, Day & Hunter, Ltd

PICTURE CREDITS

Sources for pictures in this book are listed from the top left-hand corner to the bottom right-hand corner of every page.

Front cover – Mary Evans Picture Library; The Mander & Mitchenson Theatre Collection. Back cover – The Tate Gallery, London. Front flap – Mr & Mrs C. M. Diamond. Back flap – Mr & Mrs C. M. Diamond. First endpaper – Tony Barker. Last endpaper – John Stanton.

2 – The Tate Gallery, London. 3 – London Borough of Lambeth Archives Department. 4, 5 – Sheldrake Press, courtesy Royal Institute of British Architects, photograph by Geremy Butler; Tony Barker; Tony Barker; Sheldrake Press. 6 – Sheldrake Press, courtesy The Mander & Mitchenson Theatre Collection. 7 – Mansell Collection. 8, 9 – Sheldrake Press, courtesy Guildhall Library, City of London. 10 – Sheldrake Press. 11 – Bill Manley; Mansell Collection. 12 – Islington Libraries; Islington Libraries; Guildhall Library, City of London. 13 – Guildhall Library, City of London; Tony Barker; Sylvia Keeler; Sylvia Keeler.

14, 15 – City of Manchester Art Galleries. 16 – Mansell Collection. 17 – N. C. Bryant (Ed.) *Picturesque America*, vol. II, D. Appleton & Co., New York, 1894. 18 – Mansell Collection; Mansell Collection. 19 – Tony Barker. 20 – M. Creighton, D. D., *The Story of Some English Shires*, The Religious Tract Society, London, 1897. 21 – Mansell Collection. 22 – Galerie George, London. 23 – Sheldrake Press. 24 – courtesy Bob Hook/Ivor Claydon; courtesy Bob Hook/Ivor Claydon. 25 – Florence Wykes; courtesy Bob Hook/Ivor Claydon. 26 – Tony Barker. 27 – George Hoare, Archivist, Stoll Moss Theatres, London. 28 – The Mander & Mitchenson Theatre Collection; courtesy Bob Hook/Ivor Claydon. 29 – courtesy Bob Hook/Ivor Claydon; Sheldrake Press. 30 – Mansell Collection. 31 – The Mander & Mitchenson Theatre Collection. 32 – courtesy *Country Life*. 33 – *Poems By Alfred, Lord Tennyson*, Bell and Hyman, London, 1979.

35 – Guildhall Library, City of London; Mansell Collection. 36 – Victoria and Albert Museum, London. 37 – Sheldrake Press. 38 – Sheldrake Press. 39 – Sheldrake Press. 40 – Guildhall Library, City of London. 41 – Mansell Collection. 42 – Mansell Collection. 43 – Sheldrake Press; Sheldrake Press. 44 – Tony Barker; 45 – Tony Barker; W. C. Bryant (Ed.), *Picturesque America*, vol. II, Appleton & Co., New York, 1894. 46 – Bill Manley. 47 – Aba Daba, courtesy Aline Waites. 48 – D. Roberts, *The Holy Land*, vol. I, 1842. 50 – Sheldrake Press. 51 – Mansell Collection. 53 – courtesy Bob Hook/Ivor Claydon. 54 – D. Roberts, *The Holy Land*, vol. I, 1842. 55 – The Mander & Mitchenson Theatre Collection. 56 – Aba Daba, courtesy David Wykes. 57 – Florence Wykes. 58 – Sheldrake Press. 59 – Sheldrake Press.

60, 61 – Southwark Local Studies Library, London. 62 – City of Manchester Art Galleries. 63 – Sheldrake Press. 64 – The Mander & Mitchenson Theatre Collection. 65 – Mary Evans Picture Library; Guildhall Library, City of London; Guildhall Library, City of London. 66 – Sheldrake Press, courtesy Islington Libraries, photograph by David Trace. 67 – Southwark Local Studies Library, London; Aba Daba, courtesy Aline Waites. 68 – Guildhall Library, City of London. 69 – The Mander & Mitchenson Theatre Collection. 70 – The Mander & Mitchenson Theatre Collection; Mansell Collection. 71 – Sheldrake Press, courtesy Colin Sorensen and the Livesey Museum, London, photograph by David Trace; Guildhall Library, City of London; Mansell Collection. 72 – Bill Manley; Mansell Collection. 73 – Tony Barker; Southwark Local Studies Library, London. 74 – Southwark Local Studies Library, London. 75 – The Mander & Mitchenson Theatre Collection.

76, 77 – Mansell Collection. 78 – John Stanton; John Stanton. 79 – Mansell Collection. 80 – The Players Theatre, London; The Mander & Mitchenson Theatre Collection. 81 – The BBC Hulton Picture Library; John Stanton. 82 – Bernard Kaukas. 83 – John Earle, courtesy John Stanton; Mansell Collection. 84 – Mansell Collection; T. C. Croker, *A Walk from London to Fulham*, William Tegg, London, 1860. 85 – Sheldrake Press. 86 – Mansell Collection. 87 – The Players Theatre, London. 88 – Marjorie Butcher; Bernard Kaukas. 89 – courtesy Bob Hook/Ivor Claydon.

90, 91 – The Museum of London. 92 – Bill Manley; London Borough of Lambeth Archives Department. 93 – Moët & Chandon; Guildhall Library, City of London; Tony Barker. 94 – The Mander & Mitchenson Theatre Collection; courtesy Bob Hook/Ivor Claydon. 95 – The Mander & Mitchenson Theatre Collection. 96 – Tony Barker. 97 – Mansell Collection; Tony Barker. 98 – Eleanor Lines. 99 – The Mander & Mitchenson Theatre Collection. 100 – Sally Weatherill. 101 – Sheldrake Press. 102 – Tony Barker; The Mander & Mitchenson Theatre Collection. 103 – The Mander & Mitchenson Theatre Collection. 104 – Aba Daba, courtesy David Wykes. 105 – Bill Manley. 106 – Mansell Collection; Sylvia Keeler. 107 – The Welbeck Gallery, London. 108 – The Mander & Mitchenson Theatre Collection. 109 – Mansell Collection; Tony Barker. 110 – Sheldrake Press; Mansell Collection. 111 – The Mander & Mitchenson Theatre Collection. 112 – Bill Manley. 113 – Tony Barker; The Mander & Mitchenson Theatre Collection. 114 – The Mander & Mitchenson Theatre Collection; Ironbridge Gorge Museum: Elton Collection. 115 – Ironbridge Gorge Museum: Elton Collection. 116 – Bill Manley. 117 – Southwark Local Studies Library, London. 118 – Southwark Local Studies Library, London. 119 – The Mander & Mitchenson Theatre Collection; EMI Music Publishing Ltd. 120 – Bill Manley. 121 – Tony Barker.

122, 3 – The Museum of London. 124 – Sylvia Keeler. 125 – Tony Barker; London Borough of Lambeth Archives Department. 126 – Tony Barker; Mr & Mrs C. M. Diamond; Sylvia Keeler. 127 – Mr & Mrs C. M. Diamond; London Borough of Lambeth Archives Department. 128 – John Stanton; Tony Barker. 129 – Tony Barker; Sylvia Keeler. 130 – Mr & Mrs C. M. Diamond. 131 – John Stanton; Sheldrake Press. 132 – Tony Barker. 133 – Tony Barker. 134 – John Earle. 135 – Mr & Mrs C. M. Diamond; John Earle. 136 – Southwark Local Studies Library, London; John Earle. 137 – Tony Barker. 138 – Tony Barker. 139 – Hook Norton Brewery, Oxfordshire. 140 – Tony Barker; London Borough of Lambeth Archives Department. 141-144 – The Players Theatre, London. 145 – Tony Barker; John Stanton. 146 – Tony Barker. 147 – John Stanton. 148 – The Mander & Mitchenson Theatre Collection. 149 – The BBC Hulton Picture Library. 150 – John Stanton. 151 – Tony Barker. 152 – The BBC Hulton Picture Library. 153 – The BBC Hulton Picture Library.

154, 155 – Christopher Wood Gallery. 156 – John Stanton; Guildhall Library, City of London. 157 – Tony Barker. 158 – Sheldrake Press, courtesy The British Music Hall Society and the Livesey Museum, photograph by David Trace; Sheldrake Press. 159 – London Borough of Lambeth Archives Department; Nottingham Castle Museum. 160 – Tony Barker. 161 – photograph by Bill Cash, courtesy Tony Barker. 162, 163 – The Tate Gallery, London. 164 – Tony Barker; Tony Barker. 165 – The Kirby Adair Newson Partnership; Tony Barker. 166 – The Mander & Mitchenson Theatre Collection. 167 – Tony Barker. 168 – David Cheshire; Tony Barker. 169 – Tony Barker; Tony Barker. 170 – Sheldrake Press; Mansell Collection. 171 – Sheldrake Press, courtesy The British Music Hall Society and the Livesey Museum, photograph by David Trace. 172 – Tony Barker. 173 – The BBC Hulton Picture Library; Tony Barker. 174 – Tony Barker; Mansell Collection. 175 – Tony Barker. 177 – Mansell Collection; Tony Barker.

178, 179 – National Army Museum, London. 180 – Tony Barker. 181 – Eleanor Lines. 182 – Tony Barker. 183 – Southwark Local Studies Library. 184 – Tony Barker; courtesy Bob Hook/Ivor Claydon. 185 – John Stanton; The Mander & Mitchenson Theatre Collection. 186 – The Mander & Mitchenson Theatre Collection. 187 – Tony Barker; Aba Daba, courtesy Aline Waites. 188 – Tony Barker, The Mander & Mitchenson Theatre Collection. 189 – Bill Manley. 190 – Tony Barker. 191 – Sheldrake Press. 192 – T. Archer, *Pictures and Royal Portraits*, Blackie & Son, London, 1878; courtesy Bob Hook/Ivor Claydon. 193 – The Illustrated London News Picture Library. 194 – The Mander & Mitchenson Theatre Collection. 195 – Galerie George, London; Sheldrake Press. 196 – The Mander & Mitchenson Theatre Collection. 197 – Sheldrake Press.

198, 199 – Mansell Collection. 200 – courtesy Bob Hook/Ivor Claydon. 201 – Sheldrake Press. 202 – Mansell Collection. 203 – courtesy Bob Hook/Ivor Claydon. 204 – Tony Barker; Mansell Collection. 205 – Mansell Collection; Mansell Collection; Tony Barker. 206 – Mansell Collection. 207 – Aba Daba, courtesy Aline Waites. 208 – Sheldrake Press; Sylvia Keeler. 209 – Mansell Collection. 210 – Mansell Collection. 212 – The Mander & Mitchenson Theatre Collection. 213 – Galerie George, London; Mansell Collection. 214 – Mr & Mrs C. M. Diamond. 215 – Sheldrake Press. 216 – Mansell Collection. 217 – Tony Barker.

218, 219 – Pleasures of Past Times, London, courtesy David Drummond. 220 – Tony Barker. 221 – National Portrait Gallery, London; Sheldrake Press. 222 – Merseyside County Art Galleries. 223 – Dominic le Foe. 224 – George Hoare, Archivist, Stoll Moss Theatres, London. 225 – Sheldrake Press. 226 – courtesy Bob Hook/Ivor Claydon. 227 – Sheldrake Press. 228 – Mansell Collection; Sylvia Keeler. 229 – Mansell Collection; courtesy Bob Hook/Ivor Claydon. 230 – Mansell Collection; Sheldrake Press. 231 – courtesy Bob Hook/Ivor Claydon. 232 – Mansell Collection. 233 – The BBC Hulton Picture Library. 234 – The Mander & Mitchenson Theatre Collection; The Mander & Mitchenson Theatre Collection. 236 – Mansell Collection. 237 – Tony Barker; Tony Barker; Tony Barker. 239 – Victoria and Albert Museum, London; Victoria and Albert Museum, London. 240 – Mansell Collection. 241 – Eleanor Lines. 242 – Sylvia Keeler. 243 – Bill Manley. 244 – Bill Manley. 245 – Sylvia Keeler. 246 – Sylvia Keeler. 247 – Mr & Mrs C. M. Diamond. 248 – Bill Manley. 249 – Sylvia Keeler. 250 – Mr & Mrs C. M. Diamond; City of Manchester Art Galleries. 251 – Sylvia Keeler; Sylvia Keeler.

ACKNOWLEDGEMENTS

The authors and editors owe a debt of gratitude to many people who gave unsparingly of their time, expertise and goodwill in helping to produce this book and check the accuracy of the multifarious information it contains. Raymond Mander commented extensively on the early drafts of the manuscript and provided much valuable advice on the contents until his untimely death. Nevertheless his involvement in the early stages materially influenced the shape of the book, and the illustrations and sheet music from The Raymond Mander & Joe Mitchenson Theatre Collection represent a substantial contribution. We offer our thanks as well as our sympathy to Joe Mitchenson and Colin Mabberley.

Tony Barker made himself available at all times to investigate on our behalf the primary sources in his extensive archives – a vital role in view of the conflicting evidence found in so many secondary sources on the history of music hall. He has also made a major contribution to the illustrations from his collection of music hall and theatrical memorabilia. Dr Jacky Bratton contributed authoritative research notes and provided a firm foundation of 19th-century history, guiding us towards judicious generalization in addition to fulfilling her role as an arbiter of accuracy and balance.

Julia Courtney and Barry Anthony gave us a wealth of information on Victorian social history and the story of the minstrel shows respectively, greatly broadening and enriching the scope of the book. Valerie Chandler compiled the index with her usual mastery of detail and flair for distinguishing important headings. Pat Dunn of Pat Dunn Media Associates most generously and energetically publicized the book on our behalf.

Of course, the responsibility for any errors of fact or interpretation remain the authors' and editors' alone.

We are grateful to many other people who helped us, in particular: the staff of the BBC Hulton Picture Library; Kent Baker; the staff of the British Library; Mike Bruce; David Cheshire; Peter Cotes; Mr C. M. Diamond; David Drummond; John Earle; Kathy Eason; Sylvia Eaves; Ron Finch; Mr L. W. Henderson and the staff of the Performing Right Society; Karin Hills; George Hoare, Archivist, Stoll Moss Theatres; Hook Norton Brewery Co. Ltd, Oxford; Katie Hunter-Jones; the staff of the Ironbridge Gorge Museum Trust; John Hall Antiques and Prints, London; Christine Julings; Sylvia Keeler; Dominic le Foe; the staff of the Livesey Museum; Jack Lugg; Bill Manley; the staff of the Mansell Collection; Denis Martin and Pat Lancaster of the Players Theatre; David Mason; Michael Harrington Ltd, Winchester; Christine Pilgrim; Georgina Robins; Mrs Doreen Spellman; John Stanton; Hetty Startup; the staff of the Swiss Cottage Reference Library; David Trace; Ray Waterhouse of Galerie George, London; Sally Welford; the staff of the Westminster Central Music Library; the staff of the Westminster Central Reference Library; John Whitehorn of EMI Archives; the staff of the Witt Library; Diane Wood and the staff of the BBC Radio Music Library.

·INDEX·

Titles of songs are given in italics, first lines in inverted commas. Page references in bold type refer to main entries.

792P

256